Born Frank Morrison Spillane in Brooklyn, New York City, in 1918, Mickey Spillane started writing while at high school. During the Second World War, he enlisted in the Army Air Corps and became a fighter pilot and instructor. After the war, he moved to South Carolina, having liked the look of it while flying over. He was married three times, the third time to Jane Rogers Johnson, and had four children and two stepchildren. He wrote his first novel, *I, the Jury* (1947), in order to raise the money to buy a house for himself and his first wife, Mary Ann Pearce. The novel sold six and a half million copies in the United States, and introduced Spillane's most famous character, the hard-boiled PI Mike Hammer. The many novels that followed became instant bestsellers, until in 1980 the US all-time fiction bestseller list of fifteen titles boasted seven by Mickey Spillane. More than 225 million copies of his books have sold internationally. He was uniformly disliked by critics, owing to the high content of sex and violence in his books. However, he was later praised by American mystery writers Max Alan Collins and William L. DeAndrea, as well as artist Markus Lüpertz. The novelist Ayn Rand, a friend of Spillane's, appreciated the black-and-white morality of his books. Spillane was an active Jehovah's Witness. He died in 2006 from pancreatic cancer.

D1375409

One Lonely Night

MICKEY SPILLANE

An Orion paperback

First published in the United States of America in 1951
by E. P. Dutton & Co. Inc.
This paperback edition published in 2015
by Orion Books,
an imprint of The Orion Publishing Group Ltd,
Carmelite House, 50 Victoria Embankment,
London EC4Y 0DZ

An Hachette UK company

1 3 5 7 9 10 8 6 4 2

A CIP catalogue record for this book
is available from the British Library.

ISBN 978-1-4091-5867-7

Typeset by Born Group using Book Cloud

Printed and bound by CPI Group (UK) Ltd, Croydon, CR0 4YY

The Orion Publishing Group's policy is to use papers that
are natural, renewable and recyclable products and made
from wood grown in sustainable forests. The logging and
manufacturing processes are expected to conform to the
environmental regulations of the country of origin.

www.orionbooks.co.uk

To

MARTY

CHAPTER ONE

Nobody ever walked across the bridge, not on a night like this. The rain was misty enough to be almost fog-like, a cold grey curtain that separated me from the pale ovals of white that were faces locked behind the steamed-up windows of cars that hissed by. Even the brilliance that was Manhattan by night was reduced to a few sleepy, yellow lights off in the distance.

Some place over there I had left my car and started walking, burying my head in the collar of my raincoat, with the night pulled in around me like a blanket. I walked and I smoked and I flipped the spent butts ahead of me and watched them arch to the pavement and fizzle out with one last wink. If there was life behind the windows of the buildings on either side of me, I didn't notice it. The street was mine, all mine. They gave it to me gladly and wondered why I wanted it so nice and all alone.

There were others like me, sharing the dark and the solitude, but they huddled in the recesses of the doorways not wanting to share the wet and the cold. I could feel their eyes follow me briefly before they turned inward to their thoughts again.

So I followed the hard concrete footpaths of the city through the towering canyons of the buildings and never noticed when the sheer cliffs of brick and masonry diminished and disappeared altogether, and the footpath led into a ramp then on to the spidery steel skeleton that was the bridge linking two states.

I climbed to the hump in the middle and stood there leaning on the handrail with a butt in my fingers, watching the red and green lights of the boats in the river below. They winked at me and called in low, throaty notes before disappearing into the night.

Like eyes and faces. And voices.

1

I buried my face in my hands until everything straightened itself out again, wondering what the judge would say if he could see me now. Maybe he'd laugh because I was supposed to be so damn tough, and here I was with hands that wouldn't stand still and an empty feeling inside my chest.

He was only a little judge. He was little and he was old with eyes like two berries on a bush. His hair was pure white and wavy and his skin was loose and wrinkled. But he had a voice like the Avenging Angel. The dignity and knowledge behind his face gave him the stature of a giant, the poise of Gabriel reading your sins aloud from the Great Book and condemning you to your fate.

He looked at me with a loathing louder than words, lashing me with his eyes in front of a courtroom filled with people, every empty second another stroke of the steel-tipped whip. His voice, when it did come, was edged with a gentle bitterness that was given only to the righteous.

But it didn't stay righteous long. It changed into disgusted hatred because I was a licensed investigator who knocked off somebody who needed knocking off bad and he couldn't get to me. So I was a murderer by definition and all the law could do was shake its finger at definitions.

Hell, the state would have liquidated the guy anyway . . . maybe he would have pronounced sentence himself. Maybe he thought I should have stayed there and called for the cops when the bastard had a rod in his hand and it was pointing right at my gut.

Yeah, great.

If he had let it stay there it would have been all right. I'd been called a lot of things before. But no, he had to go and strip me naked in front of myself and throw the past in my face when it should have stayed dead and buried forever. He had to go back five years to a time he knew of only second-hand and tell me how it took a war to show me the power of the gun and the obscene pleasure that was brutality and force, the spicy sweetness of murder sanctified by law.

That was me. I could have made it sound better if I'd said it. There in the muck and slime of the jungle, there in the stink that hung over the beaches rising from the bodies of the dead, there in the half-light of too many dusks and dawns laced together with the criss-crossed patterns of bullets, I had gotten a taste of death and found it palatable to the extent that I could never again eat the fruits of a normal civilization.

Goddamn, he wouldn't let me alone! He went on and on cutting me down until I was nothing but scum in the gutter, his fist slamming against the bench as he prophesied a rain of purity that was going to wash me into the sewer with the other scum leaving only the good and the meek to walk in the cleanliness of law and justice.

One day I would die and the world would be benefited by my death. And to the good there was only the perplexing question: Why did I live and breathe now . . . what could possibly be the reason for existence when there was no good in me? None at all.

So he gave me back my soul of toughness, hate and bitterness and let me dress in the armour of cynicism and dismissed me before I could sneer and make the answer I had ready.

He had called the next case up even before I reached the side of the room. It had all the earmarks of a good case, but nobody seemed to be interested. All they watched was me and their eyes were bright with that peculiar kind of horrified disgust that you see in people watching some nasty, fascinating creature in a circus cage.

Only a few of them reflected a little sympathy. Pat was there. He gave me a short wave and a nod that meant everything was okay because I was his friend. But there were things the judge had said that Pat had wanted to say plenty of times too.

Then there was Pete, a reporter too old for the fast beats and just right for the job of picking up human-interest items from the lower courts. He waved, too, with a grimace that was a combination grin for me and a sneer for the judge. Pete was a cynic too, but he liked my kind of guy. I made bonus stories for him every once in a while.

Velda! Lovely, lovely Velda! She waited for me by the door and when I walked up to her I watched her lips purse into a

3

ripe, momentary kiss. The rows and rows of eyes that had been following me jumped ahead to this vision in a low-cut dress who threw a challenge with every motion of her body. The eyes swept from her black pumps to legs and body and shoulders that were almost too good to be real and staggered when they met a face that was beauty capable of the extremes of every emotion. Her head moved just enough to swirl her black, page-boy hair and the look she sent back to all those good people and their white-haired guardian of the law was something to be remembered. For one long second she had the judge's eye, and outraged justice flinched before outraged love.

That's right, Velda was mine. It took a long time for me to find out just how much mine she was, much too long. But now I knew and I'd never forget it. She was the only decent thing about me and I was lucky.

She said, 'Let's get out of here, Mike. I hate people with little minds.'

We went outside the building to the sidewalk and climbed in my car. She knew I didn't want to talk about it and kept still. When I let her out at her apartment it was dark and starting to rain. Her hand went to mine and squeezed it. 'A good drink and you can forget about it, Mike. Sometimes people are too stupid to be grateful. Call me when you're loaded and I'll come get you.'

That was all. She knew me enough to read my mind and didn't care what I thought. If the whole damn world climbed on my back there would still be Velda ready to yank them off and stamp on their faces. I didn't even tell her goodbye. I just shut the door and started driving.

No, I didn't get drunk. Twice I looked in the mirror and saw me. I didn't look like me at all. I used to be able to look at myself and grin without giving a damn how ugly it made me look. Now I was looking at myself the same way those people did back there. I was looking at a big guy with an ugly reputation, a guy who had no earthly reason for existing in a decent, normal society. That's what the judge had said.

4

I was sweating and cold at the same time. Maybe it did happen to me over there. Maybe I did have a taste for death. Maybe I liked it too much to taste anything else. Maybe I was twisted and rotted inside. Maybe I would be washed down the sewer with the rest of all the rottenness sometime. What was stopping it from happening now? Why was I me with some kind of a lucky charm around my neck that kept me going when I was better off dead?

That's why I parked the car and started walking in the rain. I didn't want to look in that damn mirror any more. So I walked and smoked and climbed to the hump in the bridge where the boats in the river made faces and spoke to me until I had to bury my face in my hands until everything straightened itself out again.

I was a killer. I was a murderer, legalized. I had no reason for living. Yeah, he said that!

The crazy music that has been in my head ever since I came back from those dusks and dawns started again, a low steady beat overshadowed by the screaming of brassier, shriller instruments that hadn't been invented yet. They shouted and pounded a symphony of madness and destruction while I held my hands over my ears and cursed until they stopped. Only the bells were left, a hundred bells that called for me to come closer to the music, and when I wouldn't come they stopped, one by one, all except one deep, persistent bell with a low, resonant voice. It wouldn't give up. It called me to it, and when I opened my eyes I knew the bell was from a channel marker in the river, calling whenever it swayed with the tide.

It was all right once I knew where it came from. At least it was real. That judge, that damn white-headed son of a bitch got me like this. I wasn't so tough after all. It wouldn't have been so bad . . . but maybe he was right. Maybe he was dead right and I'd never be satisfied until I knew the answer myself. If there was an answer.

I don't know how long I stood there. Time was just the ticking of a watch and a blend of sound from the ramp behind

5

me. At some point after the sixth cigarette the cold mist had turned into a fine snow that licked at my face and clung to my coat. At first it melted into damp patches on the steel and concrete, then took hold and extended itself into a coverlet of white.

Now the last shred of reality was gone completely. The girders became giant trees and the bridge an eerie forest populated by whitecapped rubber-tyred monsters streaking for the end of the causeway that took them into more friendly surroundings. I leaned back into the shadow of a girder and watched them to get my mind off other things, happy to be part of the peace and quiet of the night.

It came at last, the lessening of tension. The stiffness went out of my fingers and I pulled on a smoke until it caught in my lungs the way I liked it to do. Yeah, I could grin now and watch the faces fade away until they were onto the port and starboard lights of the ships again, and the bell that called me in was only a buoy some place off in the dark.

I ought to get out of it. I ought to take Velda and my office and start up in real estate in some small community where murder and guns and dames didn't happen. Maybe I would, at that. It was wonderful to be able to think straight again. No more crazy mad hatreds that tied my insides into knots. No more hunting the scum that stood behind a trigger and shot at the world. That was official police business. The duty of organized law and order. And too slow justice. No more sticks with dirty ends on them either.

That's what the snow and the quiet did for me. It had been a long time since I had felt this good. Maybe the rottenness wasn't there at all and I was a killer only by coincidence. Maybe I didn't like to kill at all.

I stuck another Lucky in my mouth and searched my pockets for a match. Something jerked my head up before I found them and I stood there listening.

The wind blew. The snow hissed to the street. A foghorn sounded. That was all.

I shrugged and tore a match out of the book when I heard it again. A little, annoying sound that didn't belong on the bridge in the peace and quiet. They were soft, irregular sounds that faded when the wind shifted, then came back stronger. Footsteps, muted by the inch or so of snow on the walk.

I would have gotten the butt lit if the feet weren't trying to run with the desperate haste that comes with fatigue. The sound came closer and closer until it was a shadow fifty feet away that turned into a girl wrapped in a coat with a big woolly collar, her hands reaching for the support of a girder and missing.

She fell face down and tried to pull herself up to run again, but she couldn't make it. Her breathing was a long, racking series of sobs that shook her body in a convulsion of despair.

I'd seen fear before, but never like this.

She was only a few steps away and I ran to her, my hands hooking under her arms to lift her to her feet.

Her eyes were like saucers, rimmed with red, overflowing with tears that blurred her pupils. She took one look at me and choked, 'Lord . . . no, please!'

'Easy, honey, take it easy,' I said. I propped her against the girder and her eyes searched my face through the tears, unable to see me clearly. She tried to talk and I stopped her. 'No words, kid. There's plenty of time for that later. Just take it easy a minute, nobody's going to hurt you.'

As if that stirred something in her mind, her eyes went wide again and she turned her head to stare back down the ramp.

I heard it too. Footsteps, only these weren't hurried. They came evenly and softly, as if knowing full well they'd reach their objective in a few seconds.

I felt a snarl ripple across my mouth and my eyes went half shut. Maybe you can smack a dame around all you want and make her life as miserable as hell, but nobody has the right to scare the daylights out of any woman. Not like this.

She trembled so hard I had to put my arm around her shoulder to steady her. I watched her lips trying to speak, the unholy fear spreading into her face as no sound came.

7

I pulled her away from the girder. 'Come on, we'll get this straightened out in a hurry.' She was too weak to resist. I held my arm around her and started walking toward the footsteps.

He came out of the wall of white, a short, pudgy guy in a heavy belted ulster. His homburg was set on the side of his head rakishly, and even at this distance I could see the smile on his lips. Both his hands were stuck in his pockets and he walked with a swagger. He wasn't a bit surprised when he saw the two of us. One eyebrow went up a little, but that was all. Oh, yes, he had a gun in one pocket.

It was pointing at me.

Nobody had to tell me he was the one. I wouldn't even have to know he had a rod in his hand. The way the kid's body stiffened with the shock of seeing him was enough. My face couldn't have been nice to look at right then, but it didn't bother the guy.

The gun moved in the pocket so I'd know it was a gun.

His voice fit his body, short and thick. He said, 'It is not smart to be a hero. Not smart at all.' His thick lips twisted into a smile of mingled satisfaction and conceit. It was so plain in his mind that I could almost hear him speak it. The girl running along, stumbling blindly into the arms of a stranger. Her pleas for help, the guy's ready agreement to protect her, only to look down the barrel of a rod.

It didn't happen like that at all, but that's what he thought. His smile widened and he said harshly, 'So now they will find the two of you here tomorrow.' His eyes were as cold and as deadly as those of a manta ray.

He was too cocky. All he could see was his own complete mastery of the situation. He should have looked at me a little harder and maybe he would have seen the kind of eyes I had. Maybe he would have known that I was a killer in my own way too, and he would have realized that I knew he was just the type who would go to the trouble of taking the gun out of his pocket instead of ruining a good coat.

I never really gave him a chance. All I moved was my arm and before he had his gun out I had my .45 in my fist with the safety off and the trigger back. I only gave him a second to realize what it was like to die then I blew the expression clean off his face.

He never figured the hero would have a gun, too.

Before I could get it back in the holster the girl gave a lunge and backed up against the railing. Her eyes were clear now. They darted to the mess on the ground, the gun in my hand and the tight lines that made a mask of kill-lust in my face.

She screamed. Good God, how she screamed! She screamed as if I were a monster that had come up out of the pit! She screamed and made words that sounded like, 'You . . . one of them . . . no more!'

I saw what she was going to do and tried to grab her, but the brief respite she had was enough to give her the strength she needed. She twisted and slithered over the top of the rail and I felt part of her coat come away in my hand as she tumbled headlong into the white void below the bridge.

Lord, Lord, what happened? My fingers closed over the hand-rail and I stared down after her. Three hundred feet to the river. The little fool didn't have to do that! She was safe! Nothing could have hurt her, didn't she realize that? I was shouting it at the top of my lungs with nobody but a dead man to hear me. When I pulled away from the rail I was shaking like a leaf.

All because of that fat little bastard stretched out in the snow. I pulled back my foot and kicked what was left of him until he rolled over on his face.

I did it again, I killed somebody else! Now I could stand in the courtroom in front of the man with the white hair and the voice of the Avenging Angel and let him drag my soul out where everybody could see it and slap it with another coat of black paint.

Peace and quiet, it was great! I ought to have my head examined. Or the guy should maybe; his had a hell of a hole in it. The dirty son-of-a-bitch for trying to get away with that. The fat little slob walks right up to me with a rod in his hand figuring to get away with it. The way he strutted you'd think he didn't have a care in the world, yet just like that he was going to kill two people without batting an eye. He got part of what he wanted anyway. The girl was dead. He was the kind of rat who would have gotten a big laugh out of the papers tomorrow. Maybe he was supposed to be the rain of purity that was going to wash me down the gutter into the sewer with the rest of the scum. Brother, would that have been a laugh.

Okay, if he wanted a laugh, he'd get it. If his ghost could laugh I'd make it real funny for him. It would be so funny that his ghost would be the laughing-stock of hell and when mine got there it'd have something to laugh at too. I'm nothing but a stinking no-good killer, but I get there first, Judge. I get there first and live to do it again because I have eyes that see and a hand that works without being told and I don't give a damn what you do to my soul because it's so far gone nothing can be done for it! Go to hell yourself, Judge! Get a real belly laugh!

I tore his pockets inside out and stuffed his keys and wallet in my coat. I ripped out every label on his clothes right down to the laundry marks then I kicked the snow off the pavement and rubbed his fingertips against the cold concrete until there weren't any fingertips left. When I was finished he looked like the remains of a scarecrow that had been up too many seasons. I grabbed an arm and a leg and heaved him over the rail, and when I heard a faint splash many seconds later my mouth split into a grin. I kicked the pieces of cloth and his gun under the rail and let them get lost in the obscurity of the night and the river. I didn't even have to worry about the bullet. It was lying right there in the snow, all flattened out and glistening wetly.

I kicked that over the side too.

Now let them find him. Let them learn who it was and how it happened. Let everybody have a laugh while you're at it!

It was done and I lit a cigarette. The snow still coming down put a new layer over the tracks and the dark stain. It almost covered up the patch of cloth that had come from the girl's coat, but I picked that up and stuck it in with the rest of the stuff.

Now my footsteps were the only sound along the ramp. I walked back to the city telling myself it was all right, it had to happen that way. I was me and I couldn't have been anything else even if there had been no war. I was all right, the world was wrong. A police car moaned through the pay station and passed me as its siren was dying down to a low whine. I didn't even give it a second thought. They weren't going anywhere, certainly not to the top of the hump because not one car had passed during those few minutes it had happened. Nobody saw me, nobody cared. If they did the hell with them.

I reached the streets of the city and turned back for another look at the steel forest that climbed into the sky. No, nobody ever walked across the bridge on a night like this.

Hardly nobody.

CHAPTER TWO

I DIDN'T go home that night. I went to my office and sat in the big leather-covered chair behind the desk and drank without getting drunk. I held the .45 in my lap, cleaned and reloaded, watching it, feeling in it an extension of myself. How many people had it sent on the long road? My mind blocked off the thought of the past and I put the gun back in the sling under my arm and slept. I dreamt that the judge with the white hair and eyes like two berries on a bush was pointing at me, ordering me to take the long road myself and I had the .45 in my hand and my finger worked the trigger. It clicked and wouldn't go off, and with every sharp click a host of devilish voices would take up a dirge of laughter and I threw the gun at him, but it wouldn't leave my hand. It was part of me and it stuck fast.

The key turning in the lock awakened me. Throughout that dream of violent action I hadn't moved an inch, so that when I brought my head up I was looking straight at Velda. She didn't know I was there until she tossed the day's mail on the desk. For a second she froze with startled surprise, then relaxed into a grin.

'You scared the whosis out of me, Mike.' She paused and bit her lip. 'Aren't you here early?'

'I didn't go home, kid.'

'Oh! I thought you might call me. I stayed up pretty late.'

'I didn't get drunk, either.'

'No?'

'No.'

Velda frowned again. She wanted to say something, but during office hours she respected my position. I was the boss and she was my secretary. Very beautiful, of course. I loved her like hell, but she didn't know how much and she was still part of the pay roll. She decided to brighten the office with a

13

smile instead, sorted the things on my desk and started back to the reception room.

'Velda . . .!'

She stopped, her hand on the knob, and looked over her shoulder. 'Yes, Mike?'

'Come here.' I stood up and sat on the edge of the desk tapping a Lucky against my thumbnail. 'What kind of a guy am I, kitten?'

Her eyes probed into my brain and touched the discontent. For a moment her smile turned into an animal look I had seen only once before. 'Mike . . . that judge was a bastard. You're an all-right guy.'

'How do you know?' I stuck the butt between my lips and lit it.

She stood there spraddle-legged with her hands low on her hips like a man, her breasts rising and falling faster than they should, fighting the wispy thinness of the dress. 'I could love you a little or I could love you a lot, Mike. Sometimes it's both ways but mostly it's a lot. If you weren't all right I couldn't love you at all. Is that what you wanted me to say?'

'No.' I blew out a stream of smoke and looked at the ceiling. 'Tell me about myself. Tell me what other people say.'

'Why? You know it as well as I do. You read the papers. When you're right you're a hero. When you're wrong you're kill-happy. Why don't you ask the people who count, the ones who really know you? Ask Pat. He thinks you're a good cop. Ask all the worms in the holes, the ones who have reason to stay out of your way. They'll tell you too . . . if you can catch them.'

I chucked the butt into the metal basket. 'Sure, the worms'll tell me. You know why I can't catch them, Velda? Do you know why they're scared to death to tangle with me? I'll tell you why. They know damn well I'm as bad as they are . . . worse, and I operate legally.'

She reached out a hand and ran it over my hair. 'Mike, you're too damn big and tough to give a hang what people say. They're only little people with little minds, so forget it.'

'There's an awful lot of it.'

'Forget it.'

'Make me,' I said.

She came into my arms with a rush and I held her to me to get warm and let the moist softness of her lips make me forget. I had to push to get her away and I stood there holding her arms, breathing in a picture of what a man's woman should look like. It was a long time before I could manage a grin, but she brought it out of me. There's something a woman does without words that makes a man feel like a man and forget about the things he's been told.

'Did you bring in the paper?'

'It's on my desk.'

She followed me when I went out to get it. A tabloid and a full-sized job were there. The tab was opened to a news account of the trial that was one column wide and two inches long. They had my picture, too. The other rag gave me a good spread and a good going-over and they didn't have my pictures. I could start picking my friends out of the pack now.

Instead of digesting the absorbing piece of news, I scanned the pages for something else. Velda scowled at my concentration and hung over my shoulder. What I was looking for wasn't there. Not a single thing about two bodies in the river.

'Something, Mike?'

I shook my head. 'Nope. Just looking for customers.'

She didn't believe me. 'There are some excellent prospects in the letter file if you're interested. They're waiting for your answer.'

I put the paper down and reached in my pocket for a smoke. 'How are we fixed, Velda?' I didn't look at her.

'We're solvent. Two accounts paid up yesterday. The money has been banked and there's no bills. Why?'

'Maybe I'll take a vacation.'

'From what?'

'From paid jobs. I'm tired of being an employee.'

'Think of me.'

'I am,' I said. 'You can take a vacation too if you want to.'

15

She grabbed my elbow and turned me around until I was fencing with her eyes again. 'Whatever you're thinking isn't of fun on some beach, Mike.'

'It isn't?' I tried to act surprised.

'No.' She took the cigarette from my mouth, dragged on it and stuck it back. She never moved her eyes. 'Mike, don't play with me, please. Either tell me or don't, but quit making up excuses. What's on your mind?'

My mouth felt tight. 'You wouldn't believe it if I told you.'

'Yes I would.' There was nothing hidden in her answer. No laughter, no scorn. Just absolute belief in me.

'I want to find out about myself, Velda.'

She must have known what was coming. I said it quietly, almost softly, and she believed me. 'All right, Mike,' she said. 'If you need me for anything you know where to find me.'

I gave her the cigarette and went back to the office. How deep can a woman go to search a man's mind? How can they know without being told when some trivial thing can suddenly become so important? What is it that gives them that look as if they know the problem and the answer too, yet hold it back because it's something you have to discover for yourself?

I sat down in the swivel chair again and pulled all the junk out of my pockets: the keys, the wallet and the change. Two of the keys were for a car. One was an ordinary house key, another for a trunk or suitcase, and another for either a tumbler padlock or another house.

If I expected to find anything in the wallet I was mistaken. There were six fives and two singles in the bill compartment, a package of three-cent stamps and a card-calendar in one pocket, and a plain green card with the edges cut off at odd angles in the other pocket. That was all.

That was enough.

The little fat boy didn't have his name in print anywhere. It wasn't a new wallet either. Fat boy didn't want identification. I didn't blame him. What killer would?

Yeah, that was enough to make me sit back and look at the scuffed folder of calfskin and make me think. It would make you think too. Take a look at your own wallet and see what's in it.

I had the stuff spread out on the desk when I remembered the other pocket of my raincoat and pulled out the huge tweed triangle that had come from the girl's coat. I laid it out on my lap with the night before shoved into some corner of my brain and looked at it as though it were just another puzzle, not a souvenir of death.

The cloth had come apart easily. I must have grabbed her at the waist because the section of the coat included the right-hand pocket and part of the lining. I rubbed the fabric through my fingers feeling the soft texture of fine wool, taking in the details of the pattern. More out of curiosity than anything else, I stuck my hand inside the pocket and came up with a crumpled pack of cigarettes.

She didn't even have time for a last smoke, I thought. Even a condemned man gets that. She didn't. She took one look at me and saw my eyes and my face and whatever she saw there yanked a scream from her lungs and the strength to pull her over the rail.

What have I got locked up inside me that comes out at times like that? What good am I alive? Why do I have to be the one to pull the trigger and have my soul torn apart afterwards?

The cigarettes were a mashed ball of paper in my hand, a little wad of paper, cellophane and tinfoil that smelt of tobacco and death. My teeth were locked together and when I looked down at my hand my nail ripped through the paper and I saw the green underneath.

Between the cigarettes and the wrapper was another of those damnable green cards with the edges cut off at odd angles.

Two murders. Two green cards.

It was the same way backwards. Two green cards and two murders.

Which came first, the murders or the cards?

Green for death.

17

Murder at odd angles. Two murders. Eight odd angles. Yes, two murders. The fat boy got what he was after. Because of him the girl was murdered no matter how. So I got him. I was a murderer like they said, only to me it was different. I was just a killer. I wondered what the law would say and if they'd make that fine difference now. Yeah. I could have been smart about it; I could have done what I did, called the police and let them take over then take the dirty medicine the papers and the judge and the public would have handed me. No, I had to be smart. I had to go and mix it up so much that if those bodies were found and the finger pointed at me all I could expect was a trip on that long road to nowhere.

Was that why I did it . . . because I felt smart? No, that wasn't the reason. I didn't feel a bit smart. I was mad. I was kill-crazy mad at the bastards the boy with the scythe pointed out to me and goddamn mad at all the screwy little minds and the screwy big minds that had the power of telling me off later. They could go to hell, the judge and the jury and all the rest of them! I was getting too sick and disgusted of fighting their battles for them anyway! The boy with the scythe could go to hell with the rest and if he didn't like it he could come after me, personally. I'd love that. I wish there *was* a special agency called Death that could hear what I was thinking and make a try for me. I'd like to take that stinking black shadow and shove his own scythe down his bony throat and disjoint him with a couple of .45's? Come on, bony boy, let's see you do what you can! Get your white-haired judge and your good people tried and true and let's see just how good you are! I think I'm better, see? I think I can handle any one of you, and if you get the idea I'm kidding, then come and get me.

And if you're afraid to come after me, then I'm going after you. Maybe I'll know what I'm like then. Maybe I'll find out what's going on in my mind and why I keep on living when fat cold-blooded killers and nice warm-blooded killers are down there shaking hands with the devil!

I pulled the green card out of the cigarettes and matched it to the one from the wallet. They fitted – twins. I put them in my shirt pocket, grabbed my coat and hat and slammed the door after me when I left the office.

At a little after ten I pulled up outside the brick building that was the house of the law. Here was where the invisible processes went on that made cops out of men and murderers out of clues. The car in front of mine was an official sedan that carried the D.A.'s sticker, and I smoked a butt right down to the bottom before I decided to try to reach Pat even if the fair-haired boy of the course was around.

I should have waited a minute longer. I had my hand on the door when he pushed through and it looked like a cold wind hit him in the face. He screwed his mouth up into a snarl, thought better of it and squeezed a smile out.

Strictly an official smile.

He said, 'Morning.'

I said, 'Nice day.'

He got in his car and slammed the door so hard it almost fell off. I waved when he drove by. He didn't wave back. The old guy on the elevator took me upstairs and when I walked into Pat's office I was grinning.

Pat started, 'Did you . . .'

I answered with a nod. 'I did. We met at the gate. What got into the lad – is he sore at me?'

'Sit down, Mike.' Pat waved his thumb at the straight-back wooden chair reserved for official offenders about to get a reprimand. 'Look, pal, the District Attorney is only an elected official, but that's a mighty big "only". You put him over a barrel not so long ago and he isn't going to forget it. He isn't going to forget who your friends are, either.'

'Meaning you.'

'Meaning me, exactly. I'm a Civil Service servant, a Captain of Homicide. I have certain powers of jurisdiction, arrest and influence. He supersedes them. If the D.A. gets his hooks into you just once, you'll have a ring through your nose and I'll be handed the deal of whipping you around the arena just to give him a little satisfaction. Please quit antagonizing

19

the guy for my sake if not for your own. Now, what's on your mind?'

Pat leaned back and grinned at me. We were still buddies.

'What's new on the dockets, chum?'

'Nothing.' He shrugged. 'Life has been nice and dull. I come in at eight and go home at six. I like it.'

'Not even a suicide?'

'Not even. Don't tell me you're soliciting work.'

'Hardly. I'm on a vacation.'

Pat got that look. It started behind the pupils where no look was supposed to be. A look that called me a liar and waited to hear the rest of the lie. I had to lie a little myself. 'Since you have it so easy, how about taking your own vacation with me? We could have some fun.'

The look retreated and disappeared altogether. 'Hell, I'd love to, Mike, but we're still scratching trying to catch up on all the details around here. I don't think it's possible.' He screwed up his forehead. 'Don't you feel so hot?'

'Sure, I feel fine, that's why I want a vacation while I can enjoy it.' I slapped my hat back on my head and stood up. 'Well, since you won't come, I'll hit the road alone. Too bad. Ought to be lots doing.'

He rocked his chair forward and took my hand. 'Have fun, Mike.'

'I will.' I gave it a pause, then: 'Oh, by the way, I wanted to show you something before I left.' I reached in my shirt pocket and took out the two green cards and tossed them on the desk. 'Funny, aren't they?'

Pat dropped my hand like it had been hot. Sometimes he gets the damnedest expression on his face you ever saw. He held those cards in his fingers and walked around the desk to close and lock the door. What he said when he sat down makes dirty reading.

'Where'd you get these?' His voice had an edge to it that meant we were close to not being buddies any more.

'I found 'em.'

'Nuts! Sit down, damn it!' I sat down easy again and lit a smoke. It was hard to keep a grin off my mouth. 'Once more, Mike, where'd they come from?'

'I told you. I found them.'

'Okay, I'll get very simple in my questioning. *Where* did you find them?'

I was getting tired of wearing the grin. I let it do what it wanted to do and I felt the air dry my teeth. 'Look, Pat, remember me? I'm your friend. I'm a citizen and I'm a stubborn jerk who doesn't like to answer questions when he doesn't know why. Quit the cop act and ask right. So tell me I handed you a line about a vacation when all I wanted to get was some information. So tell me something you haven't told me before.'

'All right, Mike, all right. All I want to know is where you got them.'

'I killed a guy and took it off his body.'

'Stop being sarcastic.'

I must have grinned the dirtiest kind of grin there was. Pat watched me strangely, shook his head impatiently and tossed the cards back on the desk. 'Are they so important I can't hear about it, Pat?'

He ran his tongue across his lips. 'No, they're not so important in one way. I guess they could be lost easily enough. There're plenty of them in circulation.'

'Yeah?'

He nodded briefly and fingered the edge of one. 'They're Communist identification cards. One of the new fronts. The Nazi bund that used to operate in this country had cards just like 'em. They were red though. Every so often they change the cuts of the edges to try to trip up any spies. When you get in the meeting hall your card has to match up with a master card.'

'Oh, just like a lodge.' I picked one up and tucked it in my coat pocket.

He said, 'Yeah,' sourly.

'Then why all the to-do with the door. We're not in a meeting hall.'

21

Pat smacked the desk with the flat of his hand. 'I don't know, Mike. Damn it, if anybody but you came in with a couple of those cards I would have said what they were and that's all. But when it's you I go cold all over and wait for something to happen. I know it won't happen, then it does. Come on, spill it. What's behind them?' He looked tired as hell.

'Nothing, I told you that. They're curious and I found two of them. I'd never seen anything like it before and thought maybe you'd know what they were.'

'And I did.'

'That's right. Thanks.'

I put my hat back on and stood up. He let me get as far as the door. 'Mike! . . .' He was looking at his hand.

'I'm on vacation now, pal.'

He picked up a card and looked at the blank sides of it.

'Three days ago a man was murdered. He had one of these things clutched in his hand.'

I turned the knob. 'I'm still on vacation.'

'I just thought I'd tell you. Give you something to think about.'

'Swell! I'll turn it over in my mind when I'm stretched out on a beach in Florida.'

'We know who killed him.'

I let the knob slip through my fingers and tried to sound casual. 'Anybody I know?'

'Yes, you and eight million others. His name is Lee Deamer. He's running for State Senator next term.'

My breath whistled through my teeth. Lee Deamer, the people's choice. The guy who was scheduled to sweep the state clean. The guy who was kicking the politicians all over the joint. 'He's pretty big,' I said.

'Very.'

'Too big to touch?'

His eyes jumped to mine. 'Nobody is that big, Mike. Not even Deamer.'

'Then why don't you grab him?'

22

'Because he didn't do it.'

'What a pretty circle *that* is. I had you figured for a brain, Pat. He killed a guy and he didn't do it. That's great logic, especially when it comes from you.'

A slow grin started at the corner of his eyes. 'When you're on vacation you can think it over, Mike. I'll wrap it up for you, just once. A dead man is found. He has one of these cards in his hand. Three people positively identified the killer. Each one saw him under favourable conditions and were able to give a complete description and identification. They came to the police with the story and we were lucky enough to hush it up.

'Lee Deamer was identified as the killer. He was described right to the scar on his nose, his picture was snapped up the second it was shown and he was identified in person. It's the most open-and-shut case you ever saw, yet we can't touch him because when he was supposed to be pulling a murder he was a mile away talking to a group of prominent citizens. I happened to be among those present.'

I kicked the door closed with my foot and stood there. 'Hot damn.'

'Too hot to handle. Now you know why the D.A. was in such a foul mood.'

'Yeah,' I agreed. 'But it shouldn't be too tough for you, Pat. There's only four things that could have happened.'

'Tell me. See if it's what I'm thinking.'

'Sure, kid. One: twins. Two: a killer disguised as Deamer. Three: a deliberate frame-up with witnesses paid to make the wrong identification. Four: it was Deamer after all.'

'Which do you like, Mike?'

I laughed at his solemn tone. 'Beats me, I'm on vacation.' I found the knob and pulled the door open. 'See you when I get back.'

'Sure thing, Mike.' His eyes narrowed to slits. 'If you run across any more cards, tell me about them, will you?'

'Yeah, anything else?'

'Just that one question. Where did you get them?'

'I killed a guy and took it off his dead body.'

Pat was swearing softly to himself when I left. Just as the elevator door closed he must have begun to believe me because I heard his door open and he shouted, 'Mike! . . . Damn it, Mike!'

I called the *Globe* office from a hash house down the street. When I asked the switchboard operator if Marty Kooperman had called in yet she plugged into a couple of circuits, asked around and told me he was just about to go to lunch. I passed the word for him to meet me in the lobby if he wanted a free chow and hung up. I wasn't in a hurry. I never knew a reporter yet who would pass up a meal he wasn't paying for.

Marty was there straddling a chair backwards, trying to keep his eyes on two blondes and a luscious redhead who was apparently waiting for someone else. When I tapped him on the shoulder he scowled and whispered, 'Hell, I almost had that redhead nailed. Go away.'

'Come on, I'll buy you another one,' I said.

'I like this one.'

The city editor came out of the elevator, said hello to the redhead and they went out together. Marty shrugged. 'Okay, let's eat. A lousy political reporter doesn't stand a chance against that.'

One of the blondes looked at me and smiled. I winked at her and she winked back. Marty was so disgusted he spat on the polished floor. Some day he'll learn that all you have to do is ask. They'll tell you.

He tried to steer me into a hangout around the corner, but I nixed the idea and kept going up the street to a little bar that put out a good meal without any background noise. When we had a table between us and the orders on the fire, Marty flipped me a cigarette and the angle of his eyebrows told me he was waiting.

'How much about politics do you know, Marty?'

He shook the match out. 'More than I can write about.'

'Know anything about Lee Deamer?'

His eyebrows came down and he leaned on his elbows. 'You're an investigator, Mike. You're the lad with a gun under his coat. Who wants to know about Deamer?'

'Me.'

'What for?' His hand was itching to go for the pad and pencil in his pocket.

'Because of something that's no good for a story,' I said. 'What do you know about him?'

'Hell, there's nothing wrong with him. The guy is going to be the next senator from this state. He packs a big punch and everybody likes him including the opposition. He's strictly a maximum of statesman and a minimum of politician. Deamer has the cleanest record of anybody, probably because he has never been mixed up in politics too much. He is independently wealthy and out of reach as far as bribery goes. He has no use for chisellers or the spoils system, so most of the sharp boys are against him.'

'Are you against him, Marty?'

'Not me, feller. I'm a Deamer man through and through. He's what we need these days. Where do you stand?'

'I haven't voted since they dissolved the Whig party.'

'Fine citizen you are.'

'Yeah.'

'Then why the sudden curiosity?'

'Suppose I sort of hinted to you . . . strictly off the record . . . that somebody was after Deamer. Would you give me a hand? It may be another of those things you'll never get to write about.'

Marty balled his hands into fists and rubbed his knuckles together. His face wasn't nice to look at. 'You're damn right, I'll help. I'm just another little guy who's sick of being booted around the block by the bastards that get themselves elected to public office and use that office to push their own wild ideas and line their own pockets. When a good thing comes along those stinking pigs go all out to smear it. Well, not if I can help it, and not if about nine-tenths of the people in this burg can help it either. What do you need, kid?'

25

'Not much. Just a history on Deamer. All his background from as far back as you can go. Bring it right up to date. Pictures, too, if you have any.'

'I have folders of the stuff.'

'Good,' I said. Our lunch came up then and we dug into it. Throughout the meal Marty would alternately frown at his plate then glance up at me. I ate and kept my mouth shut. He could come to his own decision. He reached it over the apple pie he had for dessert. I saw his face relax and he let out a satisfied grunt.

'Do you want the stuff now?'

'Any time will do. Stick it in an envelope and send it to my office. I'm not in a hurry.'

'Okay!' He eyed me carefully. 'Can you let me in on the secret?'

I shook my head. 'I would if I could, pal. I don't know what the score is yet myself.'

'Suppose I keep my ear to the ground. Anything likely to crop up that you could use?'

'I doubt it. Let's say that Deamer is a secondary consideration to what I actually want. Knowing something about him might help both of us.'

'I see.' He struck a match under the table and held it to a cigarette. 'Mike, if there is a news angle, will you let me in on it?'

'I'd be glad to.'

'I'm not talking about publishable news.'

'No?'

Marty looked through the smoke at me, his eyes bright. 'In every man's past there's some dirt. It can be dirt that belongs to the past and not to the present. But it can be dirty enough to use to smear a person, smear him so bad that he'll have to retreat from the public gaze. You aren't tied up in politics like I am so you haven't got any idea how really rotten it is. Everybody is out for himself and to hell with the public. Oh, sure, the public has its big heroes, but they do things just to make the people think

26

of them as heroes. Just look what happens whenever Congress or some other organization uncovers some of the filthy tactics behind government . . . the next day or two the boys upstairs release some big news item they've been keeping in reserve and it sweeps the dirt right off the front page and out of your mind.

'Deamer's straight. Because he's straight he's a target. Everybody is after his hide except the people. Don't think it hasn't been tried. I've come across it and so have the others, but we went to the trouble of going down a little deeper than we were expected to and we came across the source of the so-called 'facts'. Because it was stuff that was supposed to come to light during any normal compilation of a man's background the only way it could reach the public without being suspected of smear tactics by the opposition was through the newspapers.

'Well, by tacit agreement we suppressed the stuff. In one way we're targets, too, because the big boys with the strings know how we feel. Lee Deamer's going to be in there, Mike. He's going to raise all kinds of hell with the corruption we have in our government. He'll smoke out the rats that live off the public and give this country back some of the strength that it had before we were undermined by a lot of pretty talk and pretty faces.

'That's why I want to get the story from you . . . if there is one. I want to hold a conference with the others who feel like I do and come to an honest conclusion. Hell, I don't know why I've become so damn public-spirited. Maybe it's just that I'm tired of taking all the crap that's handed out.'

I put a light to my butt and said, 'Has there been anything lately on the guy?'

'No. Not for a month, anyway. They're waiting until he gets done stumping the state before they pick him apart.'

Pat was right then. The police had kept it quiet, not because they were part of the movement of righteousness, but because they must have suspected a smear job. Deamer couldn't have been in two places at once by any means.

'Okay, Marty! I'll get in touch with you if anything lousy comes up. Do me a favour and keep my name out of any conversation, though, will you?'

'Of course. By the way, that judge handed you a dirty one the other day.'

'What the hell, he could be right, you know.'

'Sure he could, it's a matter of opinion. He's just a stickler for the letter of the law, the exact science of words. He's the guy that let a jerk off on a smoking-in-the-subway charge. The sign said NO SMOKING ALLOWED, so he claimed it allowed you not to smoke, but didn't say anything about not smoking. Don't give him another thought.'

I took a bill from my pocket and handed it to the waiter with a wave that meant to forget the change. Marty looked at his watch and said he had to get back, so we shook hands and left.

The afternoon papers were out and the headlines had to do with the Garden fight the night before. One of the kids was still out like a light. His manager was being indicted for letting him go into the ring with a brain injury.

There wasn't a word about any bodies being found in the river. I threw the paper in a waste barrel and got in my car.

I didn't feel so good. I wasn't sick, but I didn't feel so good. I drove to a parking lot, shoved the car into a corner and took a cab to Times Square and went to a horror movie. The lead feature had an actor with a split personality. One was a man, the other was an ape. When he was an ape he killed people and when he was a man he regretted it. I could imagine how he felt. When I stood it as long as I could I got up and went to a bar.

At five o'clock the evening editions had come out. This time the headlines were a little different. They had found one of the bodies.

Fat boy had been spotted by a ferryboat full of people and the police launch had dragged him out of the drink. He had no identification and no fingerprints. There was a sketch of what he might have looked like before the bullet got him smack in the kisser.

The police attributed it to a gang killing.

Now I was a one-man gang. Great. Just fine. Mike Hammer, Inc. A gang!

CHAPTER THREE

THE RAIN. The damned never-ending rain! It turned Manhattan into a city of reflections, a city you saw twice no matter where you looked. It was a slow, easy rain that took a while to collect on your hat brim before it cascaded down in front of your face. The streets had an oily shine that brought the rain-walkers out, people who went native whenever the sky cried and tore off their hats to let the tears drip through their hair.

I buttoned my coat under my neck and turned the collar up around my ears. It was good walking, but not when you were soaking wet. I took it easy and let the crowd sift past me, everybody in a hurry to get nowhere and wait. I was going south on Broadway, stopping to look in the windows of the closed stores, not too conscious of where my feet were leading me. I passed Thirty-fourth still going south, walked into the Twenties with a stop for a sandwich and coffee, then kept my course until I reached the Square.

That was where my feet led me. Union Square. Green cards and pinched-faced guys arguing desperately in the middle of little groups. Green cards and people listening to the guys. What the hell could they say that was important enough to keep anybody standing in the rain? I grinned down at my feet because they had the sense that should have been in my head. They wanted to know about the kind of people who carried green cards, the kind of people who would listen to guys who carried green cards.

Or girls.

I ambled across the walk into the yellow glare of the lights. There were no soapboxes here, just those little knots of people trying to talk at once and being shouted down by the one in the middle.

A cop went by swinging his night stick. Whenever he passed a group he automatically got a grip on the thing and looked over hopefully.

I heard some of the remarks when he passed. They weren't nice.

Coming toward me a guy who looked like a girl and a girl who looked like a guy altered their course to join one group. The girl got right into things and the guy squealed with pleasure whenever she said something clever.

Maybe there were ten groups, maybe fifteen. If it hadn't been raining there might have been more. Nobody talked about the same thing. Occasionally someone would drop out of one crowd and drift over to another.

But they all had something in common. The same thing you find in a slaughterhouse. The lump of vomit in the centre of each crowd was a Judas sheep trying to lead the rest to the axe. Then they'd go back and get more. The sheep were asking for it too. They were a seedy bunch in shapeless clothes, heavy with the smell of the rot they had asked for and gotten. They had a jackal look of discontent and cowardice, a hungry look that said you kill while we loot, then all will be well with the world.

Yeah.

Not all of them were like that, though. Here and there in the crowd was a pin-striped business suit and homburg. An expensive mink was flanked by a girl in a shabby grey-cloth job and a guy in a hand-me-down suit with his hands stuck in the pockets.

Just for the hell of it I hung on the edge of the circle and listened. A few latecomers closed in behind me and I had to stand there and hear just why anybody that fought the war was a simple-minded fool, why anybody who tolerated the foreign policy of this country was a Fascist, why anybody who didn't devote his soul and money to the enlightenment of the masses was a traitor to the people.

The goddamn fools who listened agreed with him, too. I was ready to reach out and pluck his head off his shoulders when one of the guys behind me stood on his toes and said, 'Why don't you get the hell out of this country if you don't like it?' The guy was a soldier.

I said, 'Attaboy, buddy!' but it got lost in the rumble from the crowd and the screech the guy let out. The soldier swore back at him and tried to push through the crowd to get at the guy, only two guys in trench coats blocked him.

Lovely, lovely, it was just what I wanted! The soldier went to shove the two guys apart and one gave him an elbow. I was just going to plant a beauty behind his ear when the cop stepped in. He was a good cop, that one. He didn't lift the night stick above his waist. He held it like a lance and when it hit it went in deep right where it took all the sound out of your body. I saw two punks fold up in the middle and one of the boys in the raincoats let out a gasp. The other one stepped back and swore.

The cop said, 'Better move on, soldier.'

'Ah, I'd like to take that pansy apart. Did you hear what he said?'

'I hear 'em every night, feller,' the cop told him. 'They got bats in their heads. Come on, it's better to let 'em talk.'

'Not when they say those things!'

The cop grinned patiently. 'They gotta right to say 'em. You don't *have* to listen, you know.'

'I don't give a hoot. They haven't got a right to say those things. Hell, the big mouth probably was too yeller to fight a war and too lazy to take a job. I oughta slam 'im one.'

'Uh-huh!' The cop steered him out of the crowd. I heard him say, 'That's just what they want. It makes heroes of 'em when the papers get it. We still got ways of taking care of 'em, don't worry. Every night this happens and I get in a few licks.'

I started grinning and went back to listening. One boy in a trench coat was swearing under his breath. The other was holding on to him. I shifted a little to the side so I could see what I thought I had seen the first time. When the one turned around again I knew I was right the first time.

Both of them were wearing guns under their arms.

Green cards, loud-mouthed bastards, sheep, now guns.

It came together like a dealer sweeping in the cards for shuffling. The game was getting rough. But guns, why guns? This wasn't a fighting game. Who the devil was worth killing in this motley crowd? Why guns here when there was a chance of getting picked up with them?

I pulled back out of the crowd and crossed the walk into the shadows to a bench. A guy sat on the other end of it with a paper over his face, snoring. Fifteen minutes later the rain quit playing around and one by one the crowd pulled away until only a handful was left around the nucleus. For guys who were trying to intimidate the world they certainly were afraid of a little water. All of a sudden the skies opened up and let loose with everything in sight. The guy on the end of the bench jumped up, fighting the paper that wrapped itself around his face. He made a few drunken, animal noises, swallowed hard when he saw me watching him and scurried away into the night.

I had to sit through another five minutes of it before I got up. The two men in the trench coats waited until the loose-jointed guy in the black overcoat had a fifty-foot start, then they turned around and followed him. That gave them a good reason for the rods under their arms.

Bodyguards.

Maybe it was the rain that made my guts churn. Maybe it was those words beating against my head, telling me that I was only scum. Maybe it was just me, but suddenly I wanted to grab the guy in the overcoat and slam his teeth down his throat and wait to see what his two boys would do. I'd like to catch them reaching for a gun! I'd like them to move their hands just one inch, then I'd show them what practice could do when it came to snagging a big, fat gun out of a shoulder sling! So I was a sucker for fighting a war. I was a sap for liking my country. I was a jerk for not thinking them a superior breed of lice!

The cop with the round Irish face should have used a knife in their bellies instead of the butt end of a night stick.

I waited until they were blurs in the rain then tagged along in the rear. They were a fine pair, those two, a brace of dillies. I tailed them into the subway and out again in Brooklyn. I was with them when they walked down Coney Island Avenue and beside them when they turned into a store off the avenue and they never knew I was there.

Down at the corner I crossed the street and came back up the other side. One of the boys was still in the doorway playing watchdog. I wanted to know how smart the people were who wanted to run the world. I found out. I cut across the street and walked right up to the guy without making any fuss about it. He gave me a queer look and drew his eyebrows together in a frown, trying to remember where he had seen me before. He was fumbling for words when I pulled out the green card.

He didn't try to match them up. One look was enough and he waved his head at the door. I turned the knob and went in. I'd have to remember to tell Pat about that. They weren't being so careful at all.

When I closed the door I changed my mind. The light went on, just like a refrigerator, and I saw the blackout shades on the windows and door, the felt padding beneath the sill so no light could escape under the door. And the switch. A home-made affair on the side of the door that cut the light when the door opened and threw it back on again when it closed.

The girl at the desk glanced up impatiently and held out her hand for the card. She matched them. She matched them damn carefully, too, and when she handed them back she had sucked hollows into her cheeks trying to think of the right thing to say.

'You're from . . .?'

'Philly,' I supplied. I hoped it was a good answer. It was. She nodded and turned her head toward a door in the back of the anteroom. I had to wait for her to push a button before it opened under my hand.

There were twenty-seven people in the other room. I counted them. They were all very busy. Some of them were at desks clipping things from newspapers and magazines. One guy in a corner was taking pictures of the things they clipped and it came out on microfilm. There was a little group around a map of the city over against one wall, talking too earnestly and too low for me to catch what they were saying.

I saw the other boy in the trench coat. He still had it on and he was sticking close with the guy in the overcoat. Evidently the fellow was some kind of a wheel, checking on activities here and there, offering sharp criticism or curt words of approval.

When I had been there a full five minutes people began to notice me. At first it was just a casual glance from odd spots, then long searching looks that disappeared whenever I looked back. The man in the overcoat licked his lips nervously and smiled in my direction.

I sat down at a table and crossed my legs, a smoke dangling from my mouth. I smoked and I watched, trying to make some sense out of it. Some of them even looked like Commies, the cartoon kind. There were sharp eyes that darted from side to side, too-wise women dazzled by some meagre sense of responsibility, smirking students who wore their hair long, tucked behind their heads. A few more came in while I sat and devoted themselves to some unfinished task. But sooner or later their eyes came to mine and shifted away hurriedly when I looked at them.

It became a game, that watching business. I found that if I stared at some punk who was taking his time about doing things he became overly ambitious all of a sudden. I went from one to the other and came at last to the guy in the overcoat.

He was the head man here, no doubt about it. His word was law. At twenty minutes past eleven he started his rounds of the room, pausing here and there to lay a mimeographed sheet on a desk, stopping to emphasize some obscure point.

Finally he had to pass me and for a split second he hesitated, simpered and went on. I got it and played the game to the hilt. I walked to a desk and picked up one of the sheets and read it as I sat on the edge of the desk. The scraggly blonde at the desk couldn't keep her hands from shaking.

I got the picture then. I was reading the orders for the week; I was in on the pipeline from Moscow. It was that easy. I read them all the way through, tossed the sheet down and went back to my chair.

I smiled.

Everybody smiled.

The boy in the trench coat with the gun under his arm came over and said, 'You will like some coffee now?' He had an accent I couldn't place.

I smiled again and followed him to the back of the room. I didn't see the door of the place because it was hidden behind the photography equipment.

It led into a tiny conference room that held a table, six chairs and a coffee urn. When the door closed there were seven of us in the room including two dames. Trench Coat got a tray of cups from the closet and set them on the table. For me it was a fight between grinning and stamping somebody's face in. For an after-office-hours coffee deal it certainly was a high-tension deal.

To keep from grinning I shoved another Lucky in my mouth and stuck a light to it. There they were, everyone with a coffee cup, lined up at the urn. Because I took my time with the smoke I had to join the end of the line, and it was a good thing I did. It gave me time enough to get the pitch.

Everybody had been watching me covertly anyway, saying little and satisfied with me keeping my mouth shut. When they took their coffee black and wandered off to the table the two women made a face at the bitter taste. They didn't like black coffee. They weren't used to black coffee. Yet they took black coffee and kept shooting me those sidewise glances.

How simple can people get? Did they take everybody for dummies like themselves? When I drew my cup from the urn Trench Coat stood right behind me and waited. He was the only one that bothered to breathe and he breathed down my neck.

I took sugar and milk. I took plenty of it. I turned around and lifted my cup in a mock toast and all the jerks started breathing again and the room came to life. The two women went back and got sugar and milk.

The whole play had been a signal setup a kid could have seen through.

Trench Coat smiled happily. 'It is very good you are here, comrade. We cannot be too careful, of course.'

'Of course.' It was the first time I had said anything, but you might have thought I gave the Gettysburg Address. Overcoat came over immediately, his hand reaching out for mine.

'I am Henry Gladow, you know. Certainly you know.' His chuckle was nervous and high-pitched. 'We had been expecting you, but not so quickly. Of course we realize the party works quickly, but this is almost faith-inspiring! You came with incredible speed. Why, only tonight I picked up the telegram from our messenger uptown announcing your arrival. Incredible!'

That was the reason for the bodyguards and the guns. My new chum was receiving party instructions from somebody else. That was why the Trench Coats closed in around the soldier, in case it had been a trap to intercept the message. Real cute, but dumb as hell.

'. . . happy to have you inspect our small base of operation, comrade.' I turned my attention back to him again and listened politely. 'Rarely do we have such an honour. In fact, this is the first time.' He turned to Trench Coat, still smiling. 'This is my, er, travelling companion, Martin Romberg. Very capable man, you know. And my secretary' – he indicated a girl in thick-lensed glasses who was just out of her teens – 'Martha Camisole.'

He went around the room introducing each one and with every nod I handed out I got back a smile that tried hard to be nice but was too scared to do a good job of it.

We finished the coffee, had another and a smoke before Gladow looked at his watch. I could see damn well he had another question coming up and I let him take his time about asking it. He said, 'Er, you are quite satisfied with the operation at this point, comrade? Would you care to inspect our records and documents?'

My scowl was of surprise, but he didn't know that. His eyebrows went up and he smiled craftily. 'No, comrade, not written documents. Here, in the phase, we have experts who commit the documents . . .' he tapped the side of his head, 'here.'

'Smart,' I grunted. 'What happens if they talk?'

He tried to seem overcome with the preposterous. 'Very funny, comrade. Quite, er . . . yes. Who is there to make them talk? That is where we have the advantage. In this country force is never used. The so-called third degree has been swept out. Even a truthful statement loses its truth if coercion is even hinted at. The fools, the despicable fools haven't the intelligence to govern a country properly! When the Party is in power things will be different, eh, comrade?'

'Much, much different,' I said.

Gladow nodded, pleased. 'You, er, care to see anything of special importance, comrade?' His voice had a grey tone.

'No, nothing special. Just checking around.' I dragged on the butt and blew a cloud of smoke in his face. He didn't seem to mind it.

'Then in your report you will state that everything *is* satisfactory here?'

'Sure, don't give it another thought.'

There was more sighing. Some of the fear went out of their eyes. The Camisole kid giggled nervously. 'Then may I say again that we have been deeply honoured by your visit, comrade,' Gladow said. 'Since the sudden, untimely death of our former, er, compatriot, we have been more or less uneasy. You understand these things of course. It was gratifying to see that he was not identified with the Party in any way. Even the newspapers are stupid in this country.'

I had to let my eyes sink to the floor or he would have seen the hate in them. I was an inch away from killing the bastard and he didn't know it. I turned my hand over to look at the time and saw that it was close to midnight. I'd been in the pigsty long enough. I set the empty cup down on the table and walked to the door. The crumbs couldn't even make good coffee.

All but two of the lesser satellites had left, their desks clear of all papers. The guy on the photography rig was stuffing the microfilm in a small file case while a girl burned papers in a metal waste-basket. I didn't stop to see who got the film. There was enough of it that was so plain that I didn't need any pictures drawn for me.

Gladow was hoping I'd shake hands, but he got fooled. I kept them both in my pockets because I didn't like to handle snakes, not of their variety.

The outside door slammed shut and I heard some hurried conversation and the girl at the desk say, 'Go right in.' I was standing by the inside door when she opened it.

I had to make sure I was in the right place by taking a quick look around me. This was supposed to be a Commie setup, a joint for the masses only, not a club for babes in mink coats with hats to match. She was one of those tall, willowy blondes who reached thirty with each year an improvement.

She was almost beautiful, with a body that could take your mind off beauty and put it on other things. She smiled at Gladow as soon as she saw him and gave him her hand.

His voice took on a purr when he kissed it. 'Miss Brighton, it is always a pleasure to see you.' He straightened up, still smiling. 'I didn't expect you to come at this hour.'

'I didn't expect you to be here either, Henry. I decided to take the chance anyway. I brought the donations.' Her voice was like rubbing your hand on satin. She pulled an envelope out of her pocketbook and handed it to Gladow unconcernedly. Then, for the first time, she saw me.

She squinted her eyes, trying to place me.

I grinned at her. I like to grin at a million bucks.

Ethel Brighton grinned back.

Henry Gladow coughed politely and turned to me. 'Miss Brighton is one of our most earnest comrades. She is chiefly responsible for some of our most substantial contributions.'

He made no attempt to introduce me. Apparently nobody seemed to care. Especially Ethel Brighton. A quick look flashed

40

between them that brought the scowl back to her face for a brief moment. A shadow on the wall that came from one of the Trench Coats behind me was making furious gestures.

I started to get the willies. It was the damnedest thing I had ever seen. Everybody was acting like at a fraternity initiation and for some reason I was the man of the moment. I took it as long as I could. I said, 'I'm going uptown. If you're going back you can come along.'

For a dame who had her picture in most of the Sunday supplements every few weeks, she lost her air of sophistication in a hurry. Her cheeks seemed to sink in and she looked to Gladow for approval. Evidently he gave it, for she nodded and said, 'My car . . . it's right outside.'

I didn't bother to leave any goodnights behind me. I went through the receptionist's cubicle and yanked the door open. When Ethel Brighton was out I slammed it shut. Behind me the place was as dark as the vacant hole it was supposed to be.

Without waiting to be asked I slid behind the wheel and held out my hand for the keys. She dropped them in my palm and fidgeted against the cushions. That car . . . it was a beauty. In the daylight it would have been a maroon convertible, but under the street lights it was a mass of mirrors with the chrome reflecting every bulb in the sky.

Ethel asked, 'Are you from . . . New York?'

'Nope. Philly,' I lied.

For some reason I was making her mighty nervous. It wasn't my driving because I was holding it to a steady thirty to keep inside the green lights. I tried another grin. This time she smiled back and worried the fingers of her gloves.

I couldn't get over it, Ethel Brighton a Commie! Her old man would tan her hide no matter how old she was if he ever heard about it. But what the hell, she wasn't the only one with plenty of rocks who got hung up on the red flag. I said, 'It hasn't been too easy for you to keep all this under your hat, has it?'

Her hands stopped working the glove. 'N-no. I've managed, though.'

'Yeah. You've done a good job.'

'Thank you.'

'Oh, no thanks at all, kid. For people with intelligence it's easy. When you're, er, getting these donations, don't people sorta wonder where it's going?'

She scowled again, puzzled. 'I don't think so. I thought that was explained quite fully in my report.'

'It was, it was. Don't get me wrong. We have to keep track of things, you know. Situations change.' It was a lot of crap to me, but it must have made sense to her way of thinking.

'Usually they're much too busy to listen to my explanations, and anyway, they can deduct the amounts from their income tax.'

'They ought to be pretty easy to touch, then.'

This time she smiled a little. 'They are. They think it's for charity.'

'Uh-huh! Suppose your father finds out what you've been doing?'

The way she recoiled you'd think I'd smacked her. 'Oh . . . please, you wouldn't!'

'Take it easy, kid. I'm only supposing.'

Even in the dull light of the dash I could see how pale she was. 'Daddy would . . . never forgive me. I think . . . he'd send me some place. He'd disinherit me completely.' She shuddered, her hands going back to the glove again. 'He'll never know. When he does it will be too late!'

'Your emotions are showing through, kid.'

'So would yours if . . . oh . . . oh, I didn't mean . . .' Her expression made a sudden switch from rage to that of fear. It wasn't a nice fear, it was more like that of the girl on the bridge.

I looked over slowly, an angle creeping into the corner of my mind. 'I'm not going to bite. Maybe you can't say things back there in front of the others, but sometimes I'm not like them. I can understand problems. I have plenty of my own.'

'But you . . . you're . . .'

'I'm what?'

'You know.' She bit into her lip, looking at me obliquely. I nodded as if I did.

'Will you be here long?'

'Maybe.' I shrugged. 'Why?'

The fear came back. 'Really, I wasn't asking pointed questions. Honest I wasn't. I just meant . . . I meant with the . . . other being killed and all, well . . .'

Damn it, she let her sentence trail off as if I was supposed to know everything that went on. What the hell did they take me for anyway? It was the same thing all night!

'I'll be here,' I said.

We went over the bridge and picked a path through the late traffic in Manhattan. I went north to Times Square and pulled into the kerb. 'This is as far as I go, sugar. Thanks for the ride. I'll probably be seeing you again.'

Her eyes went wide again. Brother, she could sure do things with those eyes. She gasped, 'Seeing me?'

'Sure, why not?'

'But . . . you aren't . . . I never supposed . . .'

'That I might have a personal interest in a woman?' I finished.

'Well, yes.'

'I like women, sugar. I always have and always will.'

For the first time she smiled a smile she meant. She said, 'You aren't a bit like I thought you'd be. Really. I like you. The other . . . agent . . . he was so cold that he scared me.'

'I don't scare you?'

'You could . . . but you don't.'

I opened the door. 'Good night, Ethel.'

'Good night.' She slid over under the wheel and gunned the motor. I got one last quick smile before she pulled away.

What the hell! That's all I could think of. What the hell! All right, just what the hell was going on? I walked right into a nest of Commies because I flashed a green card and they didn't say a word, not one word. They played damn fool kids' games with me that any jerk could have caught, and bowed and scraped like I was king.

Not once did anyone ask my name.

Read the papers today. See what it says about the Red Menace. See how they play up their sneaking, conniving ways. They're supposed

43

to be clever, bright as hell. They were dumb as horse manure as far as I was concerned. They were a pack of bugs thinking they could outsmart a world. Great. That coffee-urn trick was just great.

I walked down the street to a restaurant that was still open and ordered a plate of ham and eggs.

It was almost two o'clock when I got home. The rain had stopped long ago, but it was still up there, hanging low around the buildings, reluctant to let the city alone. I walked up to my apartment and shoved the key in the lock. My mind kept going back to Gladow, trying to make sense of his words, trying to fit them into a puzzle that had no other parts.

I could remember his speaking about somebody's untimely death. Evidently I was the substitute sent on in his place. But whose death? That sketch in the paper was a lousy one. Fat boy didn't look a bit like that sketch. All right then, who? There was only one other guy with a green card who was dead, the guy Lee Deamer was supposed to have killed.

Him. He's the one, I thought. I was his replacement. But what was I supposed to be?

There was just too much to think about; I was too tired to put my mind to it. You don't kill a fat man and see a girl die because of the look on your face and get involved with a Commie organization all in two days without feeling your mind sink into a soggy ooze that drew it down deeper and deeper until it relaxed of its own accord and you were asleep.

I sat slumped in the chair; the cigarette that had dropped from my fingers had burned a path through the rug at right angles with another. The bell shrilled and shrilled until I thought it would never stop. My arm going out to the phone was an involuntary movement, my voice just happened to be there.

I said hello.

It was Pat and he had to yell at me a half-dozen times before I snapped out of it. I grunted an answer and he said, 'Too late for you, Mike?'

'It's four o'clock in the morning. Are you just getting up or just going to bed?'

'Neither. I've been working.'

'At this hour?'

'Since six this evening. How's the vacation?'

'I called it off.'

'Really, now! Just couldn't bear to leave the city, could you? By the way, did you find any more green cards with the ends snipped off?'

The palms of my hands got wet all of a sudden. 'No.'

'Are you interested in them at all?'

'Cut the comedy, Pat. What're you driving at? It's too damn late for riddles.'

'Get over here, Mike,' his voice was terse. 'My apartment and make it as fast as you can.'

I came awake all at once, shaking the fatigue from my brain. 'Okay, Pat,' I said, 'give me fifteen minutes.' I hung up and slipped into my coat.

It was easier to grab a cab than wheel my car out of the garage. I shook the cabbie's shoulder and gave him Pat's address, then settled back against the cushions while we tore across town. We made it with about ten seconds to spare and I gave the cabbie a fin for his trouble.

I looked up at the sky before I went in. The clouds had broken up and let the stars come through. Maybe tomorrow will be nice, I thought. Maybe it will be a nice normal day without all the filth being raked to the top. Maybe. I pushed Pat's bell and the door buzzed almost immediately.

He was waiting outside his apartment when I got off the elevator. 'You made it fast, Mike.'

'You said to, didn't you?'

'Come on in.'

Pat had highballs in a shaker and three glasses on the coffee table. Only one had been used so far. 'Expecting company?' I asked him.

'Big company, Mike. Sit down and pour yourself a drink.'

I shucked my coat and hat and stuck a Lucky in my mouth. Pat wasn't acting right. You don't go around entertaining anybody at this hour, not even your best friends. Something had etched lines into his face and put a smudge of darkness under each eye. He looked tight as a drumhead. I sat there with a drink in my hand watching Pat trying to figure out what to say.

It came halfway through my drink. 'You were right the first time,' he said.

I put the glass down and stared at him. 'Do it over. I don't get it.'

'Twins.'

'What?'

'Twins,' Pat repeated. 'Lee Deamer had a twin brother.' He stood there swirling the mixture around in his glass.

'Why tell me? I'm not in the picture.'

Pat had his back to me, staring at nothing. I could barely hear his voice. 'Don't ask me that, Mike. I don't know why I'm telling you when it's official business, but I am. In one way we're both alike. We're cops. Sometimes I find myself waiting to know what you'd do in a situation before I do it myself. Screwy, isn't it?'

'Pretty screwy.'

'I told you once before that you have a feeling for things that I haven't got. You don't have a hundred bosses and a lot of sidelines to mess you up once you get started on a case. You're a ruthless bastard and sometimes it helps.'

'So?'

'So now I find myself in one of those situations. I'm a practical cop with a lot of training and experience, but I'm in something that has a personal meaning to me, too, and I'm afraid of tackling it alone.'

'You don't want advice from me, chum. I'm mud, and whatever I touch gets smeared with it. I don't mind dirtying myself, but I don't want any of it to rub off on to you.'

'It won't, don't worry. That's why you're here now. You think I was taken in by that vacation line? Hell! You have another bug up your behind. It has to do with those green cards and don't try to talk your way out of it.'

He spun around, his face taut. 'Where'd you get them, Mike?'

I ignored the question. 'Tell me, Pat. Tell me the story.'

He threw the drink down and filled the glass again. 'Lee Deamer . . . how much do you know about him?'

'Only that he's the up-and-coming champ. I don't know him personally.'

'I do, Mike. I know the guy and I like him. Goddamn it, Mike, if he gets squeezed out this state, this country will lose one of its greatest assets! We can't afford to have Deamer go under!'

'I've heard that story before, Pat,' I said, 'a political reporter gave it to me in detail.'

Pat reached for a cigarette and laid it in his lips. The tip of the flame from the lighter wavered when he held it up. 'I hope it made an impression. This country is too fine to be kicked around. Deamer is the man to stop it if he can get that far.'

'Politics never interested you much, Mike. You know how it starts in the wards and works itself right up to the nation. I get a chance to see just how dirty and corrupt politics can be. You should put yourself in my shoes for a while and you'd know how I feel. I get word to lay off one thing or another . . . or else. I get word that if I do or don't do a certain thing I'll be handed a fat little present. You'd think people would respect the police, but they don't. They try to use the department to push their own lousy schemes and it happens more often than you'd imagine.'

'And you, Pat, what did you do?' I leaned forward in my chair, waiting.

'I told them to go to hell. They can't touch an honest man until he makes a mistake. Then they hang him for it.'

'Any mistakes yet?'

Two streams of smoke spiralled from his nostrils. 'Not yet, kid. They're waiting though. I'm fed up with the tension. You can feel it in the air, like being inside a storage battery. Call me a reformer if you want to, but I'd love to see a little decency for a change. That's why I'm afraid for Deamer.'

'Yeah, you were telling me about him.'

'Twins. You were right, Mike. Lee Deamer was at that meeting the night he was allegedly seen killing this Charlie Moffit. He was talking to groups around the room. I was there.'

I stamped the butt out on a tray and lit another. 'You mean it was as simple as that . . . Lee Deamer had a twin brother?'

Pat nodded. 'As simple as that.'

'Then why the secrecy? Lee isn't exactly responsible for what his brother does. Even a blast in the papers couldn't smear him for that, could it?'

'No . . . not if that was all there was to it.'

'Then . . .'

Pat slammed the glass down impatiently. 'The brother's name was Oscar Deamer. He was an escaped inmate of a sanitarium where he was undergoing psychiatric treatment. Let that come out and Lee is finished.'

I let out a slow whistle. 'Who else knows about this, Pat?'

'Just you. It was too big. I couldn't keep it to myself. Lee called me tonight and said he wanted to see me. We met in a bar and he told me the story. Oscar arrived in town and told Lee that he was going to settle things for him. He demanded money to keep quiet. Lee thinks that Oscar deliberately killed this Charlie Moffit hoping to be identified as Lee, knowing that Lee wouldn't dare reveal that he had a lunatic for a brother.'

'So Lee wouldn't pay off and he got the treatment.'

'It looks that way.'

'Hell, this Oscar could have figured Lee would have an alibi and couldn't be touched. It was just a sample, something to get him entangled. That doesn't make him much of a loony if he can think like that.'

'Anybody who can kill like that is crazy, Mike.'

'Yeah, I guess so.'

Before he could answer me, the bell rang, two short burps and Pat got up to push the buzzer. 'Lee?' I asked.

Pat nodded. 'He wanted more time to think about it. I told him I'd be at home. It has him nearly crazy himself.' He went to the door and stood there holding it open as he had done for me. It was so still that I heard the elevator humming in its well, the sound of the doors opening and the slow, heavy feet of a person carrying a too-heavy weight.

I stood up myself and shook hands with Lee Deamer. He wasn't big like I had expected. There was nothing outstanding about his appearance except that he looked like a schoolteacher, a very tired, middle-aged Mr Chips.

Pat said, 'This is Mike Hammer, Lee. He's a very special, capable friend of mine.'

His handshake was firm, but his eyes were too tired to take me in all at once. He said to Pat very softly, 'He knows?'

'He knows, Lee. He can be trusted.'

I had a good look at warm grey eyes then. His hand tightened just a little around mine. 'It's nice to find people that can be trusted.'

I grinned my thanks and Pat pulled up a chair. Lee Deamer took the drink Pat offered him and settled back against the cushions, rubbing his hand across his face. He took a sip of the highball, then pulled a cigar from his pocket and pared the end off with a tiny knife on his watch chain.

'Oscar hasn't called back,' he said dully. 'I don't know what to do.' He looked first at Pat then to me. 'Are you a policeman, Mr Hammer?'

'Just call me Mike. No, I'm not a city cop. I have a Private Operator's ticket and that's all.'

'Mike's been in on a lot of big stuff, Lee,' Pat cut in. 'He knows his way around.'

'I see.' He was talking to me again. 'I suppose Pat told you that so far this whole affair has been kept quiet?' I nodded and he went on, 'I hope it can stay that way, though if it must come out, it must. I'm leaving it all to the discretion of Pat here. I – well, I'm really stumped. So much has happened in so short a time I hardly know where I'm at.'

'Can I hear it from the beginning?' I asked.

Lee Deamer bobbed his head slowly. 'Oscar and I were born in Townley, Nebraska. Although we were twins, we were worlds apart. In my younger days I thought it was because we were just separate personalities, but the truth was . . . Oscar was demented. He was a sadistic sort of person, very sly and cunning. He hated me. Yes, he hated me, his own brother. In fact, Oscar seemed to hate everyone. He was in trouble from the moment he ran off from home until he came back, then he found more trouble in our own state. He was finally committed to an institution.

'Shortly after Oscar was committed I left Nebraska and settled in New York. I did rather well in business and became active in politics. Oscar was more or less forgotten. Then I learned that he had escaped from the institution. I never heard from him again until he called me last week.'

'That's all?'

'What else can there be, Mike? Oscar probably read about me in the papers and trailed me here. He knew what it would mean if I was known to have a brother who wasn't quite . . . well, normal. He made a demand for money and told me he'd have it one way or another.'

Pat reached for the shaker and filled the glasses again. I held mine out and our eyes met. He answered my question before I could ask it. 'Lee was afraid to mention Oscar, even when he was identified as the killer of Moffit. You can understand why, can't you?'

'Now I can,' I said.

'Even the fact that Lee *was* identified, although wrongly, would have made good copy. However, the cop on the beat brought the witnesses in before they could speak to the papers and the whole thing was such an obvious mistake that nobody dared take the chance of making it public.'

'Where are the witnesses now?'

'We have them under surveillance. They've been instructed to keep quiet about it. We checked into their backgrounds and found that all of them were upright citizens, plain, ordinary people who were as befuddled as we were about the whole thing. Fortunately, we were able to secure their promise of silence by proving to them where Lee was that night. They don't understand it, but they were willing to go along with us in the cause of justice.'

I grunted and pulled on the cigarette. 'I don't like it.'

Both of them looked at me quickly. 'Hell, Pat, you ought to smell the angle as well as I do.'

'You tell me, Mike.'

'Oscar served his warning,' I said. 'He'll make another stab at it. You can trap him easily enough and you know it.'

'That's right. It leaves one thing wide open, too.'

'Sure it does. You'll have another Lee Deamer in print and pictures, this one up for a murder rap which he will skip because he's nuts.' Lee winced at the word but kept still.

'That's why I wanted you here,' Pat told me.

'Fine. What good am I?'

The ice rattled against the side of his glass. Pat tried to keep his voice calm. 'You aren't official, Mike. My mind works with the book. I know what I should do and I can't think of anything else.'

'You mean you want me to tell you that Oscar should be run down and quietly spirited away?'

'That's right.'

'And I'm the boy who could do it?'

'Right again.' He took a long swallow from the glass and set it on the table.

'What happens if it doesn't work out? To you, I mean.'

'I'll be looking for a job for not playing it properly.'

'Gentlemen, gentlemen!' Lee Deamer ran his hand through his hair nervously. 'I – I can't let you do it. I can't let you jeopardize your positions. It isn't fair. The best thing is to let it come to light and let the public decide.'

'Don't be jerky!' I spat out. Lee looked at me, but I wasn't seeing him. I was seeing Marty and Pat, hearing them say the same thing . . . and I was hearing that judge again.

There were two hot spaces where my eyes should have been. 'I'll take care of it,' I said. 'I'll need all the help I can get!' I looked at Pat. He nodded. 'Just one thing, Pat. I'm not doing this because I'm a patriot, see? I'm doing it because I'm curious and because of it I'll be on my toes. I'm curious as hell about something else and not about right and wrong and what the public thinks.'

My teeth were showing through my words and Pat had that look again. 'Why, Mike?'

'Three green cards with the edges cut off, kid. I'm curious as hell about three green cards. There's more to them than you think.'

I said good night and left them sitting there. I could hear the judge laughing at me. It wasn't a nice laugh. It had a nasty sound. Thirteen steps and thirteen loops that made the knot in the rope. Were there thirteen thousand volts in the chair too? Maybe I'd find out the hard way.

CHAPTER FOUR

I SLEPT for two hours before Velda called me. I told her I wouldn't be in for a good long while, and if anything important came up she could call, but unless it was a matter of life or death, either hers or mine, to leave me be.

Nothing came up and I slept once around the clock. It was five minutes to six when my eyes opened by themselves and didn't feel hot any more. While I showered and shaved I stuck a frozen steak under the broiler and ate in my shorts, still damp.

It was a good steak; I was hungry. I wanted to finish it but I never got the time. The phone rang and kept on ringing until I kicked the door shut so I wouldn't hear it. That didn't stop the phone. It went on like that for a full five minutes, demanding that I answer it. I threw down my knife with a curse and walked inside.

'What is it?' I yelled.

'It took you long enough to wake up, damn it!'

'Oh, Pat. I wasn't asleep. What's up this time?'

'It happened like we figured. Oscar made the contact. He called Lee and wants to see him tonight. Lee made an appointment to be at his apartment at eight.'

'Yeah?'

'Lee called me immediately. Look, Mike, we'll have to go this alone, just the three of us. I don't want to trust anybody else.'

The damp on my body seemed to turn to ice. I was cold all over, cold enough to shake just a little. 'Where'll I meet you, Pat?'

'Better make it at my place. Oscar lives over on the East Side.' He rattled off the address and I jotted it down. 'I told Lee to go ahead and keep his appointment. We'll be right behind him. Lee is taking the subway up and we'll pick him up at the kiosk. Got that?'

'I got it. I'll be over in a little while.'

We both stood waiting for the other to hang up. Finally, 'Mike . . .!'

'What?'

'You sure about this?'

'I'm sure.' I set the receiver back in its cradle and stared at it. I was sure, all right, sure to come up with the dirty end of the stick. The dam would open and let the clean water through and they could pick me out of the sewer.

I pulled on my clothes half-heartedly. I thought of the steak in the kitchen and decided I didn't want any more of it. For a while I stood in front of the mirror looking at myself, trying to decide whether or not I should wear the artillery. Habit won and I buckled on the sling after checking the load in the clip. When I buttoned up the coat I took the box from the closet shelf that held the two spare barrels and the extra shells, scooped up a handful of loose .45's and dropped them in my pocket. If I was going to do it I might as well do it right.

Velda had just gotten in when I called her. I said, 'Did you eat yet, kitten?'

'I grabbed a light bite downtown. Why, are you taking me out?'

'Yeah, but not to supper. It's business. I'll be right over. Tell you about it then.'

She said all right, kissed me over the phone and hung up. I stuck my hat on, picked up another deck of Luckies and went downstairs where I whistled for a cab.

I don't know how I looked when she opened the door. She started to smile then dropped it like a hot rivet to catch her lower lip between her teeth. Velda's so tall I didn't have to bend down far to kiss her on the cheek. It was nice standing there real close to her. She was perfume and beauty and all the good things of life.

She said, 'Come into the bedroom, Mike. You can tell me while I'm getting dressed.'

'I can talk from out here.'

Velda turned around, a grin in her eyes. 'You *have* been in a woman's bedroom before, haven't you?'

'Not yours.'

'I'm inviting you in to talk. Just talk.'

I faked a punch at her jaw. 'I'm just afraid of myself, kid. You and a bedroom could be too much. I'm saving you for something special.'

'Will it cost three dollars and can you frame it?'

I laughed for an answer and went in after her. She pointed to a satin-covered boudoir chair and went behind a screen. She came out in a black wool skirt and a white blouse. God, but she was lovely!

When she sat down in front of the vanity table and started to brush her hair I caught her eyes in the mirror. They reflected the trouble that was in mine. 'Now tell me, Mike.'

I told her. I gave her everything Pat gave me and watched her face.

She finished with the brush and put it down. Her hand was shaking. 'They want a lot of you, don't they?'

'Maybe they want too much.' I pulled out a cigarette and lit one. 'Velda, what does this Lee Deamer mean to you?'

This time she wouldn't meet my eyes. She spaced her words carefully. 'He means a lot, Mike. Would you be mad if I said that perhaps they weren't asking too much?'

'No . . . not if you think not. Okay, kid. I'll play the hand out and see what I can do with a kill-crazy maniac. Get your coat on.'

'Mike . . . you haven't told me all of it yet.'

She was at it again, looking through me into my mind. 'I know it.'

'Are you going to?'

'Not now. Maybe later.'

She stood up, a statuesque creature that had no equal, her hair a black frame to her face. 'Mike, you're a bastard. You're in trouble up to your ears and you won't let anybody help you. Why do you always have to play it alone?'

'Because I'm me.'

'And I'm me too, Mike. I *want* to help. Can you understand that?'

'Yes, I understand, but this isn't another case. It's more than that and I don't want to talk about it.'

She came to me then, resting her hands on my shoulders. 'Mike, if you *do* need me . . . ever, will you ask me to help?

'I'll ask you.'

Her mouth was full and ripe, warm with life and sparkling with a delicious wetness. I pulled her in close and tasted the fire that smouldered inside her, felt her body mould itself to mine, eager and excited.

My fingers ran into her hair and pulled her mouth away. 'No more of it, Velda. Not now.'

'Some day, Mike.'

'Some day. Get your coat on.' I shoved her away roughly, reluctant to let her go. She opened the closet and took the jacket that matched the skirt from a hanger and slipped into it. Over her shoulder she slung a shoulder-strap bag, and when it nudged the side of the dresser the gun in it made a dull clunk.

'I'm ready, Mike.'

I pushed the slip of paper with Oscar's address on it into her hand. 'Here's the place where he's holed up. The subway is a half-block away from the place. You go directly there and look the joint over. I don't know why, but there's something about it I don't like. We're going to tag after Lee when he goes in, but I want somebody covering the place while we're there.

'Remember, it's a rough neighbourhood, so be on your toes. We don't want any extra trouble. If you spot anything that doesn't seem to be on the square, walk over to the subway kiosk and meet us. You'll have about a half-hour to look around. Be careful.'

'Don't worry about me.' She pulled on her gloves, a smile playing with her mouth. Hell, I wasn't going to worry about her. That rod in her bag wasn't there for ballast.

I dropped her at the subway and waited on the kerb until a cab cruised by.

*

Pat was standing under the canopy of his apartment building when I got there. He had a cigarette cupped in the palm of his hand and dragged on it nervously. I yelled at him from the taxi and he crossed the street and got in.

It was seven-fifteen.

At ten minutes to eight we paid off the cab and walked the half-block to the kiosk. We were still fifty feet away when Lee Deamer came up. He looked neither to the right nor left, walking straight ahead as if he lived there. Pat nudged me with his elbow and I grunted an acknowledgment.

I waited to see if Velda would show, but there wasn't a sign of her.

Twice Lee stopped to look at house numbers. The third time he paused in front of an old brick building, his head going to the dim light behind the shades in the downstairs room. Briefly, he cast a quick glance behind him, then went up the three steps and disappeared into the shadowy well of the doorway.

Thirty seconds, that's all he got. Both of us were counting under our breaths, hugging the shadows of the building. The street boasted a lone light a hundred yards away, a wan, yellow eye that seemed to search for us with eerie tendrils, determined to pull us into its glare. Somewhere a voice cursed. A baby squealed and stopped abruptly. The street was too damn deserted. It should have been running with kids or something. Maybe the one light scared them off. Maybe they had a better place to hang out than a side street in nowhere.

We hit the thirty count at the same time, but too late. A door slammed above our heads and we could hear feet pounding on boards, diminishing with every step. A voice half sobbed something unintelligible and we flew up those stairs and tugged at a door that wouldn't give. Pat hit it with his shoulder, ramming it open.

Lee was standing in the doorway, hanging on to the sill, his mouth agape. He was pointing down the hall. 'He ran . . . he ran. He looked out the window . . . and he ran!'

Pat muttered, 'Damn . . . we can't let him get away!' I was ahead of him, my hands probing the darkness. I felt the wall give way to the inky blackness that was the night behind an open door and stumbled down the steps.

That was when I heard Velda's voice rise in a tense, 'Mike! . . . MIKE!'

'Over here, Pat. There's a gate in the wall. Get a light!'

Pat swore again, yelling that he had lost it. I didn't wait. I made the gate and picked my way through the litter in the alley that ran behind the buildings. My .45 was in my hand, ready to be used. Velda yelled again and I followed her voice to the end of the alley.

When I came to the street through the two-foot space that separated the buildings I couldn't have found anybody, because the street was a funnel of people running to the subway kiosk. They ran and yelled back over their shoulders and I knew that whatever it was happened down there and I was afraid to look. If anything happened to Velda I'd tear the guts out of some son-of-a-bitch! I'd nail him to a wall and take his skin off him in inch-wide strips!

A coloured fellow in a porter's outfit came up bucking the crowd yelling for someone to get a doctor. That was all I needed. I made a path through that mob pouring through the exit gates onto the station and battled my way up to the front.

Velda was all right. She was perfectly all right and I could quit shaking and let the sweat turn warm again. I shoved the gun back under my arm and walked over to her with a sad attempt of trying to look normal.

The train was almost all the way in the station. Not quite. It had to jam on the brakes too fast to make the marker farther down the platform. The driver and two trainmen were standing in front of the lead car poking at a bloody mess that was sticking out under the wheels. The driver said, 'He's dead as hell. He won't need an ambulance.'

Velda saw me out of the corner of her eye. I eased up to her, my breath still coming hard. 'Deamer?'

She nodded.

I heard Pat busting through the crowd and saw Lee at his heels, 'Beat it, kid. I'll call you later.' She stepped back and the curious crowd surged around her to fill the spot. She was gone before Pat reached me.

His pants were torn and he had a dirty black smear across his cheek. He took about two minutes to get the crowd back from the edge and when a cop from the beat upstairs came through the gang was herded back to the exits like cattle, all bawling to be in on the blood.

Pat wiped his hand across his face. 'What the hell happened?'

'I don't know, but I think that's our boy down there. Bring Lee over.'

The trainmen were tugging the remains out. One said, 'He ain't got much face left,' then he puked all over the third rail.

Lee Deamer looked over the side and turned white. 'My God!'

Pat steadied him with an arm around his waist. They had most of the corpse out from under the train now. 'That him?' Pat asked.

Lee nodded dumbly. I could see his throat working hard.

Two more cops from the local precinct sauntered over. Pat shoved his badge out and told them to take over, then motioned me to bring Lee back to one of the benches. He folded up in one like a limp sack and buried his face in his hands. What the hell could I say? So the guy was a loony, but he was still his brother. While Pat went back to talk to the trainmen I stood there and listened to him sob.

We put Lee in a cab outside before I had a chance to say anything. The street was mobbed now, the people crowding around the ambulance waiting to see what was going in on the stretcher. They were disappointed when a wicker basket came up and was shoved into a morgue wagon instead. A kid pointed to the blood dripping from one corner and a woman fainted. Nice.

I watched the wagon pull away and reached for a butt. I needed one bad. 'It was an easy way out,' I said. 'What did the driver say?'

Pat took a cigarette from my pack. 'He didn't see him. He thinks the guy must have been hiding behind a pillar then jumped out in front of the car. He sure was messed up.'

'I don't know whether to be relieved or not.'

'It's a relief to me, Mike. He's dead and his name will get published, but who will connect him with Lee? The trouble's over.'

'He have anything on him?'

Pat stuck his hand in his pocket and pulled out some stuff. Under the light it looked as if it had been stained with ink. Sticky ink. 'Here's a train ticket from Chicago. It's in a bus envelope so he must have taken a bus as far as Chi then switched to rail.' It was dated the 15th, a Friday.

I turned the envelope over and saw 'Deamer' printed across the back with a couple of schedule notations in pencil. There was another envelope with the stuff. It had been torn in half and used as a memo sheet, but the name Deamer, part of an address in Nebraska and a Nebraska postage mark were still visible. It was dated over a month ago. The rest of the stuff was some small change, two crumpled bills and a skeleton key for a door lock.

It was as nice an answer as we could have hoped for and I didn't like it. 'What's the matter now?' Pat queried.

'I don't know. It stinks.'

'You're teed off because you were done out of a kill.'

'Aw, shaddup, will you!'

'Then what's so lousy about it?'

'How the hell do I know? Can't I not like something without having to explain about it?'

'Not with me you can't, pal. I stuck my neck out when I invited you in.'

I sucked in on the cigarette. It was cold standing there and I turned my collar up. 'Get a complete identification on that corpse, Pat. Then maybe I can tell you why I think it stinks.'

'Don't worry, I intend to. I'm not taking any chances of having him laughing at us from somewhere. It would be like the crazy bastard to push someone else under that train to sidetrack us.'

'Would he have time to jam that stuff in his pockets too?' I flipped my thumb at the papers Pat was holding.

'He could have. Just the same, we'll be sure. Lee has both their birth certificates and a medical certificate on Oscar that has his full description. It won't take long to find out if that's him or not.'

'Let me know what you find.'

'I'll call you tomorrow. I wish I knew how the devil he spotted us. I nearly killed myself in that damn alley. I thought I heard somebody yelling for you, too.'

'Couldn't have been.'

'Guess not. Well, I'll see you tomorrow?'

'Uh-huh!' I took a last pull on the butt and tossed it at the kerb. Pat went back into the station and I could hear his heels clicking on the steps.

The street was more deserted now than ever. All that was left was the one yellow light. It seemed to wink at me. I walked toward it and went up the three steps into the building. The door was still standing open, enough light from the front room seeping into the hall so I could find my way.

It wasn't much of a place – just a room. There was a chair, a closet, a single bed and a washstand. The suitcase on the bed was half-filled with well-worn clothes, but I couldn't tell whether it was being packed or unpacked. I poked through the stuff and found another dollar bill stuffed in the cloth lining. Twenty pages of a mail-order catalogue were under everything. Part of them showed sporting goods including all sorts of guns. The others pictured automobile accessories. Which part was used? Did he buy a gun or a tyre? Why? Where?

I pulled out the shirts and shook them open, looking for any identifying marks. One had 'DEA' for a laundry tag next to the label, the others had nothing, so he must have done his own wash.

That was all there was to it.

Nothing.

I could breathe a little easier and tell Marty Kooperman that his boy was okay and nothing could hurt him now. Pat would be satisfied, the cops would be satisfied and everything was hunky-dory. I was the only one who still had a bug up my tail. It was a great big bug and it was kicking up a fuss. I was a hell of a way from being satisfied.

This wasn't what I was after, that's why. This didn't have to do with three green cards except that the dead man had killed a guy who carried one. What was his name . . . Moffit, Charlie Moffit. Was he dead because of a fluke or was there more to it?

I kicked at the edge of the bed in disgust and took one last look around. Pat would be here next. He'd find prints and check them against the corpse in his usual methodical way. If there was anything to be found, he'd find it and I could get it from him.

It had only been a few hours since I climbed out of the sack, but for some reason I was more tired than ever. Too much of a letdown, I guessed. You can't prime yourself for something to happen and feel right when it doesn't come off. The skin of my face felt tight and drawn, pulling away from my eyes. My back still crawled when I thought of the alley and that thing under the train.

I went into a shabby drugstore and called Velda's home. She wasn't there. I tried the office and she was. I told her to meet me in the bar downstairs and walked outside again, looking for a cab. The one that came along had a driver who had all the information about the accident in the subway second-hand and insisted on giving me a detailed account of all the gruesome details. I was glad to pay him off and get out of there.

Velda was sitting in a back booth with a Manhattan in front of her. Two guys at the bar had swung halfway around on their stools and were trying out their best leers. One said something dirty and the other laughed. Tony walked down behind the bar, but he saw me come in and stopped. The guy with the dirty mouth said something else, slid off his stool and walked over to Velda.

He set his drink down and leaned on her table, mouthing a few obscenities. Velda moved too fast for him. I saw her arm fly out, knock away the support of his hand and his face went into the table. She gave him the drink right in the eyes, glass and all.

The guy screamed, 'You dirty little . . .' then she laid the heavy glass ashtray across his temple and he had had it. He went down on his knees, his head almost on the floor. The other guy almost choked. He slammed his drink down and came off his stool with a rush. I let him go about two feet before I snagged the back of his coat collar with a jerk that put him right on his skinny behind.

Tony laughed and leaned on the bar.

I wasn't laughing. The one on the floor turned his head and I saw a pinched, weasel face with eyes that had quick death in them. Those eyes crawled over me from top to bottom, over to Velda and back again. 'A big tough guy,' he said. 'A big wise guy.'

As if a spring exploded inside him, he came up off the floor with a knife in his hand, blade up.

A .45 can make an awful nasty sound in a quiet room when you pull the hammer back. It's just a little tiny click, but it can stop a dozen guys when they hear it. Weasel face couldn't take his eyes off it. I let him have a good look and smashed it across his nose.

The knife hit the floor and broke when I stepped on it. Tony laughed again. I grabbed the guy by the neck and hauled him to his feet so I could drag the cold sharp metal of the rod across his face until he was a bright red mask mumbling for me to stop.

Tony helped me throw them in the street outside. He said, 'They never learn, do they, Mike? Because there's two of 'em and they got a shiv they're the toughest mugs in the world. It ain't nice to get took by a woman, neither. They never learn.'

'They learn, Tony. For about ten seconds they're the smartest people in the world. But then it's always too late. After ten seconds they're dead. They only learn when they finally catch a slug where it hurts.'

I walked back to the booth and sat down opposite Velda. Tony brought her another Manhattan and me a beer. 'Very good,' I said.

'Thanks. I knew you were watching.'

She lit a cigarette and her hands were steadier than mine. 'You were too rough on him.'

'Nuts! He had a knife. I have an allergy against getting cut.' I drained off half of the beer and laid it down on the table where I made patterns with the wet bottom. 'Tell me about tonight.'

Velda started to tear matches out of the book without lighting them. 'I got there about seven-thirty. A light was on in the front window. Twice I saw somebody pull aside the corner of the shade and look out. A car went around the block twice, and both times it slowed down a little in front of the house. When it left I tried the door, but it was locked so I went next door and tried that one. It was locked too; but there was a cellar-way under the stairs and I went down there. Just as I was going down the steps I saw a man coming up the block and I thought it might be Deamer.

'I had to take the chance that it was and that you were behind him. The cellar door was open and led through to the back yard. I was trying to crawl over a mound of boxes when I heard somebody in the back yard. I don't know how long it took me to get out there, possibly two minutes. Anyway, I heard a yell and somebody came out the door of the next house. I got through into the back alley and heard him running. He went too fast for me and I started yelling for you.'

'That was Oscar Deamer, all right. He saw us coming and beat it.'

'Maybe.'

'What do you mean . . . "maybe"?'

'I think there were two people in that alley ahead of me.'

'Two people?' My voice had an edge to it. 'Did you see them?'

'No.'

'Then how do you know?'

'I don't. I just think so.'

64

I finished the beer and waved to Tony. He brought another. Velda hadn't touched her drink yet. 'Something made you think that. What was it?'

She shrugged, frowning at her glass, trying to force her mind back to that brief interval. 'When I was in that cellar I thought I heard somebody in the other yard. There was a flock of cats around and I thought at the time that I was hearing them.'

'Go on.'

'Then when I was running after him I fell and while I lay there it didn't sound like just one person going down that alley.'

'One person could sound like ten if they hit any of the junk we hit. It makes a hell of a racket.'

'Maybe I'm wrong, Mike. I thought there could have been someone else and I wanted you to know about it.'

'What the hell, it doesn't matter too much now anyway. The guy is dead and that should end it. Lee Deamer can go ahead and reform all he wants to now. He hasn't got a thing to worry about. As far as two people in that alley . . . well, you saw what the place was like. Nobody lives there unless he has to. They're the kind of people who scare easily, and if Lee started running somebody else could have too. Did you see him go down the subway?'

'No, he was gone when I got there, but two kids were staring down the steps and waving to another kid to come over. I took the chance that he went down and followed. The train was skidding to a stop when I reached the platform and I didn't have to be told why. When you scooted me away I looked for those kids in the crowd upstairs but they weren't around.'

I hoisted my glass, turned it around in my hand and finished it. Velda downed her Manhattan and slipped her arms into her coat. 'What now, Mike?'

'You go home, kid,' I told her. 'I'm going to take me a nice long walk.'

We said good night to Tony and left. The two guys we had thrown in the street were gone. Velda grinned, 'Am I safe?'

'Hell, yes!'

I waved a taxi over, kissed her good night and walked off.

My heels rapped the sidewalk, a steady tap-tap that kept time with my thoughts. They reminded me of another walk I took, one that led to a bridge, and still another one that led into a deserted store that came equipped with blackout curtains, light switches on the door and coffee urns.

There lay the story behind the green cards. There was where I could find out why I had to kill a guy who had one, and see a girl die because she couldn't stand the look on my face. That was what I wanted to know . . . why it was me who was picked to pull the trigger.

I turned into a candy store and pulled the telephone directories from the rack. I found the Park Avenue Brightons and dialled the number.

Three rings later a sombre voice said, 'Mr Brighton's residence.'

I got right to the point. 'Is Ethel there?'

'Who shall I say is calling, sir?'

'You don't. Just put her on.'

'I'm sorry, sir, but . . .'

'Oh, shut up and put her on.'

There was a shocked silence and a clatter as the phone was laid on a table. Off in the distance I heard the mutter of voices, then feet coming across the room. The phone clattered again, and, 'Yes?'

'Hello, Ethel,' I said. 'I drove your car into Times Square last night. Remember?'

'Oh! Oh, but . . .' Her voice dropped almost to a whisper. 'Please, I can't talk to you here. What is . . .'

'You can talk to me outside, kid. I'll be standing on your street corner in about fifteen minutes. The north-east corner. Pick me up there.'

'I – I can't. Honestly . . . oh, please . . .' There was panic in her voice, a tone that held more than fear.

I said, 'You'd better, baby.' That was enough. I hung up and started walking toward Park Avenue. If I could read a voice right, she'd be there.

She was. I saw her while I was still a half-block away; crossing nervously back and forth, trying to seem busy. I came up behind her and said hello. For a moment she went rigid, held by the panic that I had sensed in her voice.

'Scared?'

'No – of course not.' The hell she wasn't! Her chin was wobbling and she couldn't hold her hands still. This time I was barely smiling and dames don't usually go to pieces when I do that.

I hooked my arm through hers and steered her west where there were lights and people. Sometimes the combination is good for the soul. It makes you want to talk and laugh and be part of the grand parade.

It didn't have that effect on her.

The smile might have been pasted on her face. When she wasn't looking straight ahead her eyes darted to me and back again. We went off Broadway and into a bar that had one empty end and one full end because the television wasn't centred. The lights were down low and nobody paid any attention to us on the empty end except the bartender, and he was more interested in watching the wrestling than hustling up drinks for us.

Ethel ordered an Old Fashioned and I had a beer. She held the fingers of her one hand tightly around the glass and worked a cigarette with the other. There was nothing behind the bar to see, but she stared there anyway. I had to give up carrying the conversation. When I did and sat there as quietly as she did the knuckles of her fingers went white.

She couldn't keep this up long. I took a lungful of smoke and let it come out with my words. 'Ethel . . .!' She jerked, startled. 'What's there about me that has you up a tree?'

She wet her lips. 'Really, there's . . . there's nothing.'

'You never even asked me my name.'

That brought her head up. Her eyes got wide and stared at the wall. 'I . . . I'm not concerned with names.'

'I am.'

'But you . . . I'm . . . please, what have I done? Haven't I been faithful? Must you go on . . .' She had kept it up too long. The panic couldn't stay. It left with a rush and a pleading tone took its place. There were tears in her eyes now, tears she tried hard to hold back and, being a woman, couldn't. They flooded her eyelids and ran down her cheeks.

'Ethel . . . quit being scared of me. Look in a mirror and you'll know why I called you tonight. You aren't the kind of woman a guy can see and forget. You're too damned serious.'

Dames, they can louse me up every time. The tears stopped as abruptly as they came and her mouth froze in indignation. This time she was able to look at my eyes clearly. 'We have to be serious. You, of all people, should know that!'

This was better. The words were her own, what was inside her and not words that I put there. 'Not all the time.' I grinned.

'All the time!' she said. I grinned at her and she returned it with a frown.

'You'll do, kid.'

'I can't understand you.' She hesitated, then a smile blossomed and grew. She was lovely when she smiled. 'You were testing me,' she demanded.

'Something like that.'

'But . . . why?'

'I need some help. I can't take just anybody, you know.' It was true. I did need help, plenty of it too.

'You mean . . . you want me to help you . . . find out who . . . who did it?'

Cripes, how I wanted her to open up. I wasn't in the mood for more of those damn silly games and yet I had to play them. 'That's right.'

It must have pleased her. I saw the fingers loosen up around the glass and she tasted the drink for the first time. 'Could I ask a question?'

'Sure, go ahead.'

'Why did you choose me?'

'I'm attracted to beauty.'

'But my record . . !

'I was attracted to that too. Being beautiful helped.'

'I'm not beautiful.' She was asking for more. I gave it to her.

'All I can see are your face and hands. They're beautiful, but I bet the rest of you is just as beautiful, the part I can't see.'

It was too dark to tell if she had the grace to blush or not. She wet her lips again, parting them in a small smile. 'Would you?'

'What?'

'Like to see the rest of me.' No, she couldn't have blushed.

I laughed at her, a slow laugh that brought her head around and showed me the glitter in her eyes. 'Yeah, Ethel, I want to. And I will when I want to just a little more.'

Her breath came so sharply that her coat fell open and I could see the pulse in her throat. 'It's warm here. Can we . . . leave?'

Neither of us bothered to finish our drinks.

She was laughing now, with her mouth and her eyes. I held her hand and felt the warm pressure of her fingers, the stilted reserve draining out of her at every step. Ethel led the way, not me. We walked toward her place almost as if we were in a hurry, out to enjoy the evening.

'Supposing your father . . . or somebody you know . . . should come along,' I suggested.

She shrugged defiantly. 'Let them. You know how I feel.' She held her head high, the smile crooked across her lips. 'There's not one of them I care for. Any feeling I've had for my family disappeared several years ago.'

'Then you haven't any feeling left for anyone?'

'I have! Oh, yes, I have.' Her eyes swung up to mine, half-closed, revealing a sensuous glitter. 'For the moment it's you.'

'And other times?'

'I don't have to tell *you* that. There's no need to test me any longer.'

A few doors from her building she stopped me. Her convertible was squatting there at the kerb. The car in front and behind it had a parking ticket on the windshield wiper. Hers bore only a club insignia.

'I'll drive this time,' she said.

We got in and drove. It rained a little and it snowed a little, then, abruptly, it was clear and the stars came in full and bright, framed in the hole in the sky. The radio was a chant of pleasure, snatching the wild symphonic music from the air and offering us orchestra seats though we were far beyond the city, hugging the curves of the Hudson.

When we stopped it was to turn off the highway to a winding macadam road that led beneath the overhanging branches of evergreens. The cottage nestled on top of a bluff smiling down at the world. Ethel took my hand, led me inside to the plush little playhouse that was her own special retreat and lit the heavy wax candles that hung in brass holders from the ceiling.

I had to admire the exquisite simplicity of the place. It proclaimed wealth, but in the most humble fashion. Somebody had done a good job of decorating. Ethel pointed to the little bar that was set in the corner of the log cabin. 'Drinks are there. Would you care to make us one . . . then start the fire? The fireplace has been laid up.'

I nodded, watched her leave the room, then opened the doors of the liquor cabinet. Only the best, the very best. I picked out the best of the best and poured two straight, not wanting to spoil it with any mixer, sipped mine then drank it down. I had a refill and stared at it.

A Commie! She was a jerky Red. She owned all the trimmings and she was still a Red. What the hell was she hoping for, a government order to share it all with the masses? Yeah. A joint like this would suddenly assume a new owner under a new regime. A fat little general, a ranking secret policeman, somebody. Sure, it's great to be a Commie . . . as long as you're top dog. Who the hell was supposed to be fooled by all the crap?

Yet Ethel fell for it. I shook my head at the stupid asses that are left in this world and threw a match into the fireplace. It blazed up and licked at the logs on the andirons.

Ethel came out of the other room wearing her fur coat. Her hair looked different. It seemed softer. 'Cold?'

'In there it is. I'll be warm in a moment.'

I handed her the glass and we touched the rims. Her eyes were bright, hot.

We had three or four more and the bottom was showing in the bottle. Maybe it was more than three or four. I wanted to ask her some questions. I wanted the right answers and I didn't want her to think about them beforehand. I wanted her just a little bit drunk.

I had to fumble with the catch to get the liquor cabinet open. There was more of the best of the best in the back and I dragged it out. Ethel found the switch on a built-in phonograph and stacked on a handful of records.

The fireplace was a leaping, dancing thing that threw shadows across the room and touched everything with a weird, demoniac light. Ethel came to me, holding her arms open to dance. I wanted to dance, but there were parts of me trying to do other things.

Ethel laughed. 'You're drunk.'

'I am like hell.' It wasn't exactly the truth.

'Well, *I'm* drunk. I'm very, very drunk and I love it!' She threw her arms up and spun around. I had to catch her. 'Oo, I want to sit down. Let's sit down and enjoy the fire.'

She pulled away and danced to the sofa, her hands reaching out for the black bearskin rug that was draped over the back of it. She threw it on the floor in front of the fire and turned around. 'Come on over. Sit down.'

'You'll roast in that coat,' I said.

'I won't.' She smiled slyly and flipped open the buttons that held it together. She shrugged the shoulders off first letting it fall to her waist, then swept it off and threw it aside.

Ethel didn't have anything on. Only her shoes. She kicked them off too and sunk to the softness of the bearskin, a beautiful naked creature of soft round flesh and lustrous hair that changed colour with each leap of the vivid red flame behind her.

It was much too warm then for a jacket. I heard mine hit a chair and slide off. My wallet fell out of the pocket and I didn't care. The sling on my gun rack wouldn't come loose and I broke it.

She shouldn't have done it. Damn it, she shouldn't have done it! I wanted to ask her some questions.

Now I forgot what I wanted to ask her.

My fingers hurt and she didn't care. Her lips were bright red, wet. They parted slowly and her tongue flicked out over her teeth inviting me to come closer. Her mouth was a hungry thing demanding to be tasted. The warmth that seemed to come from the flames was a radiation that flowed from the sleek length of her legs and nestled in the hollow of her stomach a moment before rising over the convex beauty of her breasts. She held her arms out invitingly and took me in them.

CHAPTER FIVE

I came awake with the dawn, my throat dry and my mind groping to make sense out of what had happened. Ethel was still there, lying curled on her side up against me. Sometime during the night the fire had gone down and she had gotten up to get a blanket and throw it over us.

Somehow I got to my feet without waking her up. I pulled on my clothes, found my gun sling and my jacket on the floor. I remembered my wallet and felt around for it, getting mad when I didn't find it. I sat on the arm of the sofa and shook my head to clear out the spiders. Bending over didn't do me much good. The next time I used my foot and scooped it out from under the end table where I must have kicked it in getting dressed.

Ethel Brighton was asleep and smiling when I left. It was a good night, but not at all what I had come for. She giggled and wrapped her arms around the blankets. Maybe Ethel would quit being mad at the world now.

I climbed into my raincoat and walked out, looking up once at the sky overhead. The clouds had closed in again, but they were thinner and it was warmer than it had been.

It took twenty minutes to reach the highway and I had to wait another twenty before a truck came along and gave me a lift into town. I treated him to breakfast and we talked about the war. He agreed that it hadn't been a bad war. He had gotten nicked too, and it gave him a good excuse to cop a day off now and then.

I called Pat about ten o'clock. He gave me a fast hello, then: 'Can you come up, Mike? I have something interesting.'

'About last night?'

'That's right.'

'I'll be up in five minutes. Stick around.'

Headquarters was right up the street and I stepped it up. The D.A. was coming out of the building again. This time he didn't see me. When I rapped on Pat's door he yelled to come in and I pushed the knob.

Pat said, 'Where the hell have you been?' He was grinning.

'No place.' I grinned back.

'If what I suspect goes on between you and Velda, then you had better get that lipstick off your face and shave.'

'That bad?'

'I can smell whisky from here too.'

'Velda won't like that,' I said.

'No dame in love with a dope does,' Pat laughed. 'Park it, Mike. I have news for you.' He opened his desk drawer and hauled out a large manila envelope that had CONFIDENTIAL printed across the back.

When he was draped across the arm of the chair he handed a fingerprint photostat to me. 'I took these off the corpse last night.'

'You didn't waste time, pal.'

'Couldn't afford to.' He dug in the envelope and brought out a three-page document that was clipped together. It had a hospital masthead I didn't catch because Pat turned it over and showed me the fingerprints on the back. 'These are Oscar Deamer's too. This is his medical case history that Lee was holding.'

I didn't need to be an expert to see that they matched. 'Same guy all right,' I remarked.

'No doubt about it. Want to look at the report?'

'Ah, I couldn't wade through all that medical baloney. What's it say?'

'In brief, that Oscar Deamer was a dangerous neurotic, paranoiac and a few other psychiatric big words.'

'Congenital?'

Pat saw what I was thinking. 'No, as a matter of fact. So rest easy that no family insanity could be passed on to Lee. It seems that Oscar had an accident when he was a child. A serious skull fracture that somehow led to his condition.'

'Any repercussions? Papers get any of it?' I handed the sheets back to Pat and he tucked them away.

'None at all, luckily. We were on tenterhooks for a while, but none of the newsboys connected the names. There was one fortunate aspect to the death of Oscar . . . his face wasn't recognizable. If the reporters had seen him there wouldn't have been a chance of covering up, and would some politicians like to have gotten that!'

I pulled a Lucky from my pack and tapped it on the arm of the chair. 'What was the medical examiner's opinion?'

'Hell, suicide without a doubt. Oscar got scared, that's all. He tried to run knowing he was trapped. I guess he knew he'd go back to the sanitarium if he was caught . . . if he didn't stand a murder trial for Moffit's murder, and he couldn't take it.'

Pat snapped his lighter open and fired my butt. 'I guess that washes it up then,' I said.

'For us . . . yes. For you, no.'

I raised my eyebrows and looked at him quizzically.

'I saw Lee before I came to work. He called,' Pat explained. 'When he spoke to Oscar over the phone Oscar hinted at something. He seems to think that Oscar might have done other things than try to have him identified for a murder he didn't do. Anyway, I told him that you had some unusual interest in the whole affair that you didn't want to speak about, even to me. He quizzed me about you, I told all and now he wants to see you.'

'I'm to run down anything left behind?'

'I imagine so. At any rate, you'll get a fat fee out of it instead of kicking around for free.'

'I don't mind. I'm on vacation anyway.'

'Nuts! Stop handing me the same old thing. Think of something different. I'd give a lot to know what you have on your mind.'

'You sure would, Pat.' Perhaps it was the way I said it. Pat went into a piece of police steel. The cords in his neck stuck out like little fingers and his lips were just a straight, thin line.

'I've never known you to hang your hat on anything but murder, Mike.'

'True, ain't it.' My voice was flat as his.

'Mike, after the way I've been pitching with you, if you get in another smear you'll be taking me with you.'

'I won't get smeared.'

'Mike, you bastard, you have a murder tucked away somewhere.'

'Sure, two of 'em. Try again.'

He let his eyes relax and forced a grin. 'If there were any recent kills on the pad I'd go over them one by one and scour your hide until you told me which one it was.'

'You mean,' I said sarcastically, 'that the Finest haven't got one single unsolved murder on their hands?'

Pat got red and squirmed. 'Not recently.'

'What about that laddie you hauled out of the drink?'

He scowled as he remembered. 'Oh, that gang job. Body still unidentified and we're tracking down his dental work. No prints on file.'

'Think you'll tag him?'

'It ought to be easy. That bridgework was unusual. One false tooth was made of stainless steel. Never heard of that before.'

The bells started in my head again. Bells, drums, the whole damn works. The cigarette dropped out of my fingers and I bent to pick it up, hoping the blood pounding in my veins would pound out the crazy music.

It did. That maddening blast of silent sound went away. Slowly.

Maybe Pat never heard of stainless-steel teeth before, but I had.

I said, 'Is Lee expecting me?'

'I told him you'd be over some time this morning.'

'Okay!' I stood up and shoved my hat on. 'One other thing, what about the guy Oscar bumped?'

'Charlie Moffit?'

'Yeah.'

'Age thirty-four, light skin, dark hair. He had a scar over one eye. During the war he was 4-F. No criminal record and not much known about him. He lived in a room on Ninety-first Street, the same one he's had for a year. He worked in a pie factory.'

'Where?'

'A pie factory,' Pat repeated, 'where they make pies. Mother Switcher's Pie Shoppe. You can find it in the directory.'

'Was that card all the identification he had on him?'

'No, he had a driver's licence and a few other things. During the scuffle one pocket of his coat was torn out, but I doubt if he would have carried anything there anyway. Now, Mike . . . why?'

'The green cards, remember?'

'Hell, quit worrying about the Reds. We have agencies who can handle them.'

I looked past Pat outside into the morning. 'How many Commies are there floating around, Pat?'

'Couple hundred thousand, I think,' he said.

'How many men have we got in those agencies you mentioned?'

'Oh . . . maybe a few hundred. What's that got to do with it?'

'Nothing . . . just that that's the reason I'm worried.'

'Forget it. Let me know how you make out with Lee.'

'Sure.'

'And Mike . . . be discreet as hell about this, will you? Everybody with a press card knows your reputation and if you're spotted tagging around Lee there might be some questions asked that will be hard to answer.'

'I'll wear a disguise,' I said.

Lee Deamer's office was on the third floor of a modest building just off Fifth Avenue. There was nothing pretentious about the place aside from the switchboard operator. She was special. She had one of those faces that belonged in a chorus and a body she was making more effort to show than to conceal. I heard her voice and it was beautiful. But she was chewing gum like a cow and that took away any sign of pretentiousness she might have had.

There was a small anteroom that led to another office where two stenos were busy over typewriters. One wall of that room was all glass with a speaking partition built in at waist level. I had to lean down to my belt buckle to talk and gave it up as a bad job. The girl behind it laughed pleasantly and came out the door to see me.

She was a well-tailored woman in her early thirties, nice to look at and speak to. She wore an emerald ring that looked a generation older than she was. She smiled and said, 'Good morning, can I do something for you?'

I remembered to be polite. 'I'd like to see Mr Deamer, please.'

'Is he expecting you?'

'He sent word for me to come up.'

'I see.' She tapped her teeth with a pencil and frowned. 'Are you in a hurry?'

'Not particularly, but I think Mr Deamer is.'

'Oh, well . . . the doctor is inside with him. He may be there awhile, so . . .'

'Doctor?' I interrupted.

The girl nodded, a worried little look tugging at her eyes. 'He seemed to be quite upset this morning and I called in the doctor. Mr Deamer hasn't been too well since he had that attack awhile back.'

'What kind of attack?'

'Heart. He had a telephone call one day that agitated him terribly. I was about to suggest that he go home and at that moment he collapsed. I . . . I was awfully frightened. You see, it had never happened before, and . . .'

'What did the doctor say?'

'Apparently it wasn't a severe attack. Mr Deamer was instructed to take it easy, but for a man of his energy it's hard to do.'

'You say he had a phone call? That did it?'

'I'm sure it did. At first I thought it was the excitement of watching the Legion parade down the avenue, but Ann told me it happened right after the call came in.'

Oscar's call must have hit him harder than either Pat or I thought. Lee wasn't a young man any more; a thing like that could raise a lot of hell with a guy's ticker. I was about to say something when the doctor came out of the office. He was a little guy with a white goatee out of another era.

He nodded to us both, but turned his smile on the girl. 'I'm sure he'll be fine. I left a prescription. See that it's filled at once, please.'

'Thank you, I will. Is it all right for him to have visitors?'

'Certainly. Apparently he has been thinking of something that disturbed him and had a slight relapse. Nothing to worry about as long as he takes it easy. Good day.'

We said so-long and she turned to me with another smile, bigger this time. 'I guess you can go ahead in then. But please . . . don't excite him.'

I grinned and said I wouldn't. Her smile made her prettier. I pushed through the door, passed the steno and knocked on the door with Deamer's name on it.

He rose to greet me but I waved him down. His face was a little flushed and his breathing fast. 'Feeling better now? I saw the doctor when he came out.'

'Much better, Mike. I had to fabricate a story to tell him . . . I couldn't tell the truth.'

I sat in the chair next to his and he pushed a box of cigars toward me. I said no and took out a Lucky instead. 'Best to keep things to yourself. One word and the papers'll have it on page one. Pat said you wanted to see me.'

Lee sat back and wiped his face with a damp handkerchief. 'Yes, Mike. He told me you were interested somehow.'

'I am.'

'Are you one of my . . . political advocates?'

'Frankly, I don't know a hoot about politics except that it's a dirty game from any angle.'

'I hope to do something about that. I hope I can, Mike, I sincerely hope I can. Now I'm afraid.'

'The heart?'

He nodded. 'It happened after Oscar called. I never suspected that I have a . . . condition. I'm afraid now the voters must be told. It wouldn't be fair to elect a man not physically capable of carrying out the duties of his office.' He smiled wistfully, sadly. I felt sorry for the old boy.

'Anyway, I'm not concerned with the politics of the affair.'

'Really? But what . . .'

'Just a loose end, Lee. They bother me.'

'I see. I don't understand, but I see . . . if you can make sense of that.'

I waved the smoke away from in front of him. 'I know what you mean. Now about why you wanted to see me. Pat gave me part of it already, enough so I can see the rest.'

'Yes. You see, Oscar intimated that no matter what happened, he was going to see to it that I was broken, completely broken. He mentioned some documents he had prepared.'

I crushed the butt out and looked at him. 'What kind of documents?'

Lee shook his head slowly. 'The only possible thing he could compound would be our relationship as brothers. How, I don't know, because I have all the family papers. But if he could establish that I was the brother of a man committed to a mental institution, it would be a powerful weapon in the hands of the opposition.'

'There's nothing else,' I asked, 'that could stick you?'

He spread his hands apart in appeal. 'If there was it would have been brought to light long ago. No, I've never been in jail or in trouble of any sort. I'm afraid that my attention to business precluded any trouble.'

'Uh-huh! How come this awful hatred?'

'I don't know, actually. As I told Pat and you previously, it may have been a matter of ideals, or because, though we were twins, we weren't at all alike. Oscar was almost, well . . . sadistic in his ways. We had little to do with each other. As younger men I became established in business while Oscar got into all sorts of scrapes. I've tried to help him, but he wouldn't accept help from me at all. He hated me fiercely. I'm inclined to believe that this time Oscar had intended to bleed me for all the money he could, then make trouble for me anyway.'

'You were lucky you took the attitude you did. You can't pay off, it only makes matters worse.'

'I don't know, Mike; as much as he hated me I certainly didn't want that to happen to him.'

'He's better off.'

'Perhaps.'

I reached for another cigarette. 'You want me to find out what he left then, that's it.'

'If there is anything to be found, yes.'

When I filled my lungs with smoke I let it go slowly, watching it swirl up toward the ceiling. 'Lee,' I said, 'you don't know me so I'll tell you something. I hate phonies. Suppose I *do* find something that ties you up into a nice little ball. Something real juicy. What do you think I should do with it?'

It wasn't the reaction I expected. He leaned forward across the desk with his fingers interlocked. His face was a study in emotions. 'Mike,' he said in a voice that had the crisp clarity of static electricity, 'if you do, I charge you to make it public at once. Is that clear?'

I grinned and stood up. 'Okay, Lee. I'm glad you said that.' I reached out my hand and he took it warmly. I've seen evangelists with faces like that, unswerving, devoted to their duty. We looked at each other then he opened his desk drawer and brought out a lovely sheaf of green paper. They had big, beautiful numbers in the corners.

'Here is a thousand dollars, Mike. Shall we call it a retainer?'

I took the bills and folded them tenderly away. 'Let's call it payment in full. You'll get your money's worth.'

'I'm sure of it. If you need any additional information, call on me.'

'Right! Want a receipt?'

'No need of it. I'm sure your word is good enough.'

'Thanks. I'll send you a report if anything turns up.' I flipped a card out of my pocket and laid it on his desk. 'In case you want to call me. The bottom one is my home phone. It's unlisted.'

We shook hands again and he walked me to the door. On the way out the cud-chewing, switchboard sugar smiled between chomps and then went back to her magazine. The receptionist said so-long and I waved back.

Before I went to the office I grabbed a quick shave, a trim around the ears and took a shower that scraped the hide off me along with the traces of Ethel's perfume. I changed my shirt and suit but kept old Betsy in place under my arm.

Velda was working at the filing cabinet when I breezed in with a snappy hello and a grin that said I had money in my pocket. I got a quick once-over for lipstick stains, whisky aromas and what not, passed and threw the stack of bills on the desk.

'Bank it, kid.'

'Mike! What did *you* do?'

'Lee Deamer. We're employed.' I gave it to her in short order and she listened blankly.

When I finished she said, 'You'll never find a thing, Mike. I know you won't. You shouldn't have taken it.'

'You're wrong, chick. It wasn't stealing. If Oscar left anything that will tie Lee up wouldn't you want me to get it?'

'Oh, Mike, you must! How long do we have to put up with the slime they call politics? Lee Deamer is the only one . . . the only one we can look to. Please, Mike, you *can't* let anything happen to him!'

I couldn't take the fear in her voice. I opened my arms out and she stepped into them. 'Nobody will hurt the little guy, Velda. If there's anything I'll get it. Stop sniffling.'

'I can't. It's all so nasty. You never stop to think what goes on in this country, but I do.'

'Seems to me that I helped fight a war, didn't I?'

'You shouldn't have let it stop there. That's the matter with things. People forget, even the ones who *shouldn't* forget! They

82

let others come walking in and run things any way they please, and what are they after – the welfare of the people they represent? Not a bit. All they want is to line their own pockets. Lee isn't like that, Mike. He isn't strong like the others, and he isn't smart politically. All he has to offer is his honesty and that isn't much.'

'The hell it isn't. He's made a pretty big splash in this state.'

'I know, and it has to stick, Mike. Do you understand?'

'I understand.'

'Promise me you'll help him, Mike, promise me your word.'

Her face turned up to mine, drawn yet eager to hear. 'I promise,' I said softly. 'I'll never go back on a promise to you, nor to myself.'

It made her feel better in a hurry. The tears stopped and the sniffing died away. We had a laugh over it, but behind the laughter there was a dead seriousness. The gun under my arm felt heavy.

I said, 'I have a job for you. Get me a background on Charlie Moffit. He's the one Oscar Deamer bumped.'

Velda stopped her filing. 'Yes, I know.'

'Go to his home and his job. See what kind of a guy he was. Pat didn't mention a family so he probably didn't have any. Take what cash you need to cover expenses.'

She shoved the drawer in and fingered the bills on the desk. 'How soon?'

'I want it by tonight if you can. If not, tomorrow will do.'

I could see her curiosity coming out, but there are times when I want to keep things to myself and this was one of them. She knew it and stayed curious without asking questions.

Before she slipped the bills inside the bank book I took out two hundred in fifties. She didn't say anything then, either, but she smelt a toot coming up and I had to kiss the tip of her nose to get the scowl off her puss.

As soon as Velda left I picked up the phone and dialled Ethel Brighton's number. The flunky recognized my voice from last night and was a little more polite. He told me Ethel hadn't come in yet and hung up almost as hard as he could but not quite.

I tapped out a brief history of the case for the records, stuck it in the file and called again. Ethel had just gotten in. She grabbed the phone and made music in it, not giving a damn who heard her. 'You beast! You walked right out of the cave and left me to the wolves.'

'That bearskin would scare them away. You looked nice wrapped up in it.'

'You liked . . . all of me, then. The parts you could see?'

'All of you, Ethel. Soft and sweet.'

'We'll have to go back.'

'Maybe,' I said.

'Please,' softly whispered.

I changed the subject. 'Busy today?'

'Very busy. I have a few people to see. They promised me sizeable . . . donations. Tonight I have to deliver them to Com . . . Henry Gladow.'

'Yeah. Suppose I go with you?'

'If *you* think it's all right I'm sure no one will object.'

'Why me?' That was one of the questions I wanted an answer to.

She didn't tell me. 'Come now,' she laughed. 'Supposing I meet you in the Oboe Club at seven. Will that do?'

'Fine, Ethel. I'll save a table so we can eat.'

She said so-long with a pleasant laugh and waited for me to hang up. I did, then sat there with a cigarette in my fingers trying to think. The light hitting the wall broke around something on the desk making two little bright spots against the pale green.

Like two berries on a bush. The judge's eyes. They looked at me.

Something happened to the light and the eyes disappeared. I picked the phone up again and called the *Globe*. Marty was just going out on a story, but had time to talk to me. I asked him, 'Remember the Brighton family? Park Avenue stuff.'

'Sure, Mike. That's social, but I know a little about them. Why?'

'Ethel Brighton's on the outs with her father. Did it ever make the papers?'

I heard him chuckle a second. 'Getting toney, aren't you, kid? Well, part of the story was in the papers some years ago. It seems that Ethel Brighton publicly announced her engagement to a certain young man. Shortly afterwards the engagement was broken.'

'Is that all?'

'Nope,' he grunted, 'the best is yet to come. A little prying by our diligent Miss Carpenter who writes the social chatter uncovered an interesting phase that was handled just as interestingly. The young man in question was a down-and-out artist who made speeches for the Communist Party and was quite willing to become a capitalist by marriage. He was a conscientious objector during the war though he probably could have made 4-F without trouble. The old man raised the roof, but there was nothing he could do. When he threatened to cut Ethel off without a cent she said she'd marry him anyway.

'So the old man connived. He worked it so that he'd give his blessing so long as the guy enlisted in the army. They needed men bad so they took him, and as soon as he was out of training camp he was shipped overseas. He was killed in action, though the truth was that he went AWOL during a battle and deserved what he got. Later Ethel found out that her father was responsible for everything but the guy's getting knocked off and he had hoped for that too. She had a couple of rows with him in public, then it died down to where they just never spoke.'

'Nice girl,' I mused.

'Lovely to look at anyway.'

'You'll never know. Well, thanks, pal.'

He stopped me before I could hang up. 'Is this part of what you were driving at the other day . . . something to do with Lee Deamer?' His voice had a rasp.

'Not this,' I said. 'It's personal.'

'Oh, well call me any time, Mike.' He sounded relieved.

And so the saga of one Ethel Brighton. Nice girl turned dimwit because her old man did her out of a marriage. She was lucky and didn't know it.

I looked at my watch, remembered that I had meant to buy Velda lunch and forgot, then went downstairs and ate by myself. When I finished the dessert I sat back with a cigarette and tried to think of what it was that fought like the hammers of hell to come through my mind. Something was eating its way out and I couldn't help it. I gave up finally and paid my check. There was a movie poster behind the register advertising the latest show at the house a block over, so I ambled over and plunked in a seat before the show started. It wasn't good enough to keep me awake. I was on the second time around when I glanced at the time and hustled into the street.

The Oboe Club had been just another second-rate saloon on a side street until a wandering reporter happened in and mentioned it in his column as a good place to relax if you liked solitude and quiet. The next day it became a first-rate night-club where you could find anything but solitude and quiet. Advertising helped plenty.

I knew the head waiter to nod to and it was still early enough to get a table without any green passing between handshakes. The bar was lined with the usual after-office crowd having one for the road. There wasn't anyone to speak to, so I sat at the table and ordered a highball. I was on my fourth when Ethel Brighton came in, preceded by the head waiter and a few lesser luminaries.

He bowed her into her seat, then bowed himself out. The other one helped her adjust her coat over the back of the chair. 'Eat?' I asked.

'I'll have a highball first. Like yours.' I signalled the waiter and called for a couple more.

'How'd the donations come?'

'Fine,' she said, 'even better than I expected. The best part is, there's more where that came from.'

'The Party will be proud of you.' She looked up from her drink with a nervous little smile.

'I . . . hope so.'

'They should. You've brought in a lot of mazuma.'

'One must do all one can.' Her voice was a flat drone, almost machine-like. She picked up her glass and took a long pull. The waiter came and took our orders, leaving another highball with us.

I caught her attention and got back on the subject. 'Do you ever wonder where it all goes to?'

'You mean . . . the money?' I nodded between bites. 'Why . . . no. It isn't for me to think about those things. I only do as I'm told.' She licked her lips nervously and went back to her plate.

I prodded her again. 'I'd be curious if I were in your shoes. Give a guess, anyway.'

This time there was nothing but fear in her face. It tugged at her eyes and mouth and made her fork rattle against the china. 'Please . . .'

'You don't have to be afraid of me, Ethel. I'm not entirely like the others. You should know that.'

The fear was still there, but something else overshadowed it. 'I can't understand you . . . you're different. It's – well . . .'

'About the money, give a guess. Nobody should be entirely ignorant of Party affairs. After all, isn't that the principle of the thing . . . everybody for everybody? Then you'd have to know everything about everybody to be able to really do the Party justice.'

'That's true.' She squinted and a smile parted her lips. 'I see what you mean. Well, I'd guess that most of the money goes to foster the schools we operate . . . and for propaganda, of course. Then there are a lot of small things that come up like office expenses here and there.'

'Pretty good so far. Anything else?'

'I'm not too well informed on the business side of it so that's about as far as I can go.'

'What does Gladow do for a living?'

'Isn't he a clerk in a department store?'

I nodded as if I had known all along. 'Ever see his car?'

Ethel frowned again. 'Yes. He has a new Packard; why?'

'Ever see his house?'

'I've been there twice,' she said. 'It's a big place up in Yonkers.'

'And all that on a department store clerk's salary.'

Her face went positively white. She had to swallow hard to get her drink down and refused to meet my eyes until I told her to look at me. She did, but hesitantly. Ethel Brighton was scared silly . . . of me. I grinned, but it was lost. I talked and it went over her head. She gave all the right answers and even a laugh at one of my jokes, but Ethel was scared and she wasn't coming out of it too quickly.

She took the cigarette I offered her. The tip shook when she bent into the flame of my lighter. 'What time do you have to be there?' I asked.

'Nine o'clock. There's . . . a meeting.'

'We'd better go then. It'll take time getting over to Brooklyn.'

'All right.'

The waiter came over and took away a ten spot for his trouble while the head-boy saw us to the door. Half the bar turned around to look at Ethel as she brushed by. I got a couple of glances that said I was a lucky guy to have all that mink on my arm. Real lucky.

We had to call the parking lot to get her car brought over then we drove the guy back again. It was a quarter after eight before we pointed the car toward the borough across the stream. Ethel was behind the wheel, driving with a fixed intensity. She wouldn't talk unless I said something that required an answer. After a while it got tiresome so I turned on the radio and slumped back against the seat with my hat down over my eyes.

Only then did she seem to ease up. Twice I caught her head turning my way, but I couldn't see her eyes nor read the expression on her face. Fear. It was always there. Communism and Fear. Green Cards and Fear. Terror on the face of the girl on the bridge; stark, unreasoning fear when she looked at my face. Fear so bad it threw her over the rail to her death.

I'd have to remember to ask Pat about that, I thought. The body had to come up sometime.

The street was the same as before, dark, smelly, unaware of the tumour it was breeding in its belly. Trench Coat was standing outside the door seemingly enjoying the night. Past appearance didn't count. You showed your card and went in the door and showed it again. There was the same girl behind the desk and she made more of me than the card I held. Her voice was a nervous squeak and she couldn't sit still. Deliberately, I shot her the meanest grin I could dig up, letting her see my face when I pulled my lips back over my teeth. She didn't like it. Whatever it was scared her, too.

Henry Gladow was a jittery little man. He frittered around the room, stopped when he saw us and came over with a rush. 'Good evening, good evening, comrades.' He spoke directly to me. 'I am happy to see you again, comrade. It is an honour.'

It had been an honour before, too.

'There is news?' I screwed my eyebrows together and he pulled back, searching for words until he found them. 'Of course. I am merely being inquisitive. Ha, ha! We are all so very concerned, you know.'

'I know,' I said.

Ethel handed him another of those envelopes and excused herself. I watched her walk to a table and take a seat next to two students where she began to correct some mimeographed sheets. 'Wonderful worker, Miss Brighton.' Gladow smiled. 'You would scarcely think that she represents all that we hate.'

I made an unintelligible answer.

'You are staying for the meeting?' he asked me.

'Yeah, I want to poke around a little.'

This time he edged close to me, looking around to see if there was anyone close enough to hear. 'Comrade, if I am not getting too inquisitive again, is there a possibility that . . . the person could be here?'

There it was again. Just what I wanted to know and I didn't dare ask the question. It was going to take some pretty careful handling. 'It's possible,' I said tentatively.

He was aghast. 'Comrade! It is unthinkable!' He reflected a moment, then: 'Yet it had to come from somewhere. I simply can't understand it. Everything is so carefully screened, every member so carefully selected that it seems impossible for there to be a leak anywhere. And those filthy warmongers, doing a thing like that . . . so cold-blooded! It is simply incredible. How I wish the Party was in power at this moment. Why, the one who did that would be uncovered before the sun could set!'

Gladow cursed through his teeth and pounded a puny, carefully tended fist into his palm. 'Don't worry,' I said slowly.

It took ten seconds for my words to sink in. Gladow's little eyes narrowed in pleasure like a hog seeing a trough full of slops. The underside of his top lip showed when he smiled. 'No, comrade. I won't worry. The Party is too clever to let a direct representative's death go unpunished. No, I won't worry because I realize that the punishment that comes will more than equal the crime.' He beamed at me fatuously. 'I am happy to realize that the higher echelon has sent a man of your capacity, comrade.'

I didn't even thank him. I was thinking and this time the words made sense. They made more than sense . . . they made murder! Only death is cold-blooded, and who was dead? Three people. One hadn't been found. One was found and not identified, even by a lousy sketch. The other was dead and identified. He was cold-bloodedly murdered and he was a direct representative of the Party and I was the guy looking for his killer.

Good Lord, the insane bastards thought I was an MVD man!

My hands started to shake and I kept them in my pockets. And who was the dead man but Charlie Moffit! My predecessor. A goddamned Commie Gestapo man. A hatchet-man, a torpedo, a lot of things you want to call him. Lee ought to be proud of his brother, damn proud. All by himself he went out and knocked off a skunk.

But I was the prize, I was the MVD guy that came to take his place and run the killer down. Oh, brother! No wonder the jerks were afraid of me! No wonder they didn't ask my name! No wonder I was supposed to know it all.

I felt a grin trying to pull my mouth out of shape because so much of it was funny. They thought they were clever as hell and here I was right in the middle of things with an *in* that couldn't be better. Any good Red would give his shirt to be where I was right this minute.

Everything started to come out right then, even the screwy test they put me through. A small-time setup like this was hardly worth the direct attention of a Moscow man unless something was wrong, so I had to prove myself.

Smart? Sure, just like road apples that happen behind horses.

Now I knew and now I could play the game. I could be one of the boys and show them some fun. There were going to be a lot of broken backs around town before I got done.

There was only one catch I could think of. Some place was another MVD laddie, a real one. I'd have to be careful of him. At least careful that he didn't see me first, because when I met up with that stinkpot I was going to split him right down the middle with a .45!

I had been down too deep in my thoughts to catch the arrival of the party that came in behind me. I heard Gladow extending a welcome that wasn't handed out to just anybody. When I turned around to look I saw one little fat man, one big fat man and a guy who was in the newspapers every so often. His name was General Osilov and he was attached to the Russian Embassy in Washington. The big and little fat men were his aides and they did all the smiling. If anything went on in the head of the bald-headed general it didn't show in his flat, wide face.

Whatever it was Henry Gladow said swung the three heads in my direction. Two swung back again fast leaving only the general staring at me. It was a stare-down that I won. The general coughed without covering his mouth and stuck his hands in the pocket of his suitcoat. None of them seemed anxious to make my acquaintance.

From then on there was a steady flow of traffic in through the door. They came singly and in pairs, spaced about five minutes apart. Before the hour was out the place was packed. It was filled with the kind of people you'd expect to find there and it would hit you that when the cartoonists did a character of a pack of shabby Reds lurking in the shadow of democracy they did a good job.

A few of them dragged out seats and the meeting was on. I saw Ethel Brighton slide into the last chair in the last row and waited until she was settled before I sat down beside her. She smiled, let that brief look of fear mask her face, then turned her head to the front. When I put my hand over hers I felt it tremble.

Gladow spoke. The aides spoke. Then the general spoke. He pulled his tux jacket down when he rose and glared at the audience. I had to sit there and listen to it. It was propaganda right off the latest Moscow cable and it turned me inside out. I wanted to feel the butt of an M-l against my shoulder pointing at those bastards up there on the rostrum and feel the pleasant impact as it spit slugs into their guts.

Sure, you can sit down at night and read about the hogwash they hand out. Maybe you're fairly intelligent and can laugh at it. Believe me, it isn't funny. They use the very thing we built up, our own government and our own laws, to undermine the things we want.

It wasn't a very complicated speech the general made. It was plain, bitter poison and they cheered him noiselessly. He was making plain one thing. There were still too many people who didn't go for Communism and not enough who did and he gave a plan of organization that had worked in a dozen countries already. One armed Communist was worth twenty capitalists without guns. It was Hitler all over again. A powerful Communist government already formed would be there to take over when the big upset came, and according to him it was coming soon. Here, and he swept the room with his arm, was one phase of that government ready to go into action.

I didn't hear the rest of it. I sat there fiddling with my fingernails because I was getting ready to bust loose and spoil their plans. If I let any more words go in my ears there was going to be blood on the floor and it wasn't time for that yet. I caught snatches of things that went on, repeated intimations of how the top men were already in the core of the present government eating its vitals out so the upset would be an easy one.

For a long time I sat there working up more hatred than I had ever had at any time and I wasn't conscious of how tightly Ethel Brighton was squeezing my hand. When I looked at her tears were running down her face. That's the kind of thing the general and his party could do to decent people.

I took a long look at him, making sure that I wouldn't forget his face, because some day he'd be passing a dark alley or forget to lock his door when he went to bed. That's when he'd catch it. And I didn't want to get tagged for it either. That would be like getting the chair for squashing a spider.

The meeting ended with handshakes all around. The audience lined up along the walls taking handfuls of booklets and printed sheets to distribute later, then grouped in bunches around the room talking things over in excited murmurs. Henry Gladow and Martin Romberg were up on the rostrum having their own conference. The general said something to Henry and he must have ordered his bodyguard down into the crowd to look for his trench coat or something. Martin Romberg looked hurt. Tough.

While the seats were folded and stacked I lost track of Ethel. I saw her a few minutes later coming from the washroom and she looked a little better. She had a smile for me this time, a big one. I would have made something of it if a pimply-faced kid about twenty didn't come crawling over and tell me that the general wanted to know if I had time to speak to him.

Rather than answer I picked a hole in the crowd that had started to head for the door and walked up to the rostrum. The general stood alone, his hands behind his back. He nodded briefly and said something in a guttural tongue.

I let my eyes slide to the few who remained near by. There wasn't any respect in my tone when I said, 'English. You know better than that.'

The general paled a little and his mouth worked. 'Yes . . . yes. I didn't expect to find anyone here. Do you have a report for me?'

I shook a cigarette out of the pack and stuck it in my mouth. 'When I have you'll know about it.'

His head bobbed anxiously and I knew I had the bull on him. Even a general had to be leery of the MVD. That made it nice for me. 'Of course. But there should be some word to bring back to the committee.'

'Then tell 'em things are looking up. It won't be long.'

The general's hands came out in front where he squeezed them happily. 'Then you *do* have word! The courier . . . he did have the documents? You know where they are?'

I didn't say a word. All I did was look at him and he got that same look on his face as the other had. He was thinking what I thought he was thinking, that he had taken me for granted and it was his mistake and one word in the right sources and he'd feel the axe.

He tried his first smile. 'It is very all right, you know. Comrade Gladow told me.'

I dragged on the cigarette and blew it in his face wishing it was some mustard gas. 'You'll know soon enough,' I said. I left him standing there and walked back to Ethel. She was slipping into her mink and nobody seemed to care a hoot what she wore.

'Going home?'

'Yes . . . are you?'

'Might as well. You can drop me off if you don't mind.'

'I don't mind.'

One of the men paused to have a word with her before she left. She excused herself to talk to him and I used the time to look around and be sure there weren't any faces there that I'd ever forget. When the time came I wanted to be able to put the finger on them and put it on good.

Maybe it was the way I stared at the babe from the desk at the door or maybe it was because I looked at her too long. Her lashes made like bird's wings for a second and everything in the room seemed to get interesting all of a sudden. Her eyes jerked around but kept coming back to mine and each time there was a little more of a blush crowding her hairline.

I kept my grin hidden because she thought I was on the make. It could have been pathetic if it wasn't so damn funny. She wasn't the kind of woman a guy would bother with if there was anything else around. Strictly the last-resort type. From the way she wore her clothes you couldn't tell what was underneath and suspected probably nothing. Her face looked like nature had been tired when it made it and whatever she did to her hair certainly didn't improve things any.

Plain was the word. Stuffy was the type. And here she thought a man saw something interesting in her.

I guessed that all women were born with some conceit in them so I put on a sort of smile and walked over to her casually. A little flattery could make a woman useful sometimes.

I held out my deck of butts. 'Smoke?'

It must have been her first cigarette. She choked on it, but came up smiling. 'Thank you.'

I said, 'You've, er . . . belonged some time, Miss . . .'

'Linda Holbright.' She got real fluttery then. 'Oh, yes, for years you know. And I . . . try to do anything I can for the Party.'

'Good, good!' I said. 'You seem to be . . . very capable. Pretty, too.'

Her first blush had been nothing. This one went right down to her shoes. Her eyes got big and blue and round and gave me the damnedest look you ever saw. Just for the hell of it I gave her one back with a punch in it. What she made of it stopped her from breathing for a second.

I heard Ethel finish her little conversation behind me and I said, 'Good night, Linda. I'll see you soon.' I gave her that look again. 'Real soon.'

95

Her voice sounded a little bit strained. 'I . . . meant to ask you. If there is anything . . . important you should know . . . where can I reach you?'

I ripped the back off a book of matches and wrote down my address. 'Here it is. Apartment 5B.'

Ethel was waiting for me, so I said good night again and started for the door behind the mink coat. It made nice wiggles when she walked. I liked that.

I let her go out first then followed her. The street was empty enough so you wouldn't think anything unusual about the few couples who were making their ways to the subways. Trench Coat was still at the door holding a cigarette in his mouth. His belt was too tight and the gun showed underneath it. One day a cop would spot that and there'd be more trouble.

Yeah, they sure were smart.

Going back was better than going down. This time Ethel turned into a vivid conversationalist, commenting on everything she saw. I tried to get in a remark about the meeting and she brushed it off with some fast talk. I let her get it out of her system, sitting there with my mouth shut, grinning at the right places and chiming in with a grunt whenever she laughed.

About a block from my apartment I pointed to the corner and said, 'I'll get off under the light, kid.'

She edged into the kerb and stopped. 'Good night, then,' she smiled. 'I hope you enjoyed the meeting.'

'As a matter of fact, I thought they stunk.' Ethel's mouth dropped open. I kissed it and she closed it, fast. 'Do you know what I'd do if I were you, Ethel?'

She shook her head watching me strangely.

'I'd go back to being a woman and less of a dabbler in politics.'

This time her eyes and mouth came open together. I kissed her again before she could get it shut. She looked at me as if I were a puzzle that couldn't be solved and let out a short, sharp laugh that had real pleasure in it.

'Aren't you a bit curious about my name, Ethel?'

Her face went soft. 'Only for my own sake.'

'It's Mike. Mike Hammer and it's a good name to remember.'

'Mike . . .' very softly. 'After last night . . . how could I forget.'

I grinned at her and opened the door. 'Will I be seeing you again?'

'Do you want to?'

'Very much.'

'Then you'll be seeing me again. You know where I live.'

I couldn't forget her, either. On that bearskin rug with the fire behind her she was something a man never forgets. I stuck my hands in my pockets and started to whistle my way down the street.

I got as far as the door next to mine when the sedan across the street came to life. If the guy at the wheel hadn't let the clutch out so fast I wouldn't have looked up and seen the snout of the rifle that hung out the back window. What happened then came in a blur of motion and a mad blasting of sound. The long streak of flame from the rifle, the screaming of the ricochetted slug, the howl of the car engine. I dove flat out, rolling before I hit the concrete, my hand pulling the gun out, my thumb grabbing for the hammer. The rifle barked again and gouged a hunk out of the sidewalk in front of my face, but by that time the .45 in my hand was bucking out the bullets as fast as my finger could pull the trigger, and in the light of the street lamp overhead I saw the dimples pop into the back of the car and the rear window spiderweb suddenly and smash to the ground. Somebody in the car screamed like a banshee gone mad and there were no more shots. Around me the windows were slamming up before the car had made the turn at the corner.

I kept saying it over and over to myself. 'Those goddamned bastards. They got wise! Those goddamn bastards!'

A woman shrieked from a window that somebody was dead and when I looked up I saw she was pointing to me. When I climbed back on my feet she shrieked again and fell away from the window.

It hadn't been a full twenty seconds since that car had started up, and a police car was wheeling around the corner. The driver slammed on the brakes and the two of them came out with Police Specials in their hands, both of them pointed at me. I was trying to shove a fresh load into the clip when the cop snarled, 'Drop that gun, damn it!'

I wasn't doing any arguing with them. I tossed the gun so it landed on my foot then shoved it away gently. The other cop picked it up. Before they told me to put my hands on my head and stood there while they flashed the beam of light in my face.

'There's a ticket for that rod in my wallet along with a Private Operator's licence.'

The cop didn't lose any time frisking me for another rod before yanking my wallet out. He had a sceptical look on his face until he saw the ticket. 'Okay, put 'em down,' he said. I dropped my hands and reached for my .45. 'I didn't say to pick that up yet,' he added. I let it stay there. The cop who drove the buggy looked the ticket over then looked at me. He said something to his partner and motioned for me to get the gun.

'All clear?' I blew the dust off old Betsy and stowed it away. A crowd was beginning to collect and one of the cops started to herd them away.

'What happened?' He wasn't a man of many words.

'There you got me, feller. I was on my way home when the shooting started. Either it's the old yam of mistaken identity which isn't too probable or somebody whom I thought was a friend, isn't.'

'Maybe you better come with us.'

'Sure, but in the meantime a black Buick sedan with no back window and a few bullets in its behind is making tracks to the nearest garage. I think I got one of the guys in the car and you can start checking the doctors.'

The cop peered at me under his visor and took my word for it. The call went out on the police wires without any more talk. They were all for dragging me with them until I had a call put in to Pat and his answer relayed back to the squad car. Pat told them I was available at any time and they gave me the green light through the crowd.

I got a lot of unfriendly looks that night.

When I stood in front of my door with the key in my hand it hit me just like that. My little love scene with Ethel Brighton had had repercussions. My wallet on the floor. It wasn't in the same place in the morning. When she had gotten up for that blanket she had seen it, and my P.I. card in the holder. Tonight she passed the word.

I was lucky to get out of there with a whole skin.

Ethel, I thought, you're a cute little devil. You looked so nice in your bare skin with the fire behind you. Maybe I'll see you stripped again. Soon. When I do I'm going to take my belt off and lash your butt like it should have been lashed when you first broke into this game.

In fact, I looked forward to doing it.

CHAPTER SIX

I FINISHED a quart bottle of beer before calling Velda. I got her at home and asked her what she found. She said, 'There wasn't much *to* find, Mike. His landlady said he was on the quiet side because he was too stupid to talk. He never complained about a thing and in all the time he was living there he never once had company.'

No, he wouldn't talk too much if he was an MVD agent. And he wouldn't have company for that matter either. His kind of company was met at night and in the dark recesses of a building somewhere.

'Did you try the pie factory where he worked?'

'I did, but I didn't get anywhere. The last few months he had been on deliveries and most of the guys who knew him were out selling pies. The manager told me he was a stupid egg who had to write everything down in order to remember it, but he did his job fairly well. The only driver I did see said something nasty when I mentioned Moffit and tried to date me.'

The boy put on a good act. People aren't likely to get too friendly with somebody who's pretty stupid. I said, 'When do the drivers leave the plant?'

'Eight a.m., Mike. Are you going back?'

'I think I'd better. Supposing you come along with me. I'll meet you on the street in front of the office about seven and that'll give us time to get over there and see some of them.'

'Mike . . . what's so important about Charlie Moffit?'

'I'll tell you tomorrow.'

Velda grunted her displeasure and said good night. I had hardly hung up when I heard the feet in the hall and my doorbell started to yammer. Just in case, I yanked the .45 out and dropped it in my pocket where I could keep my hand around it.

The gun wasn't necessary at all. It was the boys from the papers, four of them. Three were on the police beat and the fourth was Marty Kooperman. He wore a faint, sardonic smile that was ready to disbelieve any lie I told.

'Well, the Fourth Estate! Come on in and don't stay too long.' I threw the door open.

Bill Cowan of the *News* grinned and pointed to my pocket. 'Nice way to greet old friends, Mike.'

'Isn't it. Come on in.'

They made a straight line for the refrigerator, found it empty, but uncovered a fresh bottle of whisky that I had been saving and helped themselves. All but Marty. He closed the door himself and stood behind me.

'We hear you got shot at, Mike.'

'You heard right, friend. They missed.'

'I'm thinking that I could say "too bad" and mean it.'

'What's your bitch, Marty! I've been shot at before. How come you're on the police run?'

'I'm not. I came along for the ride when I heard what happened.' He paused. 'Mike . . . for once come clean. Has this got to do with Lee Deamer?'

The boys in the kitchen were banging their first drinks down. I had that much time at least. I said, 'Marty, don't worry about your idol. Let's say that this happened as a result of my poking into something that I *thought* was connected with Deamer. He doesn't figure into it in any way.'

Marty took in a breath and let it out slowly. He twisted his hat in his hands then flipped it on the coat rack. 'Okay, Mike, I'll take your word for it.'

'Suppose it had to do with Lee, what then, chum?'

His lips tightened over a soft voice. 'We'd have to know. They're out to get Lee any way they can and there aren't many of us who can stop them.'

I scowled at him. 'Who's us?'

'Your Fourth Estate, Mike. Your neighbours. Maybe even you if you knew what we knew.'

That was all we had time for. The boys came charging back with fresh drinks and pencils ready. I let them inside to the living-room and sat down. 'Shoot, laddies. What's on your mind?'

'The shooting, Mike. Good news item, ya know.'

'Yeah, great news. Tomorrow the public gets my picture and another lurid account of how that Hammer character conducts a private war on a public thoroughfare and I'll get an eviction notice from my landlord and a sudden lack of clients.'

Bill laughed and polished his drink off. 'Just the same, it's news. We got some of it from headquarters, but we want the story straight from you. Hell, man, look how lucky you are. You get to tell your side of it while the others can't say a word. Come on, give.'

'Sure, I'll give.' I lit up a Lucky and took a deep drag on it. 'I was walking home and . . .'

'Where were you?'

'Movies. So just as I . . .'

'What movie?'

I showed him my teeth in a lopsided grin. That was an easy one. 'Laurance Theatre. Bum show.'

Marty showed me his teeth back. 'What was playing, Mike?' He was the only one not ready to take notes.

I started in on as much of the picture as I had seen and he stopped me with his hand. 'That's enough. I saw it myself. Incidentally, have you still got your stub?'

Marty should have been a cop. He knew damn well that most men have an unconscious habit of dropping the things in their pockets. I pulled out an assortment and handed him one. He took it while the other boys watched, wondering what the hell it was all about. He picked up the phone, called the theatre and gave them the number on the ticket, asking if it had been sold that day. They said it had been and Marty hung up sheepishly. I let go my breath, glad that he hadn't asked what time. He wasn't such a good detective after all.

'Go on,' he said.

103

'That's all. I was coming home when the punks in the car started to blast. I didn't get a look at any of them.'

Bill said, 'You on a case now?'

'If I was I wouldn't say so anyhow. What else?'

One of the boys from a tabloid wrinkled his nose at my story. 'Come on, Mike, break down. Nobody took a shot at you without a reason.'

'Look, pal, I have more enemies than I have friends. The kind of enemies I make go around loaded. Take a check on most known criminals and you'll find people who don't like me.'

'In other words, we don't get a story,' Bill said.

'In other words,' I told him, '. . . yes. Want another drink?'

At least that was satisfactory. When they had the bottom of the bottle showing I whistled to stop their jabbering and got them together so I could get in a last word. 'Don't any of you guys try tagging me around hoping for a lead about this. I'm not taking anything without paying it back. If a story crops up I'll let you in on it, meantime stick to chasing ambulances.'

'Aw, Mike.'

'No "Aw," pally. I'm not kidding around about it, so stay out of my way.'

As long as the bottle was empty and I wouldn't give with a yarn, they decided that there wasn't much sense in sticking around. They went out the door in a bunch with Marty trailing along in the rear. He said so-long ruefully, his eyes warning me to be careful.

I spread the slats of the blinds apart and watched them all climb into a beat-up coupé and when I was sure they were gone for the night I took off my clothes and climbed into the shower.

I took a hot and a cold, brushed my teeth, started to put away my tools and the bell rang again. I damned a few things in general and the Fourth Estate in particular for not making sure all the boys were there when they started their inquisition. Probably a lone reporter who got the flash late and wanted to know all about it. I wrapped a towel around my lower half and made wet tracks from the bathroom to the front door.

She stood there in the dim light of the hall not knowing whether to be startled, surprised or shocked. I said, 'Goddamn!'

She smiled hesitantly until I told her to come in and made a quick trip back for a bathrobe. Something had happened to Linda Holbright since the last time I had seen her and I didn't want to stand there in a towel while I found out what it was.

When I got back to the living-room she was sitting in the big chair with her coat thrown over the back. This time she didn't have on a sack suit and you knew what was underneath it. It wasn't 'probably nothing' either. It was a whole lot of something that showed and she wasn't making any bones about it. The angles seemed to be gone from her face and her hair was different. Before, it was hair. Now it was a smooth wavy mass that trailed across her shoulders. She still wasn't pretty, but a guy didn't give a damn about that when there was a body like hers under her face.

Because of a smile she had gone to a hell of a lot of trouble. She must have taken her one asset to a perfectionist and let him build a dress around it. I think it was a dress. Paint would have done the same thing. There wasn't anything on underneath to spoil the effect and that showed. She was excited as hell and that showed too.

I was thinking that it could be very nice if she had only come a little sooner, before I knew that Ethel had told what she had found in my wallet. Linda smiled at me tentatively as I sat down opposite her and lit up a smoke. I smiled back and started thinking again. This time there was a different answer. Maybe they were playing real cute and sent her in for the kicker. Maybe they had figured that their little shooting deal might get messed up and sent her around to get the score on me.

It made nice thinking because that was the way they worked and I didn't feel sorry for her any more. I got up and moved to the couch and told her to come over. I made her a drink and it must have been her first drink because she choked on it.

I kissed her and it must have been her first kiss, but she didn't choke on it. She grabbed me like the devil was inside her, bit me twice on the neck then pushed back to look at me to be sure this was happening to her.

There was no softness to her body. It was tense with the pain that was pleasure, oddly resilient under my hands. She closed her eyes, smothering the leaping fire to glowing coals. She fought to open them halfway and when she saw that I had been burned by their flame she smiled a twisted smile as if she was laughing at herself.

If she was going to, she should have asked me then. Any woman should know when a man is nothing but a man and when he'll promise or tell anything. I knew all those things too and it didn't do me any good because I was still a man.

She asked nothing. She said, 'This . . . is the first time . . . I ever . . .' and stopped there with the words choking to a hoarse whisper in her throat. She made me feel like a goddamn heel. She hadn't known about Ethel's little stunt because she had been too busy getting prettied up for me.

I was going to make her put her coat on and tell her to get the hell out of there and learn more about being a woman before she tried to act like one. I would have done just that until I thought a little further and remembered that she was new to the game and didn't know when to ask the questions but figured on trying anyway. So I didn't say a damn thing.

Her hand did something at her back and the dress that looked like paint peeled off like paint with a deliberate slowness that made me go warm all over.

And she still asked nothing except to be shown how to be a woman.

She wouldn't let me go to the door with her later. She wanted to be part of the darkness and alone. Her feet were a soft whisper against the carpet and the closing of the door an almost inaudible click.

I made myself a drink, had half of it and threw the rest away. I had been right the first time and went back to feeling like a heel. Then it occurred to me that now that she had a little taste of life maybe she'd go out and seek some different company for a change.

106

I stopped feeling like a heel, made another drink, finished it and went to bed.

The alarm woke me up at six, giving me time to shower and shave before getting dressed. I grabbed a plate of bacon and eggs in a diner around the corner, then hopped in my car and drove downtown to pick up Velda. She was standing in front of the building tucked inside a dark grey business suit, holding her coat open with her hand on her hips.

A newsboy was having trouble trying to watch her and hawk his editions too. I pulled in at the kerb and tooted the horn. 'Let's go, sugar.'

When she climbed in next to me the newsboy sighed.

'Early, isn't it?' She grinned.

'Too damned.'

'You were going to tell me something today, Mike.'

'I didn't say when.'

'One of those deals. You're a fine one.' She turned her head and looked out the window.

I tugged at her arm and made her look back at me. 'I'm sorry, Velda. It doesn't make nice conversation. I'll give it to you all at once when we get back. It's important to me not to talk about it right now. Mind?'

Maybe she saw the seriousness in my eyes. She smiled and said all right, then turned on the radio so we could have some music on our way across the bridge to Brooklyn where Mother Switcher had her pie factory.

Mother Switcher turned out to be a short, squat guy with long handlebar lip whiskers and eyebrows that went up and down like window shades. I asked him if I could speak to a few of his drivers and he said, 'If you're a union organizer it's no good. All my boys already belong to a union and get paid better'n union wages besides.'

I said I was no union organizer. 'So what is it, then?'

'I want to find out about a guy named Moffit. He worked for you.'

'That dope! He owe you money?'

'Not exactly.'

'Sure! Go talk to the boys, only don't stop their work.'

I said thanks and took Velda with me when I went around behind the building where the trucks were lined up for their quota of pies. We waited until the first truck was filled then buttonholed the driver. He gave Velda a big smile and tipped his cap.

She took it from there. 'You knew Charlie Moffit, didn't you?'

'Yeah, sure, lady. What's he done now, crawled out of his grave?'

'I imagine he's still there, but tell me, what was he like?'

The guy frowned and looked at me for the first time. 'I don't get it,' he grunted.

I flashed my buzzer. So did Velda. 'Now I get it,' he said. 'Was he in trouble?'

'That's what we want to find out. What was he like?'

He leaned against his truck and chewed on a match. 'Well, I'll tell ya. Charlie was a queer duck.' He tapped his head and made a screwy face. 'Not all there, ya know. We were forever playing all kinds of gags on him. The dope would fall for 'em too. He was always losing something. Once it was his change bag and once it was a whole load of pies. He said some kids got him in a ball game and while he played they swiped his pies. Ever hear of anything like that?'

'No, I didn't,' Velda laughed.

'That wasn't all, either. He was a mean bast . . . son-of-a-gun. Once we caught him trying to set fire to a cat. One of the boys slugged him.'

It didn't sound right, that picture of Charlie Moffit. I was thinking while Velda popped the questions. Some of the other men came over and added a little something that distorted the picture even more. Charlie liked women and booze. Charlie molested kids in the street. Charlie was real bright for long periods then he'd get drunk and seem to fall into a conscious coma when he'd act like a kid. He wasn't right in his dome. He had rocks in his head. He sure liked the women, though.

I took Velda out of there and started back to Manhattan, my head aching from thoughts that were too big for it. I had to squint to watch the traffic and hunch over the wheel to be sure I knew where I was going. Away in the back of my mind that devilish unseen conductor was warming up his orchestra for another of those wild symphonies. I must be mad, I thought. I must be mad. I don't think like I used to. The little things won't come through any more and it was the little things falling into place that made big things.

My mind rambled on until Velda said, 'We're here.'

The attendant was waving me into the parking lot. I took my ticket and handed him my keys while she flagged a cab. All the way to the office I sat with my eyes closed and kept the curtains down on the orchestra that was trying so hard to play. Whoever was at the drums wouldn't give up. He kept up a steady beat, thumping his drum with a muted stick, trying to make me open the curtain.

Velda brought out the bottle and handed it to me. I stared at the glass, filled it and drank it down. She offered me another and I shook my head. I had to sit down. I wanted to sit down and pull something over my head to shut out the light and the sound.

'Mike.' Velda ran her fingers through my hair.

'What is it, kid?' My voice didn't sound right.

'If you tell me I might be able to help you.' I opened my eyes and looked at her. She had her coat off and her breasts rose high against the folds of the blouse. She pulled up the big chair and sat down, her legs flashing in the light that streamed through the window. They were beautiful legs, long, alive with smooth muscles that played through the tight fabric of her dress as she moved. It was so easy to love that woman. I ought to try it more often. It was mine whenever I wanted it.

I closed my eyes again.

There wasn't any answer or any special way to tell her. I sat there with my eyes closed and gave it to her as it happened, bit by bit. I told her how I killed on the bridge. I told her about

Marty and almost all about Ethel. I told her everything that happened and waited to see what she would say.

A minute went by. I opened my eyes and saw that Velda was watching me and there was no shame, no terror in her face. She believed in me. She said, 'It doesn't make sense, Mike.'

'It doesn't at that,' I said tiredly. 'There's a flaw in it that I can see. Do you see it too?'

'Yes. Charlie Moffit.'

'That's right. The man with a present and no past. Nobody knows him nor knows where he comes from. He's just a present.'

'Almost ideal for an MVD operative.'

'That's right again. Almost. Where's the flaw?'

Velda's fingers made a little tap-tap against the arm of the chair. 'The act was too nearly perfect. It was too good to be anything but true.'

'Roger! Charlie Moffit was anything but MVD. I thought those Reds were figuring me to be the man who took his place. I was wrong. I was impersonating the wrong dead man. The boy on the bridge was MVD. Pat handed it to me on a platter, but I let it slip by. His only identifiable mark was his bridgework because he had a stainless-steel tooth. There's only one country where they use stainless steel for teeth . . . the U.S.S.R. Fat boy was an imported killer, a checkrein on other agents in this country. Do you know how they knew he was dead?'

'Not from the sketch in the papers. He didn't have any fingerprints, either.'

'They wouldn't have found them if they did. I forgot to tell you, but I wore his fingertips to the bone on the concrete before I threw him over.'

Velda bit her lip and shuddered. She said, 'Mike!' too softly.

'No, the reason they knew he was dead was because he dropped out of sight. I don't think they got the connection until later when some smart apple started to check the unidentified bodies in the morgue. Pat said they sent dental charts out. One of those that received them could have recognized what that stainless-steel tooth meant and there it was.'

'But they knew he was dead the next night . . . or so you supposed.'

'Uh-huh! Fat boy didn't check in. They must have a system for those things. There was only one answer if he didn't check in. He was dead. The dental charts only verified it.'

'What must they think? Why . . .'

I kept my voice low so I wouldn't get boiling mad again. 'They think it was a dirty democratic conspiracy. It was all too secret to be normal. They think it was our government playing them dirty. They're the only ones who are supposed to be able to kick you under the table.'

Velda said something dirty and she wasn't smiling.

I went on: 'The other night there was a new note in the Party. Something happened to a courier of theirs, something about documents. They are missing. The Party is very upset, the poor devils.'

Velda came up out of her seat, her face tight as a drumhead. 'They're at it again, Mike. Government documents and double-dealing. Damn it, Mike, why do these things have to happen?'

'They happen because we're soft. We're honourable.'

'Did they say what they were?'

'No. I gathered they were pretty important.'

'They must be.'

'Velda, there's a lot of things that are important that we give away for free. Do you know what they were doing one night? They had a pile of technical journals and flying mags you can pick up on any news-stand. They were photographing the stuff onto microfilm for shipment back. A good intelligence man can pick out a lot of data from photos. They take a bit here and a bit there until the picture is complete and bingo, they have something we're trying to keep under the hat.'

'But documents, Mike. That's government stuff! That's something the FBI should know about.'

'I know, I know. Maybe they do. Maybe they know they're missing and suspect where they've gone. Maybe they don't know because the documents were photostats. They're gone and that's what counts. I'm in a muddle because they found me out and now I can't do any more snooping. They'll be looking for me with a vengeance now. They tried to kill me last night and . . .'

'Mike!'

'Oh, you didn't hear about that. You should read the papers. There's six lines about it on page four. They didn't even print my picture. Yeah, they know me now and it's every man for himself. The next time I'll start the shooting and I won't miss.'

Velda had her hand over her mouth, her teeth clamped on a fingernail. 'God, you get into some of the most horrible scrapes! I do wish you'd be careful.' Her eyes got a little wet and she got mad at herself. 'You won't tell anybody anything and you won't ask for help when you need it most. Mike . . . please . . . there are times when you have to let somebody else in on things.'

I could feel my lip curling. 'Sure, Velda, sure. I'll tell everybody that I go around killing people just like that. It's easy to say, but I'm the guy who's supposed to be a menace to society. Hell, I'll take it my way and the public can lump it.'

She wiped away a tear that was feeling its way down her cheek. 'He shouldn't have done that to you, Mike.'

'Who?'

'The judge.'

I swore violently and my voice was hoarse.

'Are you . . . going to keep looking?'

I nodded my head. 'Indirectly, yes. I'm still on a case for Lee Deamer.'

Velda's head snapped up. 'Mike . . . that's it!'

'What?'

'The documents! Charlie Moffit was the courier they spoke about! He was carrying those documents the night Oscar attacked and killed him! Oscar must have taken them from him.'

'Damn!' The word exploded out of me. Of course, of course! The pocket that was ripped out of his coat! I shot Velda a grin that had 'thanks' written on it. 'It comes clear, kid, real clear. Oscar came to town to bleed Lee and he wouldn't bleed. So he goes out and kills a guy hoping to be identified as Lee, knowing damn well Lee would have an alibi and it would just make sensational reading for the public. He figured that would bring Lee to heel when he asked for money again. The gimmick came when he killed the guy. The papers must have stuck out of his pocket and Oscar grabbed them. When he realized what they were he saw the ideal way to bring Lee around. That's what he hinted at to Lee over the phone. If Lee brought in the cops and anything happened to him, the presence of those papers were to be attributed to Lee.'

Velda was white, dead-white and her breathing came too fast. 'It's rotten, Mike. Good heavens, if it ever gets out . . .'

'Yeah, Lee is finished even if he *can* prove himself innocent.'

'Oh, no!'

'Beautiful! No matter what happens the Commies win. If they get the documents they probably have something juicy for cruddy Uncle Joe. If they don't and somebody else finds them, their worst enemy is yanked off their necks.'

'Mike . . . it can't happen!'

'Now, do I go it alone, Velda? Now, do I take it by myself?'

'Yes. You . . . and me. The bastards! The dirty, filthy Red bastards!' They should see her now, I was thinking. Gladow, the general, the boys in the Kremlin should see her now and they'd know what they were getting into. They'd see the face of beauty that had a kill-lust in every beautiful line and they'd stick inside their cold, walled-in city and shake in their shoes!

'When do we start, Mike?'

'Tonight. Be here at nine sharp. We'll see if we can find what Oscar did with those papers.' She sat back in the chair and stared at the wall.

I picked up the phone and dialled Pat's number. He came on with, 'Homicide, Captain Chambers speaking.'

'Mike, pal. Any new corpses today?'

'Not yet. You didn't shoot straight enough. When are you coming in to explain about last night? I went to bat for you and I want a report and not a lot of subterfuge.'

'I'm practically on my way now. I'll drop by your office and pick you up for lunch.'

'Okay! Make it snappy.'

I said I would and cradled the receiver. Velda was waiting for orders. 'Stay here,' I told her. 'I have to see Pat and I'll call you when I'm finished. In case I don't call or come back, be here at nine.'

'That's all?'

'That's all,' I repeated. I tried to look stern like a boss should, but she grinned and spoiled it. I had to kiss her goodbye before she'd let me go. 'There's no telling if I'll see you alive again,' she laughed. Then she slapped her hand over her mouth and her eyes went wide. 'What am I saying?'

'I still have a couple of lives left, kid. I'll save one for you, so don't worry.' I grinned again and went out the door.

Downstairs I got tired of waiting for a cab so I walked the half-mile to the lot. A car in the city could be a pain in the butt sometimes. But what the hell, it was a nice day for a change and the air felt fairly fresh if a bus or something didn't go by.

I picked up my keys when I handed over the ticket and found my heap. I was in second heading toward the gate when I saw that the boy had cleaned off my windows, and jammed on my brakes to flip him a quarter. That two-bits saved my skin. The truck that had been idling up the street had jumped ahead to intercept me broadside, saw I was stopping and tried to get me by swerving onto the driveway and off again.

Metal being ripped out by the roots set up a shriek and the car leaped ahead before there was a nasty snap that disengaged it from the body of the truck. I let out a string of curses because the jolt had wedged me up against the wheel and I couldn't get my rod out. By the time I was back in the seat the truck was lost in the traffic.

The attendant yanked the door open, his face ashen. 'Gawd, mister, you hurt?'

'No, not this time.'

'Them crazy fools! Gawd, they coulda killed ya!' His teeth started to chatter violently.

114

'They sure coulda.' I got out of the car and walked around the front. One side of the bumper had been ripped clear off the frame and stuck out like an oversize L.

'Boy, that was close, awright. I seen 'em come up the street, but I never give 'em a thought. Them crazy fools musta been fooling around the cab and hit the gas. They never stopped. You want I should call a cop?'

I kicked the bumper and it all but fell loose. 'Forget it. They got away by now. Think you can get this bumper off?'

'Sure, I got some tools. Only two bolts holding it on anyway.'

'Okay, take it off and pick up one for this model at a garage somewhere. I'll fix you up for your trouble.'

He said, 'Yessir, mister. Sure,' and ran after his tools. I sat on the fender and smoked a cigarette until he finished then passed him two bucks and told him not to forget a new bumper. He said he wouldn't forget.

When I pulled away I looked up and down that one-way street just to be sure. It happened twice. I said it wouldn't, but it happened again anyway. They must have had a tail on me when I came out of the office and saw a beautiful chance to nail me cold. That truck would have made hash of me if it had connected right.

They were going to all kinds of trouble, weren't they? That made me important. You have to be important if you were better off dead. The judge should like that.

Pat was sitting with his back to the door looking out the window at the city when I came in. He swung around in his chair and nodded hello. I pulled a chair up and sat down with my feet propped up on his desk. 'I'm all set, Captain. Where are the bright lights?'

'Cut it out, Mike. Start talking.'

'Pat, so help me, you know almost everything right now.'

'Almost. Give me the rest.'

'They tried again a little while ago. This time it was a truck and not bullets.'

The pencil in Pat's hand tapped the desk. 'Mike, I'm not a complete fool. I play along with you because we're friends, but

I'm a cop, I've been a cop a long time, and I know my business. You're not telling me people are shooting you up in the streets without a reason.'

'Hell, they gotta have a reason.'

'Do you know what it is?' He was drawing to the end of his patience.

I took my feet off the desk and leaned toward him. 'We've been through this before, Pat. I'm not a complete fool either. In your mind every crime belongs to the police, but there are times when an apparent crime is a personal affront and it isn't very satisfying not to take care of it yourself. That's how I feel about it.'

'So you know then.'

'I think I know. There's nothing you can do about it so quit being a cop and let's get back to being friends.'

Pat tried to grin, but didn't put it over too well. 'Are you straightened out with Lee?'

My feet went up on the desk again. 'He gave me a tidy sum to poke around. I'm busy at it.'

'Good, Mike. Be sure you make a clean sweep.' He dropped his head and passed his hand over his hair. 'Been reading the papers lately?'

'Not too much. I noticed one thing . . . they're pulling for Deamer in nearly every editorial column. One sheet reprints all his speeches.'

'He's giving another tonight. You should go hear him.'

'I'll leave that stuff up to you, chum. There's too much dribble and not enough pep talk at those meetings.'

'The devil there isn't! Take the last one I was at. We had supper with the customary speeches afterward, but it was the small talk later that counted. Lee Deamer made the rounds speaking to small groups and he gave them the real stuff. It was easier for him to talk that way. Most of us had never met him until that time, but when he spoke we were sold completely. We have to have that guy in, Mike. No two ways about it. He's strong. He can't be pushed or bullied. You wouldn't know it to look at him, but he's the strength that this nation will be relying on some day.'

'That was the same night Oscar pulled the stops out, wasn't it?'

'That's right. That's why we didn't want any of it to reach the public. Even a lie can be told to give the people the wrong impression.'

'You've sure gotten a big interest in politics, Pat.'

'Hell, why not? I'll be glad to go back to being a cop again instead of a tool in some politician's workshop. Lee gave a talk over the radio last night. You know what he did?'

I said no. I had been too busy to listen.

'He's brought some of his business sense into politics. He sat down with an adding machine and figured things up. He wanted to know why it cost the state ten million to have a job done when any private contractor could do it for six. He quoted names and places and figures and told the public that if he was elected his first order would be to sign warrants of arrest for certain political joes who are draining the state dry.'

'And . . .?'

Pat looked at the desk and glared. 'And today I heard that the big push comes soon. Lee has to be smeared any way at all.'

'It won't happen, Pat.'

I shouldn't have used that tone. His head jerked up and his eyes were tiny bright spots watching me from tight folds of skin. His hand closed into a fist slowly and tightened until the cords bulged out. 'You know something, Mike, by God, you know something!'

'I do?' I couldn't make it sound funny.

Pat was ready to split wide open. 'Mike, you're in on it. Damn it, you went and found something. Oh, I know you . . . no talking until you're ready, but this isn't a murder that involved only a handful of people . . . this is something that takes in a whole population and you better not tip the apples over.'

He stood up, his hands on the edge of the desk for support. He spat the words out between his teeth and meant every one.

117

'We've been friends, Mike. You and I have been in and out of a lot of things together and I've always valued your friendship. And your judgment. Just remember this, if I'm guessing right and you're in on something that might hurt Lee and won't talk about it, and if that something *does* hurt Lee, then we can forget about being friends. Is that clear?'

'That's clear, Pat. Would it make you feel better if I told you that your line of reasoning is a little off? You're getting teed off at me when you ought to be teeing off on some of the goddamn Commies we got loose in this city.'

His face had a shrewd set to it. 'So they're part of it too.' Muscles stuck out in lumps along his jaws. Let him think how he liked.

'Nothing will happen to Lee,' I said. 'At least nothing that I'm concerned with.' This time I got some conviction in my voice. Pat stopped glaring and sat down.

He didn't forget the subject. 'You still have those green cards on your mind?'

'Yeah, I have. I don't like what they mean, and you shouldn't either.'

'I hate everything they stand for. I'm sorry we have to tolerate it. We ought to do what they would have done a hundred years ago.'

'Stop talking nonsense. You're in America now.'

'Sure I am, and I want to stay here. If you want a democracy you have to fight for it. Why not now before it's too late? That's the trouble, we're getting soft. They push us all around the block and we let them get away with it!'

'Calm down, will you.' I hadn't realized that I was banging on his desk until he rapped my knuckles. I sat down.

'What did you do about Oscar?' I asked.

'What could we do? Nothing. It's over, finished.'

'And his personal effects?'

'We went through them and there was nothing to be found. I posted a man to check his place in case any mail came in. I had the idea that Oscar might have mailed something to himself. I took the man off today when nothing showed.'

I had to struggle to hold my face straight. Pat had the place watched! Neat, very neat. If we weren't the only ones who wanted to go through that apartment then we wouldn't be going in on a cold deal. Nobody else could have gotten there either!

I reached for a butt and lit it. 'Let's go out to eat, Pat.'

He grabbed his coat off the rack and locked the door to the office. On the way out I thought of something I should have thought of before and had him open it up again. I picked up the phone and called the office. Velda answered with a silky hello.

I said, 'Mike, honey. Look, have you emptied the wastebasket by my desk yet?'

'No, there wasn't anything to empty.'

'Go look if there's a cigarette pack there. Don't touch it.'

She dropped the phone and I heard her heels clicking along the floor. In a moment she was back. 'It's there, Mike.'

'Swell! Take it out of there without touching it if you can. Put it in a box and have a boy run it down to Pat right away.'

Pat watched me curiously. When I hung up he said, 'What is it?'

'An almost empty pack of butts. Do me a favour and lift the prints off it. You'll find a lot of mine on them and if I'm lucky you'll find some others too.'

'Whose?'

'Hell, how do I know? That's why I want you to get the prints. I need an identification. That is, if we're still friends.'

'Still friends, Mike,' he grinned. I socked him on the arm and started for the door again.

CHAPTER SEVEN

THAT night the nation got the report on the 6.15 p.m. news broadcast. There had been a leak in the State Department and the cat was out of the bag. It seemed that we had had a secret. Somebody else was in on it now. The latest development in the process for the annihilation of man had been stolen. Supposedly secret files had been rifled and indications pointed to the duplication of the secret papers. The FBI was making every effort to track down the guilty parties.

I threw my cigarette against the wall and started swearing until I ran out of words. Then I started over again. The commentator droned on repeating what he had already said and I felt like screaming at him to tell the world who took those damn papers. Tell 'em it was the same outfit who tried to make a mockery of our courts and who squirmed into the government and tried to bring it down around our necks. Tell everybody who did it. You know you want to say it; what are you afraid of?

There wasn't any doubt of it now, those documents the general had been so anxious to get hold of were the ones we were looking for ourselves! My guts were all knotted up in a ball and my head felt like a machine-shop was going on inside it. Here I had the whole lousy situation right in my hands and I had to keep it there.

Me, Mike Hammer. I was up in the big leagues now. No more plain and simple murders. I was playing ball with the big boys and they played rough. The end justified the means, that was their theory. Lie, steal, kill, do anything that was necessary to push a political philosophy that would enslave the world if we let it. Great!

Nice picture. Judge, a beautiful picture of a world in flames. You must be one of the normal people who get the trembles when they read the papers. A philosophy like that must give you the willies. What are you thinking now . . . how that same secret that was stolen might be the cause of your death? And what would you say if you knew that I was the only one who might be able to stop it in time? Okay, Judge, sit your fanny in a chair and relax. I have a little philosophy of my own. Like you said, it's as bad as theirs. I don't give a damn for a human life any more, even my own. Want to hear that philosophy? It's simple enough. Go after the big boys. Oh, don't arrest them, don't treat them to the dignity of the democratic process of courts and law . . . do the same thing to them that they'd do to you! Treat 'em to the unglorious taste of sudden death. Get the big boys and show them the long road to nowhere and then none of those stinking little people with little minds will want to get big. Death is funny, Judge, people are afraid of it. Kill 'em left and right, show 'em that we aren't so soft after all. Kill, kill, kill, kill! They'll keep away from us then!

Hell, it was no use trying to smoke. I'd light up a butt and take a drag then throw it away because my fingers weren't steady enough to hold it. I went inside to the bedroom and took my .45 off the top of the dresser to clean it for the second time. It felt good, feeling the cold butt setting up against the palm of my hand. The deadly noses of the slugs showing in the clip looked so nice and efficient.

They liked to play dirty, I was thinking. Let's make it real dirty. I thumbed the slugs out, laying them in a neat row, then took a penknife and clipped the ends off the noses. That was real dirty. They wouldn't make too much of a hole where they went in, but the hole on the other side would be a beaut. You could stick your head in and look around without getting blood on your ears. I put the gun together, shoved the slugs back in the clip and strapped on the sling. I was ready.

It was a night to give you the meemies. Something happened to the sky and a slow, sticky fog was rolling in from the river. The cold was penetrating, undecisive as to whether to stay winter or turn into spring. I turned the collar of my coat up around my ears and started walking down the street. I didn't lose myself in any thoughts this time. My eyes looked straight ahead, but they saw behind me and to either side. They picked up figures hurrying to wherever it was they were going, and the twin yellow eyes of the cars that rolled in the street, boring holes in the fog. My ears picked up footsteps, timed their pace and direction then discarded them for other sounds.

I was waiting for them to try again.

When I reached the corner I crossed over to my car, passed it, then walked back again. I opened the door, felt for the handle that unlocked the hood and took a quick check of the engine. I wasn't in the mood to get myself blown all over the neighbourhood when I started the car. The engine was clean. So was the rest of the heap.

A car came by and I drew out behind it, getting in line to start the jaunt downtown to the office. The fog was thicker there and the traffic thinner. The subways were getting a big play. I found a place to park right outside the office and scraped my wheels against the kerb then cut the engine. I sat there until a quarter to nine trying to smoke my way through a deck of Luckies. I still had a few to go when I went inside, put my name in the night register and had the elevator operator haul me up to my office floor.

At exactly nine p.m. a key turned in the lock and Velda came in. I swung my feet off the desk and walked out to the outside office and said hello. She smiled, but her heart wasn't in it. 'Did you catch the news broadcast, kid?'

Her lips peeled back. 'I heard it. I didn't like it.'

'Neither did I, Velda. We have to get them back.'

She opened her coat and perched on the edge of the desk. Her eyes were on the floor, staring at a spot on the carpet. She wasn't just a woman now. An aurora of the jungle hung around her, turning her into a female animal scenting a game run and anxious to be in on the kill. 'It can't stop there, Mike.'

I dropped my butt and ground it into the carpet. 'No, it can't.' I knew what she was thinking and didn't like it.

'The papers aren't all. As far as they can go is to checkmate us. They'll try again.'

'Will they?'

Her eyes moved up to meet mine, but that was all. 'We can stop them, Mike.'

'I can, sugar. Not you. I'm not shoving you into any front lines.'

Her eyes still held mine. 'There's somebody in this country who directs operations for them. It isn't anyone we know or the FBI knows or the Party knows. It's somebody who can go and come like anybody else and not be interfered with. There are others who take orders and are equally dangerous because they represent the top of the chain of command and can back up their orders with force if necessary. How long will it take us to get them all, the known and the unknown?'

'It might take *me* a long time. Me, I said.'

'There's a better way, Mike. We can get all those we know and any we suspect and the rest will run. They'll get the hell out of here and be afraid to come back.'

It was almost funny, the way her reasoning followed mine. 'Just me, Velda,' I said.

Her head came up slowly and all I could think of was a big cat, a great big, luxurious cat leaning against the desk. A cat with gleaming black hair darker than the night and a hidden body of smooth skin that covered a wealth of rippling, deadly muscles that were poised for the kill. The desk light made her teeth an even row of merciless ivory, ready to rip and tear. She was still grinning, but a cat looks like it's grinning until you see its ears laid flat back against its head.

'Mike, there are men and women in this country. They made it together even when it was worse than now. Women learned how to shoot and shoot straight. They learned fast, and knew how to use a gun or a knife and use it right when the time came. I said we'd do it together. Either that or I take the whole thing to Pat.'

I waited a long minute before I said, 'Okay, it's us. I want it that way anyhow.'

Velda slid off the desk and reached for my hand. I squeezed it hard, happy as hell I had the sense to realize that I knew what I wanted at last. She said it very simply. 'I love you, Mike.'

I had her in my arms, searched for her mouth and found it, a warm mouth with full, ripe lips that burned into my soul as they fused with mine. I tasted the love she offered and gave it back with all I had to give, crushing her until her breath came in short, quick jerks.

I held her face in my hands and kissed her eyes and her cheeks, listened to her moan softly and press herself closer and closer. I was lucky as hell and I knew it.

She opened her eyes when I held her off. I dropped my hand in my pocket and took out the box that I had picked up that afternoon. When I pressed the button the lid flew up and the sapphire threw back a perfect star. My fingers felt big and clumsy when I took it out and slipped it over her finger.

You don't have to speak at a time like that. Everything has been said and if anything remains it's written there in a silent promise your heart makes and that's all there is to it. Velda looked at it with a strange wonder for a long time before she kissed me again.

It was better than the last time.

It told her everything she wanted to know and no matter what happened now nothing would ever change.

'We have to go,' I said.

She snapped out the lights while I waited at the door and we went down the elevator together. The watchman gave me the okay sign, so I knew nobody had been near my car while I was gone. When we were back in the fog I told her about Pat's having kept a man on Oscar's house and she picked it right up.

'Maybe . . . maybe we'll be the first.'

'I'm hoping that,' I said.

'What will they look like?'

'I don't know. If Moffit had them in his pocket, then they were in a package or an envelope big enough to fit in there. It may be that we're barking up the wrong tree. They may have been on microfilm.'

'Let's hope we're right.'

About two blocks away I ran the car in between a couple of parked trucks and waved her out. 'We're taking the long way around this time.'

'Through the alley?'

'Uh-huh! I don't like the idea of using the front door. When we reach the opening between the buildings duck in and keep on going.'

Velda felt for my hand and held on to it. For all the world we might have been just a couple of dopes out for a walk. The fog was a white tube all around us, but it could be hiding a lot of things beside us. We crossed the street, came up around the subway kiosk and walked in the protection of the wall, the two of us searching for the narrow passageway that led behind the buildings.

As it was, we almost passed it. I stepped in holding Velda's hand and the darkness swallowed us up. For two or three minutes we stood there letting our eyes accustom themselves to this deeper gloom, then edged forward slowly, picking our way through the trash that had accumulated over the years. Animals and people had made a barely perceptible path through the centre of the litter and we followed it until we stood behind the building and could feel our way along the alley by sticking close to the rotted planking that formed the wall of the yards behind the houses.

Velda was fishing in her handbag and I told her, 'No lights. Just keep looking for a pile of bottles. There's a door in the wall behind it and that's the place.'

I tried to judge the distance from that other night and found little to remember. Soft furry things would squeal and run across our feet whenever we disturbed the junk lying around. Tiny pairs of eyes would glare at us balefully and retreat when we came closer. A cat moved in the darkness and trapped a pair of eyes that had been paying too much attention to us and the jungle echoed with a mad death cry.

Velda tugged my hand and pointed to the ground, 'Here're the bottles, Mike.' She dropped my hand to walk around them. 'The door is still open.'

I pushed her through into the yard and we held still, taking in the black shadow of the building. The back door still swung open on one hinge. How many people lived here? I thought. How long ago was it when this dirty pile of brick and mortar was a home besides being a house? I went up the short flight of steps and took the flashlight from my pocket.

Velda flashed hers on the wall beside the door, illuminating a printed square of cardboard tacked to the framework. It read, THIS BUILDING HAS BEEN CONDEMNED FOR OCCUPANCY. A paragraph explained why and a rubber-stamp signature made it official.

Ha!

The air had a musty odour of decay that collected in the long hall and clung to the walls. There was a door that led to the cellar, but the stairs were impenetrable, piled high with an unbelievable collection of scrap. Velda opened the door to the room that faced the backyard and threw her spot around the walls. I looked in over her shoulder and saw a black, charred mass and the remains of some furniture. It must have been a year or more since that room had started to burn, and nobody had been in it since. It was amazing to me that the house still stood.

Halfway down the hall there was a door-frame but no door and the room was stacked with old bed-frames, a few mattresses left to the fleas and nothing worth stealing. The next room was, or had been, Oscar's. I had my hand on the knob when Velda grabbed me and we froze there.

From somewhere in the upper recesses of the house came a harsh, racking cough and the sound of someone vomiting.

I heard Velda take a deep breath of relief. 'Drunk,' she said.

'Yeah.' I went back to the door. A plain skeleton key unlocked it and we stepped inside, locking it again behind us. Velda went to the windows and tucked the shade in so there would be no chance of our lights being seen from the outside. Then we started to take that room apart.

Oscar's effects were collecting dust in the police storeroom, but it was unlikely that they had been in his bag or among his clothes. If they had been I would have found them the first time. We peeled the covers off the bed, found nothing and put them back. We felt in the corners and under things. I even tore the moulding off the wall and shoved my hand behind it. There was nothing there, either.

Velda was working her way along the rear wall. She called softly, 'Mike, come here a minute.'

I followed the track of light to where she was fiddling with some aged draperies that had been tacked to the wall in a vain attempt to give a tapestry effect. She had one side pulled away and was pointing to it. 'There used to be a door here. It led to that storeroom on the other side.'

'Umm! This house was a one-family job at one time.'

'Do you suppose . . .'

'That it's in there?' I finished. She nodded. 'We better look. This room is as bare as a baby's spanked tail.'

The two of us wormed out into the hall and shut the door. Velda led the way with her light and took a cautious step over the sill into the room beyond. From upstairs the coughing came again. I banged my shin against an iron bedpost and swore softly.

It only took ten minutes to go over that room, but it was long enough to see that nothing had been put in or taken out in months. A layer of dust covered everything; the junk was attached to the walls with thousands of spider webs. The only prints in the grime on the floor were those we had made ourselves.

I hated to say it; Velda hated to hear it. 'Not a damn thing. Oscar never had those papers.'

'Oh, Mike!' There was a sob in her voice.

'Come on, kid, we're only wasting time now.'

The flashlight hung in her hand, the penny-sized beam a small, lonely spot on the floor, listlessly trying to add a bit of brightness to a night that was darker than ever now.

'All right, Mike,' she said. 'There must be other places for it to be.'

The guy upstairs coughed again. We would have paid no attention to him except that we heard the thump of his feet hitting the floor then the heavy thud as he fell. The guy started cursing then was still.

It wasn't a conscious thing that held us back; we just stood there and listened, not scared, not worried, just curious and cautious. If we hadn't stopped where we were at the moment we did we would have walked right into the mouth of hell.

The front door opened and for a brief interval the Trench Coats were dimly silhouetted against the grey of the fog outside. Then the door closed and they were inside, motionless against the wall.

I did two things fast. I grabbed Velda and pulled out the .45.

Why did I breathe so fast? I hadn't done a thing and yet I wanted to pant my lungs out. They were on fire, my throat was on fire, my brain was on fire. The gun that I used to be able to hold so still was shaking hard and Velda felt it too. She slid her hand over mine, the one that squeezed her arm so hard it must have hurt, and I felt some of the tension leave me.

Velda wasn't shaking at all. Trench Coats moved and I heard a whispered voice. Something Velda did made a metallic snap. My brain was telling me that now it had come, the moment I had waited for. Trench Coats. Gladow and Company. The hammer-and-sickle backed up with guns. The general's boys.

They came for me! Even in the fog they had managed to follow me here and now they were ready to try again. *The third time they won't miss.* That was the common superstition, wasn't it? It was to be at close quarters and a crossfire with me in the middle.

I could feel my teeth grinding together. A hot wave of hate, so violent that it shook me from top to bottom, swept through my body. Who the hell were they supposed to be? Did they expect to come in and find me with my back to the door? Was I supposed to be another sap . . . the kind of guy who'd give people like them the old fighting chance . . . a gesture of sportsmanship? I should take a chance on dying like that?

They went in the room then, softly, but not so softly that my ears couldn't follow every step they took. I could hear their breathing coming hard, the scuffle of leather against wood. I even heard the catch of the flashlight when it snapped on.

Very slowly I jacked the hammer of the .45 back. My hand told Velda to stay there. Just stay there and shut up. I bent down and unlaced my shoes, stepped out of them and into the hall. I lay on my stomach looking into the room, the .45 propped on my forearm. The light of the flash made a circuit of the wall then stopped on the draperies that covered up the opening to the other room. Trench Coat, who didn't have a flash, stepped forward to pull the drapes down.

And Velda was in there waiting for me.

I said, 'Looking for me, Martin?' The sudden shift of the flash and the lance of flame that spit from his gun came at the same time. I heard the bullets smack the wall over my head. He fired at the door where my belly should have been, mouthing guttural, obscene curses.

Then I shot him. I aimed a little below and inside the red eye of his gun barrel and over the blast of the .45 I heard his breath leave him in a wheezing shriek that died in a bubble of blood that came to his mouth. His rod went off once, a bullet ripped into the floor, and Trench Coat dropped.

The other one didn't stay in the room. I heard cloth rip, feet stumble and a heavy body slam against the wood. The other killer had gone into the room with Velda!

I was on my feet trying to decide. I had to decide! Good God, I had to get him before he saw her. If I went in through either door he'd get me and I had to go! I could feel him waiting for me, the darkness screening him completely. He knew I'd come and he knew he'd get me.

I walked toward the door. I didn't bother trying to be quiet.

I stepped into the doorway.

The crack of the gun was a flat noise that echoed once and was gone. There was no streak of flame, only that sudden, sharp sound and a peculiar hiss that seemed out of place. I felt no shock, no pain, only a sudden tensing of the muscles and a stillness that was nearly audible.

I must have caught it, I thought. It wasn't like this before. The last time it hurt. I tried to raise my hand and it came up slowly, effortlessly. In the room a gun clattered on the bare planking and was followed immediately by a soft thunk.

She seemed far away, so far away. 'Mike?'

I couldn't get the breath out of my lungs at first. 'You . . . all right, Velda?'

'I killed him, Mike.'

Dear God what was there to say? I reached for her and folded her against my chest feeling her sob softly. I grabbed her flash and threw it on Trench Coat. Martin Romberg lay on his face with a hole in his back. She must have held it right against his spine when she pulled the trigger. That's why I didn't see the flash.

I straightened Velda up and pulled her toward the door. 'Come on. We can't stay here.' I found my shoes and yanked them on without bothering to tie them.

It was easier going out. It always is. The fog was still there, rolling in over the walls, sifting down between the building. Our eyes, so long in the dark, could see things that were hidden before and we raced down that back alley heading for that narrow slip a block away from the house.

The curious had already started their pilgrimage toward the sound of the shooting. A police car whined through the night, its light a blinking eye that cleared the way. We lost ourselves in the throng, came out of it and found the car. Two more police cars passed us as we started to cut back to the land of the living on the other side of town.

Velda sat stiff and straight staring out the window. When I looked down she still held the gun in her hand. I took it away from her and laid it on the seat. 'You can file another notch on it, kid. That makes two.'

I gave it to her brutally hoping it might snap her out of it. She turned her head and I saw that her mouth had taken on a smile. She picked up that nasty little .32 automatic and dropped it in her handbag. The snap catch made the same metallic sound that I had heard back there in the room. 'My conscience doesn't hurt me, Mike,' she said softly.

I patted her hand.

'I was afraid I wouldn't be quick enough. He never saw me. He stood in the centre of the room covering both entrances and I knew what he was waiting for and I knew you'd come after him. He would have killed you, Mike.'

'I know, honey.'

'He was standing close enough so I could reach out and put the gun right against him.' Her lips tightened. 'Is this how . . . you feel, Mike? Is it all right for me to feel like this? Not having a sensation of guilt?'

'I feel happy.'

'So do I. Perhaps I shouldn't, Mike. Maybe I should feel ashamed and sinful, but I don't. I'm glad I shot him. I'm glad I had the chance to do it and not you. I wanted to, do you understand that?'

'I understand completely. I know how you feel because it's how I feel. There's no shame or sin in killing a killer. David did it when he knocked off Goliath. Saul did it when he slew his tens of thousands. There's no shame to killing an evil thing. As long as you have to live with the fact you might as well enjoy it.'

This time Velda laughed easily. My mind turned to the judge and I could picture his face, disappointed and angry that my time still hadn't come. And we had the best alibi in the world. Self-defence. We had a gun licence and they didn't. If it reached us we were still clear.

Velda said, 'They were there after the same thing, weren't they?'

'What?'

She repeated it. I slammed the wheel with my hand and said something I shouldn't have. Velda looked at me, her forehead furrowed. 'They were . . . weren't they?'

I shook my head in disgust at myself. 'What a sap I am. Of course they were! I thought they were after me again and they were searching for those damn documents!'

'Mike! But how would they know? The papers never carried any news of Charlie Moffit's murder. They reported it, but that was all. How could they know?'

'The same way the public knew the documents were stolen. Look, it's been a good time since he was knocked off. Just about long enough for somebody to get a loose tongue and spill something. That's how they knew . . . there was a leak. Somebody said something they shouldn't have!'

'The witnesses. They'd be the ones. Didn't Pat say they were warned to keep quiet about it?'

'"Advised" is the word,' I said. 'That doesn't make them liable to any official action. Damn it, why can't people keep their big mouths shut!'

Velda fidgeted in her seat. 'It was too big to keep, Mike. You don't witness a murder and just forget about it.'

'Ah, maybe you're right. Maybe I give people credit for having more sense than they actually have. Hell, the leak could just as well have come out of police headquarters too. It's too late now to worry about it. The damage is done.'

Velda lost herself in her thoughts for a good five minutes. I stayed hunched over the wheel trying to see through the fog. 'It wasn't there, Mike. If it wasn't there then it has to be somewhere else.'

'Yeah.'

'You looked around the place right after Oscar died. It wasn't among his things. The police must have looked too. Then we looked again. Do you think it could possibly be that Oscar didn't have them?'

'What else is there to think. Either that or he hid them outside his room.'

'Doubtful, Mike. Remember one thing, if Oscar showed himself anywhere he would have been mistaken for Lee. He couldn't have done much fooling around.'

I had to grin because the girl who was wearing my ring was so smart I began to feel foolish around her. I did pretty good for myself. I picked a woman who could shoot a guy just like that and still think straight. 'Go on, Velda.'

'So maybe Oscar never got those documents. Charlie's ripped pocket just happened when he fell. If Charlie was the courier, and if the documents he was carrying are missing, then Charlie must have them tucked away somewhere. Remember what the men at the pie factory said . . . that he was dopey for certain periods of time? He was forgetful? Couldn't he have . . .'

I stopped her and took it from there myself. She had tapped it right on the nose.

'When, Mike?'

I glanced at her quickly. 'When what?'

'When do we go through his apartment?'

She was asking for more! Once in a night wasn't enough. 'Not now,' I told her. 'Tomorrow's another day. Our dead friends won't be making a report tonight and the Party won't be too anxious to make any more quick moves until they figure this one out first. We have time, plenty of time.'

'No we don't.'

I convinced her that we had by talking my head off all the way up to her apartment. When I let her out I only had one more thing to say. She waited, knowing well enough what was coming. 'In case anyone asks, I was with you in your place all night, understand?'

'Can't we partially tell the truth?'

'Nope, we're engaged.'

'Oh! Now I have to wait some more.'

'Not long, kid, not too long. When this is all finished there'll be time for other things.'

'I can wait.'

'Good! Now hop upstairs and get to bed, but first take that gun of yours and hide it somewhere. Put it where it can't be found until I tell you to take it out.'

She leaned over and kissed me, a soft, light kiss that left my mouth tingling with the thought of what lay behind this girl who could be so completely lovable and so completely deadly. There were fires burning in her eyes that nothing could ever quench, but they asked me to try . . . to try hard.

I looked at her legs as she got out of the car and decided that I'd never seen enough of them. They had been there all the time, mine any time I had wanted to ask and until now I never had the sense to ask. I had been stupid, all right. I was much smarter now. I waited until she was in the door before I turned the car around and crawled back to my own place.

It was late and I was tired. There had been too much in this one night again, I thought to myself. You get wound up like a watch spring, tighter and tighter until the limit is reached and you let go with a bang that leaves you empty and gasping.

When I locked the door I went directly to the closet and took down the box of parts and shells for the gun. I laid them out on the kitchen table and took the .45 apart piece by piece, cleaning and oiling every bit of it. I unwrapped the new barrel and put it in place, throwing the rest of the gun together around it. On second thought I changed the firing pin too. A microscope could pick up a lot of details from empty shell cases.

It took a half-hour to get the gun ready to go again. I shoved the old barrel and pin in a quart beer can, stuffed in some paper to keep it from rattling and dumped the works down the incinerator.

I was feeling pretty good when I crawled into the sack. Now let's see what would happen.

The alarum was about to give up when I finally woke up. There was nothing I wanted more than staying in bed, but I forced myself into a sitting position, fought a brief battle with the sheets and got my feet on the floor. A cold shower took the sleep out of my eyes and a plate of bacon and eggs put some life into my body.

I dressed and called Velda. She wasn't at home so I tried the office. She was there. I said, 'How the devil do you do it?'

She laughed and came right back at me. 'I'm still a working girl, Mike. Office hours are from eight to five, remember?'

'Any customers?'

'Nope.'

'Any bills?'

'Nope.'

'Love me?'

'Yup. Love me?'

'Yup. What a conversation. Any calls?'

'Yup. Pat called. He wants to see you. Lee Deamer called. He wants to see you, too.'

I brightened up fast. 'If they call back, tell them I'll check in. How about the papers?'

'Headlines, Mike. Big black headlines. It seems that a couple of rival gangs met up with each other in an old building over on the East Side. They forgot to carry their dead off when the battle was finished.'

'Don't sound so smug. Did Pat mention anything about it?'

'No, but he will. He was pretty edgy with me.'

'Okay, give him my love. I'll see you shortly.' I hung up and laid out my working suit for the day. When I finished dressing I looked out the window and swore to myself. The fog was gone, but a drizzle had come in on its heels and the people on the street were bundled into coats trying to keep warm. The winter was dying a hard death.

On the way to the office I stopped off at a saloon and saw a friend of mine. I told him I wanted an unlicensed automatic of a certain make and .32 calibre, one that hadn't done anything except decorate somebody's dresser drawer since it was bought. My friend went to the phone and made two calls. He came back, told me to wait a few minutes, served a few customers at the bar, then went into the kitchen in the rear and I heard his voice arguing for a while. He came back with a package in his hand and said, 'Twenty bucks, Mike.'

I peeled off twenty, took the gun apart and removed the barrel and the pin. The rest I told my friend to dump in with his trash, thanked him and left. I stopped off at the office long enough to hand the two parts to Velda and tell her to slip them in her gun during her lunch hour. Then I went down to see Pat.

As Velda said, he wasn't happy. He said, 'Hell, Mike,' but his eyes raked me up and down. 'Sit,' he said.

I sat down and picked the paper off his desk. The headlines were big and black. There was a picture of the outside of the house with an interior shot in the middle section with white dotted lines to indicate where the bodies had been found. 'Real trouble, huh, Pat?'

'Yeah, I thought maybe you could explain some of it.'

'Don't be silly.'

'Been shooting your gun lately?'

'Yesterday, as a matter of fact. I fired one into some waste right in my own apartment to check the ejector action. Why?'

'A paraffin test is out of order then. Mind if I see your gun?'

I said no and handed it over. Pat pressed a button on his desk and one of the technicians came in. Pat handed him the gun. 'Get me a photograph of one of the slugs, Art.'

'You're assuming a lot, aren't you, Pat?'

'I think so. Want to talk about it?'

'No, wait until you get your photograph.'

He sat back and smiled and I read the papers. The two men were identified as Martin Romberg and Harold Valleck. They were good and dead. Both had prison records for various crimes and were suspected of being killed in a gang brawl. The police were expecting early developments in the crime. The reporters didn't have much to go on.

Art came back before I finished the funnies and handed Pat an enlarged sheet that was covered with angle shots of the slug. He laid the gun on the desk. Pat smiled again and pulled another sheet from his desk drawer. There wasn't anything funny about the way he smiled. I looked at him with a frown covering up the grin that was trying to break through, lit a butt and went back to the paper and finished the funnies.

Pat said, 'You're too smart to be dumb, Mike. That or you're clean and I'm stupid as hell.' His face looked empty.

I had a nice little speech all ready to take him down a peg or two when I realized that he was on the spot. 'You mean they were supposed to match, is that it?'

He nodded. 'Something like that. A .45 killed one of them. There were only three of us who knew about Oscar's being there.'

'Were they after Oscar or just there?'

'Hell, I don't know, Mike. Murder isn't uncommon in that neighbourhood. Ordinarily I wouldn't give a hoot about it, but this isn't an ordinary thing. I feel about as effective as a clam right now.'

'What for? Cripes, you can't help yourself if somebody gets shot. The place was empty. It was a good place for a hideout. Maybe those two eggs were holed up in there when they got caught up with.'

Pat leaned back and rubbed his hands across his eyes. 'Look, Mike, I'm not dumb. Anybody can change barrels in a gun. I'll bet you the shell cases won't match your pin either.'

'How'd you guess?'

'You're treating me like a kid now, feller. You're the one who's forgetting that we're friends. I know you like a book and I don't want to tear any pages out of that book because if I do I'm afraid of what the ending will be like. I know it was you, I don't know who handled the .32, I'm scared to ask questions and I hate to have you lie to me. Little lies I don't like.'

I folded the paper and put it back on his desk. Pat wouldn't look at me. 'Why the finger pointing at me, Pat?'

'Nuts! Just plain nuts. You should know why.'

'I don't.'

'One of those boys had a green Commie card on him. Now do you know why?'

'Yeah,' I said. I had forgotten all about that. I lifted the cigarette and dragged the smoke down into my chest. "Now what?'

'I want to know what you're after. I want to know everything, Mike. Whenever I think about things I get cold all over and want to smash things. You've been playing cute and there's no way I can touch you. I have to absorb myself in police work and routine detail when I know I'm on the outside hoping for a look in.'

'That's the trouble with the police. They have to wait until something happens. A crime has to be committed before they can make a move.'

Pat watched me thoughtfully, his hands locked behind his head. 'Things have happened.'

'Roger, but, as you stated, they have been played very cute.'

'I'm still on the outside looking in.'

I snubbed the butt out and stared at the shreds of tobacco hanging out the end. 'Pat . . . more things are going to happen. I know you like a book, too, but there's something else I have to know.'

'Go on.'

'How far can I trust you?'

'It depends on a lot of things. Never forget that I'm still a cop.'

'You're still a plain citizen who likes his country and likes to see it stay the way it is, aren't you?'

'Naturally.'

'All right. You're all snagged up in the ritual of written law and order. You have to follow the rules and play it square. There's a weight around your neck and you know it. If I told you what I knew you'd bust a gut trying to get something done that couldn't be done and the rats would get out of the trap.

'I'm only one guy, Pat, but I'm quite a guy and you know it. I make my own rules as I go along and I don't have to account to anybody. There's something big being kicked around and it's exactly as you said . . . it's bigger than you or me or anybody and I'm the only one who can handle it. Don't go handing me the stuff about the agencies that are equipped to handle every conceivable detail of this and that. I'm not messing with detail . . . I'm messing with people and letting them see that I'm nobody to mess with and there are a lot more like me if you want to look for them.

'What's going on isn't a case for a crime laboratory and it isn't a case for the police. The whole thing is in the hands of the people, only they don't know it yet. I'm going to show it to them because I'm the only one who has the whole works wrapped up tight trying to bring it together so we can see what it is. You can stop worrying about your law and your order and about Lee Deamer, because when I'm finished Lee can win his election and go ahead and wipe out the corruption without ever knowing that he had a greater enemy than crime plain and simple.'

I picked up my gun and stuck it in the sling. Pat hadn't moved. His head bobbed slightly when I said so-long, but that was all.

I was still seeing the tired smile on Pat's face, telling me that he understood and to go ahead, when I called Lee Deamer's office. His secretary told me that he was speaking at a luncheon of U.N. delegates in a midtown hotel and had already left. I got the name of the hotel, thanked her and hung up.

He must be getting anxious and I didn't blame him a bit. It was a little before noon, so I hopped in the heap and tooled it up Broadway and angled over to the hotel where it cost me a buck to park in an unloading zone with a guy to cover for me.

The clerk at the desk directed me to the hall where the luncheon was to be held and had hardly finished before I saw Lee come in the door. He swung a briefcase at his side and one of the girls from his office trailed behind him carrying another. Before I could reach him a swarm of reporters came out of nowhere and took down his remarks while the photogs snapped his picture.

A covey of important-looking joes stood on the outside of the circle impatient to speak to Deamer, yet unwilling to offend the Press by breaking up the party. It was Lee himself who told the boys to see him after the luncheon and walked through their midst. He had spotted me leaning against the desk and went directly into the manager's office. That little man went in

140

after him, came out in a minute and scanned the desk. I didn't have to be told that he was looking for me.

I nodded and strode in as casually as I could. The manager smiled at me, then took up a position near the door to give us a few minutes in private. Lee Deamer was sitting in a leather-covered chair next to the desk and his face was a study in anxiety.

'Hello, Lee.'

'Mike, how are you? I've been worried sick ever since I saw the papers this morning.'

I offered him a butt and he shook his head. 'There's nothing to worry about, Lee. Everything is fine.'

'But last night. I . . . you mean you weren't connected with the doings in Oscar's place?' I grinned and lit the smoke.

'I don't know what to think. I called Captain Chambers and he led me to believe that he thought the same thing.'

'He did. I talked him out of it.' I raked another chair up with my foot and sat down. Murder is murder. It can be legal and it can't. No matter what it is it's still murder and the less people know about it the better. I said, 'I went through Oscar's place right after the accident. Pat went through it himself. Later I took another check and I'm satisfied that if Oscar *did* leave any incriminating junk lying around, he didn't leave it in his room.'

Lee sighed, relieved. 'I'm glad to hear that, Mike, but I'm more than glad to hear that you didn't have anything to do with those . . . deaths. It's ugly.'

'Murder is always ugly.'

'Then there's nothing further to be said, I imagine. That takes a great load off my mind. Truly, Mike, I was terribly worried.'

'I should think so. Well, keep your mind at rest. I'm going to backtrack on Oscar a little bit and see what comes up. It's still my opinion that he was bluffing. It's not the easiest thing in the world to frame somebody who can't be framed. If anything comes up I'll let you know, meanwhile no news is good news, so they say.'

'Fine, Mike, I'll leave everything to you. Captain Chambers will co-operate as he sees possible. I want nothing hanging over my head. If it becomes necessary I would rather the public knew about my relationship with Oscar and the facts of the case before the election.'

'Forget that stuff,' I told him brusquely, 'there's plenty the public shouldn't know. If you went into George Washington's background you'd probably kick up a lot of dirt too. You're the one that counts, not Oscar. Remember that.'

I put the chair back in place and doused the butt in a flower pot. I told Lee to give me a few minutes before he left, said so-long and took off. Lee looked ten years younger than he had when he came in. I liked that guy.

There was a public phone in the lobby and I called Velda to ask her if she had switched parts in her gun. She said she had, then told me Pat had just been on the wire. I said, 'But I just saw him a little while ago.'

'I know, but he told me to have you contact him right away if I could reach you.'

'Okay, I'll call him back. Look, I'll probably be out most of the day, so I'll pick you up sometime tonight at your place.'

'Charlie Moffit?'

'Yeah, we'll take his joint.'

'I'll be ready, Mike.'

I hung up, threw in another nickel and spun Pat's number when I got the dial tone. The last time I had seen him he looked tired. This time his voice was dancing.

Like on hot coals.

'Pat, feller, why the sudden rush?'

'I'll tell you why later. Get your tail down here chop-chop. I have things to talk over with you. Privately.'

'Am I in trouble?'

'There's a damn good chance that you'll be in jail if you don't hurry.'

'Get off my back, Pat. Get a table in Louie's and I'll be down for lunch. The check is yours this time.'

'I'll give you fifteen minutes.'

I made it just in time. Louie was behind the bar and thumbed

142

me toward the booths in the rear. Pat was in the last one on the aisle sucking on a cigarette as hard as he could.

Did you ever see a guy who was burned up at his wife? He was like a bomb trying hard to go off and couldn't because the powder was wet. That's what Pat reminded me of. Police efficiency was leaking out his ears and his usual suavity hung on him like a bag. If you could call those narrow slits eyes, then you could say he was looking at me with intent to kill.

I walked back to the bar and had Louie make me up a drink before the session started.

He waited until I was comfortable against the back of the booth and started on my drink before he yanked an envelope out of his pocket and flipped it across the table at me. I slid the contents out and looked at them.

They were photographs of fingerprints. Most were mine.

Four weren't.

Attached to the four that weren't was a typewritten sheet, single spaced and carefully paragraphed. 'They came off that cigarette pack,' Pat said.

I nodded and read through the report.

Her name was Paula Riis. She was thirty-four years old, a college grad, a trained nurse and a former employee in a large Western insane asylum. Since it was a state job her prints were on file there and in Washington.

Pat let me stuff the sheets back in the envelope before he spoke. I hardly heard him say unnecessarily, 'She worked in the same place that Oscar had been assigned to.' A cloud of smoke circled his head again.

The music started in my head. It was different this time. It wasn't loud and it had a definite tune and rhythm. It was soft, melodious music that tried to lullaby me into drowsiness with subtle tones. It tried to keep me from thinking and I fought it back into the obscurity from which it came.

I looked at his eyes and I looked deep into twin fires that had a maddening desire to make me talk and talk fast. 'What, Pat?'

'Where is she?' His voice sounded queer.

I said, 'She's dead. She committed suicide by jumping off a bridge into the river. She's dead as hell.'

'I don't believe you, Mike.'

'That's tough. That's just too damn bad because you have to believe me. You can scour the city or the country from now to doomsday and you won't find her unless you dredge the river and by now maybe even that's too late. She's out at sea somewhere. So what?'

'I'm asking the same thing. So what, Mike? She isn't an accident, a freak coincidence that you can explain off. I want to know why and how. This thing is too big for you to have alone. You'd better start talking or I'm going to have to think one thing. You aren't the Mike Hammer I knew once. You used to have sense enough to realize that the police are set up to handle these things. You used to know that we weren't a bunch of saps. If you still want to keep still then I'm going to think those things and the friendship I had for a certain guy is ended because that guy isn't the same guy any more.'

That was it. He had me and he was right. I took another sip of the drink and made circles with the wet bottom on the table.

'Her name was Paula. Like I said, she's dead. Remember when I came to you with those green cards, Pat? I took them from her. I was walking across the bridge one night when this kid was going into her dutch act. I tried to stop her. All I got was the pocket of her coat where she had the pack of butts and the cards.

'It made me mad because she jumped. I had just been dragged over the coals by that damned judge and I was feeling sour enough not to report the thing. Just the same, I wanted to know what the cards meant. When I found out she was a Commie, and that Charlie Moffit was a Commie, I got interested. I couldn't help it.

'Now the picture is starting to take form. I think you've put it together already. Oscar was insane. He had to be. He and that nurse planned an escape and probably went into hiding in their little love nest a long time ago. When money became scarce they saw a way to get some through using Oscar's physical similarity to Lee.

144

'The first thing that happened was that Oscar killed a guy, a Commie. Now: either he took those cards off Moffit's body for some reason, or he and this Paula Riis actually were Commies themselves. Anyway when Oscar killed Moffit, Paula realized that the guy was more insane than she thought and got scared. She was afraid to do anything about it so she went over the bridge.'

It was a wonderful story. It made a lot of sense. The two people that could spoil it were dead. It made a lot of sense without telling about the fat boy on the bridge and setting myself up for a murder charge.

Pat was on the last of his smokes. The dead butts littered the table and his coat was covered with ashes. The fires in his eyes had gone down . . . a little anyway. 'Very neat, Mike. It fits like a glove. I'm wondering what it would fit like if there was more to it that you didn't tell me.'

'Now you're getting nasty,' I said.

'No, just careful. If it's the way you told it the issue's dead. If it isn't there will be a lot of hell coming your way.'

'I've seen my share,' I grunted.

'You'll see a lot more. I'm going to get some people on this job to poke around. They're other friends of mine and though it won't be official it will be a thorough job. These boys carry little gold badges with three words you can condense to FBI. I hope you're right, Mike. I hope you aren't giving me the business.'

I grinned at him. 'The only one who can get shafted is me. You . . . hell, you're worried about Lee. I told you I wouldn't line him up for a smear. He's my client and I'm mighty particular about clients. Let's order some lunch and forget about it.'

Pat reached for the menu. The fires were still in his eyes.

CHAPTER EIGHT

I LEFT Pat at two o'clock and picked up a paper on the corner. The headlines had turned back to the cold war and the spy trials going on in New York and Washington. I read the sheet through and tossed it in a basket then got in my car.

I made a turn at the corner and cut over to an express street to head back to my place when I noticed the blue coupé behind me. The last time I had seen it it had been parked across from mine outside Pat's office. I turned off the avenue and went down a block to the next avenue and paralleled my course. The blue coupé stuck with me.

When I tried the same thing again it happened all over. This time I picked out a one-way street, crept along it behind a truck until I saw room enough at the kerb to park the car. I went into the space head first and sat there at the wheel waiting. The coupé had no choice, it had to pass me.

The driver was a young kid in a pork-pie hat and he didn't give me a glance. There was a chance that I could be wrong, but just for the hell of it I jotted down his licence number as he went by and swung out behind him. Only once did I see his eyes looking into his mirror, and that was when he turned on Broadway. I stuck with him a way to see what he'd do.

Five minutes later I gave it up as a bad job. He wasn't going anywhere. I made a left turn and he kept going straight ahead. I scowled at my reflection in the dirty windshield.

I was getting the jumps, I thought. I never used to get like that. Maybe Pat had put his finger on it . . . I'd changed.

When I stopped for the red light I saw the headlines on the papers laid out on a stand. More about the trials and the cold war. Politics. I felt like an ignorant bastard for not knowing what it was all about. There's no time like the present then. I swung the wheel and cut back in the other direction. I parked the car and walked up to the grey stone building where the pickets carried banners protesting the persecution of the 'citizens' inside.

One of the punks carrying a placard was at the meeting in Brooklyn the other night. I crossed the line by shoving him almost on his fanny. An attendant carried my note in to Marty Kooperman and he came out to lead me back to the press seats.

Hell, you read the papers, you know what went on in there. It made me as sick to watch it as it did you to read about it. Those damn Reds pulled every trick they knew to get the case thrown out of court. They were a scurvy bunch of lice who tried to turn the court into a burlesque show.

But there was a calm patience in this judge and jury, and in the spectators, too, that told you what the outcome would be. Oh, the defendants didn't see it. They were too cocksure of themselves. They were the Party. They were Powerful. They represented the People.

They should have turned around and seen the faces of the people. They would have had their pants scared off. All at once I felt good. I felt swell!

Then I saw the two guys in the second row. They were dressed in ordinary business suits and they looked too damn smug. They were the boys who came in with General Osilov that night. I sat through two more hours of it before the judge broke it up for the day. The press boys made a beeline for the phones and the crowd started to scramble for the doors.

A lot of the people covered it up, but I had time to see the general's aides pass a fat briefcase to another guy who saw that it reached one of the defendants.

All I could think of was the nerve they had, the gall of them to come into a court of law and directly confirm their relationship with a group accused of a crime against the people. Maybe that's why they could get ahead so fast. They were brazen. That briefcase would hold one thing. Money. Cash in bills. Dough to support the trial and the accompanying propaganda.

Nuts!

I waited until they went through the doors and stayed on their heels. At least they had the sense not to come in an official car; that would have been overdoing it. They walked down a block, waved a cab to the kerb and climbed in. By that time I was in a cab myself and right behind them. One nice thing about taking a taxi in New York. There're so many cabs you can't tell if you're being followed or not.

The one in the front of us pulled to a stop in front of the hotel I had left not so long before. I paid off my driver and tagged after them into the lobby. The place was still jammed with reporters and the usual collection of the curious. General Osilov was standing off in a corner explaining things to four reporters through an interpreter. The two went directly up to him, interrupted and shook his hand as if they hadn't seen him in years. It was all very clubby.

The girl at the news-stand was bored. I bought a pack of Luckies and held out my hand for the change. 'What's the Rusky doing?'

'Him? He was a speaker at the luncheon upstairs. You should have heard him. They piped all the speeches into the lobby over the loudspeaker and he had to be translated every other sentence.'

Sure, he couldn't speak English. Like hell!

I said, 'Anything important come out?'

She handed me my change. 'Nah, same old dribble every time. All except Lee Deamer. He jumped on that Cossack for a dozen things and called him every name that could sneak by in print. You should have heard the way the people in the lobby cheered. Gosh, the manager was fit to be tied. He tried to quiet them down, but they wouldn't shut up.'

Good going, Lee. You tear the bastards apart in public and I'll do it in private. Just be careful, they're like poisonous snakes . . . quiet, stealthy and deadly. Be careful, for Pete's sake!

I opened the Luckies and shook one out. I hung it in my mouth and fumbled for a match. A hand draped with mink held a flame up to it and a voice said, 'Light, mister?'

149

It was a silly notion, but I wondered if I could be contaminated by the fire. I said, 'Hello, Ethel,' and took the light.

There was something different about her face. I didn't know what it was, but it wasn't the same any more. Fine, nearly invisible lines drew it tight, giving an oriental slant to her eyes. The mouth that had kissed so nice and spoke the word that put the finger on me seemed to be set too firm. It pulled the curve of her lips out of shape.

She had a lesson coming to her, this one. Bare skin and a leather belt. Either she was playing it bold or she didn't think I had guessed. Maybe she thought she couldn't have made it out the door without my seeing her and decided to make the first move herself. Whatever her reason, I couldn't read it in her voice or her face.

I was going to ask her what she was doing here and I saw why. The reputable Mr Brighton of Park Avenue and Big Business was holding court next to a fluted column. A lone reporter was taking notes. A couple of big boys, whose faces I recognized from newspapers, were listening intently, adding a word now and then. They all smiled but two.

The sour pusses were General Osilov and his interpreter. The little guy beside the general talked fast and gesticulated freely, but the general was catching it all as it came straight from Brighton himself.

A couple of hundred words later Ethel's old man said something and they all laughed, even the general. They shook hands and split up into new groups that were forming every time a discussion got started.

I took Ethel's arm and started for the door. 'It's been a long time, kid. I've missed you.'

She tried a smile and it didn't look good on her. 'I've missed you too, Mike. I halfway expected you to call me.'

'Well, you know how things are.'

'Yes, I know.' I threw my eyes over her face, but she was expressionless.

'Were you at the luncheon?' I asked.

'Oh! . . .' she came out of it with a start. 'No, I stayed in the lobby. Father was one of the speakers, you know.'

'Really? No need for you to stick around, is there?'

'Oh, no, none at all. I can . . . oh, Mike, just a moment. I forgot something, do you mind?'

We paused at the door and she glanced back over her shoulder. I turned her around and walked back. 'Want me to go with you?'

'No, I'll be right back. Wait for me, will you?'

I watched her go and the girl at the counter smiled. I said, 'There's a ten in it if you see what she does, sister.' She was out of there like a shot and closed up on Ethel. I stood by the stand smoking, looking at the mirrors scattered around the walls. I could see myself in a half-dozen of them. If Ethel watched to see whether or not I moved she must have been satisfied.

She was gone less than a minute. Her face looked tighter than ever.

I walked up to meet her and the girl scrambled behind her counter. I took out a dime, flipped it in my hand and went over and got a pack of gum. While the girl gave me my nickel change I dropped the ten on the counter. 'She spoke to a couple of guys back in the hall. Nothing else. They were young.'

I took my gum back and offered Ethel a piece. She said she didn't want any. No wonder she looked so damned grim. She had fingered me again. Naked skin and ten extra lashes. She was going to be a sorry girl.

When we got into the cab two boys in almost identical blue suits opened the doors of a black Chevvy sedan and came out behind us. I didn't look around again until we had reached the lot where I left my car. The black Chevvy was down the street. Ethel kept up a running conversation that gave me a chance to look at her, and back over my shoulder occasionally.

If I had been paying any attention I would have gotten what she was driving at. She kept hinting for me to take her up to my place. MAN MURDERED IN OWN APARTMENT. More nice

151

headlines. I ignored her hints and cruised around Manhattan with the black sedan always a few hundred feet behind.

Dusk came early. It drove in with the fog that seemed to like this town, a grey blind that reduced visibility to a minimum. I said to her, 'Can we go back to your cabin, kid? It was pretty nice there.'

I might have been mistaken, but I thought I saw the glint of tears. 'It *was* nice there, wasn't it?'

'It was you, not the cabin, Ethel.'

I wasn't mistaken, the tears were there. She dropped her eyes and stared at her hands. 'I had forgotten . . . what it was like to live.' She paused, then: 'Mike . . .'

'What?'

'Nothing. We can go to the cabin if you'd like to.'

The Chevvy behind us pulled around a car and clung a little closer. I loosened the .45 with my forearm and a shrug. The dusk deepened to dark and it was easy to watch the lights in the mirror. They sat there, glowering, watching, waiting for the right moment to come.

How would it be? Ethel wanted it in my apartment. Why? So she would be out of the line of fire? Now what. They'd draw alongside and open up and they wouldn't give a hoot whether they got the both of us or not. It was a question of whether I was important enough to kill at the same time sacrificing a good party worker. Hell, there were always suckers who would rake in the dough for them. Those two headlights behind me trying to act casual said that.

We were out of the city on a wide open road that wound into the dark like a beckoning finger. The houses thinned out and there were fewer roads intersecting the main drag.

Any time now, I thought. It can happen any time. The .45 was right where I could get at it in a hurry and I was ready to haul the wheel right into them. The lights behind me flicked on bright, back to dim and on bright again, a signal they were going to pass.

I signalled an okay with my lights and gripped the wheel. The lights came closer.

I didn't watch the mirror. I had my eyes going between the road and the light-beams on the outside lane that got brighter as they came closer when all of a sudden the beams swerved and weren't there any more. When I looked they were going in a crazy rolling pattern end over end into the field alongside the road.

I half whispered, 'Cripes!' and slammed on the brakes. A handful of cars shot by the accident and began to pull in to a stop in front of me.

Ethel was rigid in her seat, her hands pushing her away from the windshield where the quick stop had thrown her. 'Mike! What . . .'

I yanked the emergency up. 'Stay here. A car went over behind us.'

She gasped and said something I didn't catch because I was out and running back toward the car. It was upside down and both doors were open. The horn blasted, a man screamed and the lights still punched holes in the night. I was the first one there, a hundred yards ahead of anyone else.

I had time to see the tommy-gun on the grass and the wallet inside the car. So that was it. That was how it was to be pulled off. One quick blast from a chatter gun that would sweep my car and it was all over. Somebody groaned in the darkness and I didn't bother to see who it was. They deserved everything they got. I grabbed that tommy-gun and the wallet and ducked behind the car in the darkness and ran back down the road. The others had just reached the wreck and were hollering for somebody to get a doctor.

Ethel screamed when I threw the trunk open and I yelled for her to shut up. I tossed the tommy-gun on the spare tyre and shut the lid. There were more cars coasting up, threading through the jam along the road. A siren screamed its way up and two state cops started the procession moving again. I joined the line and got away from there.

'Who was it, Mike? What happened back there?'

'Just an accident,' I grinned. 'A couple of guys were going too fast and they rolled over.'

'Were they . . . hurt?'

'I didn't stay to look. They weren't dead . . . yet.' I grinned again and her face tightened. She looked at me with an intense loathing and the tears started again.

'Don't worry, baby. Don't be so damn soft-hearted. You know what the Party policies are. You have to be cold and hard. You aren't forgetting, are you?'

The 'no' came through her teeth.

'Hell, the ground was soft and the car wasn't banged up much. They were probably just knocked out. You know, you have to get over being squeamish about such things.'

Ethel shifted in her seat and wouldn't look at me again. We came to the drive and the trees that hung over it. We pulled up to the front of the cabin that nestled on the bluff atop the river and sat there in the dark watching the lights of the river boats.

Red and green eyes. No, they were boats. From far away came a dull booming, like a giant kettledrum. I had heard it once before, calling that way. It was only a channel marker, only a steel bell on a float that clanged when the tide and the waves swung it. I felt a shudder cross my shoulders and I said, 'Shall we go in?'

She answered by opening the door. I went into the cabin behind her.

I closed the door and reached behind my back and turned the key in the lock. Ethel heard the ominous click and stopped. She looked over her shoulder at me once, smiled and went on. I watched her throw her mink on the sofa then put a match to the tapers in the holders.

She thought it was a love nest. We were locked in against the world where we could practise the human frailties without interruption. She thought I didn't know and was going to give her all for the Party so as not to arouse my suspicions. She was crying softly as if the sudden passion was too much for her.

I put the key in my pocket and crossed the room to where she was and put my hands on her shoulders. She spun around, her hands locking behind my waist, her mouth reaching up

154

for mine. I kissed her with a brutal force she'd remember and while I kissed her my fingers hooked in the fabric of her dress.

She ripped her mouth away from mine and pressed it against my cheek. She was crying hard and she said, 'I love you, Mike. I never wanted to love again and I did. I love you.' It was so low I hardly heard it.

My teeth were showing in a grin. I raised my hand until it was against her breast and pushed. Ethel staggered back a step and I yanked with the hand that held her dress and it came off in one piece with a quick loud tear, leaving her gasping and hurt with vivid red marks on her skin where the fabric had twisted and caught.

She gasped, pressed the back of her hand to her mouth and looked at me through eyes wide with fear. 'Mike . . . you didn't have to . . .'

'Shut up!' I took a step forward and she backed off, slowly, slowly, until the wall was at her back and she could retreat no more. 'Am I going to rip 'em right off your hide, Ethel?'

Her head shook, unbelieving what was happening to her. It only lasted a moment, and her hands that trembled so bent up behind her back and the bra fell away and landed at her feet. Her eyes were on mine as she slid her hands inside the fragile silk of the shorts and pushed them down.

When she stepped out of them I slid my belt off and let it dangle from my hand. I watched her face. I saw the gamut of emotions flash by in swift succession, leaving a startled expression of pure animal terror.

'Maybe you should know why you're getting this, Ethel. It's something you should have gotten a long time ago. Your father should have given it to you when you started fooling around one of those Commie bastards who was after the dough you could throw his way instead of yourself. I'm going to lace the hell out of you and you can scream all you want and nobody will be around to hear you but me and that's what I want to hear.

'You put the finger on me twice now. You fingered me when you saw the badge inside my wallet and the Party put a man on my back. They put a lot of men, I guess. Two of 'em are dead already. It didn't go so good and you saw a chance to finger me again in the lobby back there. What did you expect for it, a promotion or something?'

I started to swing the belt back and forth very gently. Ethel pressed against the wall, her face a pale oval. 'Mike . . . it wasn't . . .'

'Keep quiet,' I said.

A naked woman and a leather belt. I looked at her, so bare and so pretty, hands pressed for support against the panelling, legs spread apart to hold a precarious balance, a flat stomach hollowed under the fear that burned her body a faint pink, lovely smooth breasts, firm with terrible excitement, rising and falling with every gasping breath. A gorgeous woman who had been touched by the hand of the devil.

I raised the belt and swung it and heard the sharp crack of the leather against her thighs and her scream and that horrible blasting roar all at once. Her body twisted and fell while I was running for the window with the .45 in my hand pumping slugs into the night and shouting at the top of my voice.

And there in the darkness I heard a body crashing through the brush, running for the road. I ran to the door that I had locked myself and cursed my own stupidity while I fumbled for the key in my pocket.

The door came open, but there was only silence outside, a dead, empty silence. I jammed a fresh clip into the gun and held it steady, deliberately standing outlined in the light of the door asking to be made a target.

I heard it again, the heavy pounding of feet going away. They were too far to catch. When they stopped a motor roared into life and he was gone. My hands had the shakes again and I had to drop the rod back in the sling. The prints of his feet were there in the grass, winding around the house. I followed them to the window and bent over to pick up the hat.

A pork-pie hat. It had a U-shaped nick taken out of the crown. The boy in the blue Chevvy. Mr MVD himself, a guy who looked like a schoolboy and could pass in a crowd for anything but what he was. I grinned because he was one thing he shouldn't have been, a lousy shot. I was duck soup there in that room with my back toward him and he missed. Maybe I was supposed to be his first corpse and he got nervous. Yeah. I turned and looked in the window.

Ethel was still on the floor and a trickle of red drained from her body.

I ran back to her, stumbling over things in the darkness. I turned her over and saw the hole under her shoulder, a tiny blue thing that oozed blood slowly and was beginning to swell at the edges.

I said, 'Ethel . . . Ethel, honey!'

Her eyes came open and she looked tired, so tired. 'It . . . doesn't hurt, Mike.'

'I know. It won't for a while. Ethel . . . I'm sorry. God, I feel awful.'

'Mike . . . don't.'

She closed her eyes when I ran my hand over her cheek. 'You said . . . a badge, Mike. You're not one of them, are you?'

'No. I'm a cop.'

'I'm . . . glad. After . . . I met you I saw . . . the truth, Mike. I knew . . . I had been a fool.'

'No more talking, Ethel. I'm going for a doctor. Don't talk.'

She found my hand and hung on. 'Let me, Mike . . . please. Will I die?'

'I don't know, Ethel. Let me go for a doctor.'

'No . . . I want to tell you . . . I loved you. I'm glad it happened. I had to love somebody . . . else.'

I forced her finger off my hand and pushed her arm away gently. There was a phone on the bar and I lifted it to my ear. I dialled the operator and had a hard time keeping my voice level. I said I wanted a doctor and wanted one quick. She told me to wait and connected me with a crisp voice that sounded steady and alert. I told him where we were and to get here fast. He said he would hurry and broke the connection.

157

I knelt beside her and stroked her hair until her eyes came open, silently protesting the pain that had started. Her shoulder twitched once and the blood started again. I tried to be gentle. I got my arms under her and carried her to the couch. The wound was a deeper blue and I prayed that there was no internal haemorrhage.

I sat beside her holding her hand. I cursed everything and everybody. I prayed a little and I swore again. I had thoughts that tried to drive me mad.

It was a long while before I realized that she was looking at me. She struggled to find words, her mind clouding from the shock of the bullet. I let her talk and heard her say, 'I'm not . . . one of them any more. I told . . . everything . . . I told . . .'

Her eyes had a glazed look. 'Please don't try to talk, kid, please.'

She never heard me. Her lips parted, moved. 'I never . . . told them about you . . . Mike. I never saw . . . your badge. Tonight . . . those men . . .' It was too much for her. She closed her eyes and was still, only the cover I had thrown over her moved enough to tell that she was still alive.

I never heard the doctor come in. He was a tall man with a face that had looked on much of the world. He stepped past me and leaned over her, his hand opening the bag he carried. I sat and waited, smoking one cigarette after another. The air reeked with a sharp chemical smell and the doctor was a tall shadow passing back and forth across my line of vision, doing things I wasn't aware of, desperate in his haste.

His voice came at me several times before I answered him. He said, 'She will need an ambulance.'

I came out of the chair and went to the phone. The operator said she would call and I hung up. I turned around. 'How is she, doc?'

'We won't know for a while yet. There's a slight chance that she'll pull through.' His whole body expressed what he felt. Disgust. Anger. His voice had a demanding, exasperated tone. 'What happened?'

Perhaps it was the sharpness of his question that startled me into a logical line of reasoning. There was a sudden clarity about the whole thing I hadn't noticed before. I heard Ethel telling me that she had pulled out of the Party and it left me with an answer that said this time it wasn't me they were after . . . it was her . . . and Pork-Pie *had* been a good shot. He would have been a dead shot, only Ethel had twisted when I laid the strap across her and the bullet that was intended for her heart had missed by a fraction and might give her life back to her.

The soft kill-music that I always hear at the wrong times took up a beat and was joined by a multitude of ghostly instruments that plucked at my mind to drive away any reason that I had left.

I walked to the doctor and stared at his eyes so he could see that I had looked on the world too, and could see the despair, the lust, the same dirty thoughts that he had seen in so many others and said, 'Do you know who I am, doctor?'

He looked long this time, searching me. 'Your face is familiar.'

'It should be, doctor. You've seen it in the papers. You've read about it many times. It's been described a hundred different ways and there's always that reference to a certain kill-look that I have. My name is Mike Hammer. I'm a private detective. I've killed a lot of people.'

He knew me then; his eyes asked if I were trying to buy his silence with the price of death. 'Did you do that to her too?'

'No, doctor. Somebody else did that, and for it that somebody is going to die a thousand times. It wasn't just one person who wanted that girl dead. One person ordered it, but many demanded it. I'm not going to tell you the story of what lies behind this, but I will tell you one thing. It's so damned important that it touches your life and mine and the lives of everyone in this country and unless you want to see the same thing happen again and again you'll have to hold up your report.

'You know who I am and I can show you my papers so there will never be any trouble in finding me if you think it should be done. But listen . . . if ever you believed anything, believe this . . . if I get connected with this I'll be tied up in that crazy web of police detail and a lot of other people will die. Do you understand me?'

'No.' Just like that, no. I tried to keep from grabbing his neck in my hands and forcing my words down his throat. My face went wild and I couldn't control it. The doctor didn't scare, he just stood there and watched me make myself keep from killing him too.

'Perhaps I do after all.' His face became sober and stern. I swallowed hard with the relief I felt. 'I don't understand it at all,' he said. 'I'll never understand these things. I do know this though, a powerful influence motivates murder. It is never simple enough to understand. I can't understand war, either. I'll do what I can, Mr Hammer. I do have a good understanding of people and I think that you are telling me a truth that could have some very unpleasant aspects, whatever they are.'

I squeezed his hand hard and got out of there. So much to be done, I thought, so much that's still left to do. My watch said it was after ten and Velda would be waiting. Tonight we had a mission planned and after that another and another until we found the ending.

I touched the starter and the engine caught with a roar. The night had sped by and there never was enough time to do what I wanted. First Pork-Pie Hat, then those men, then Ethel. I stopped and retraced my thoughts. Ethel and those men. She was going to tell me about them; she almost did. I reached in my pocket and took out the wallet.

The card was behind some others in one of the pockets. It was an official card with all the works. The words I saw stood out as though they were written in flame. FEDERAL BUREAU OF INVESTIGATION. Good Lord, Ethel had fingered me to the FBI! She had turned on the Party and even on me! Now it *was* clear . . . Those two Feds had tailed me hoping to be led to my apartment and perhaps a secret cache of papers that could lead to those missing documents! They tailed me, but they in turn were being tailed by somebody else who knew what had happened. Pork-Pie Hat ran them off the road and came after us with the intention of killing Ethel before she could spill anything else she knew!

I let the music in my head play and play. I laughed at it and it played harder than ever, but this time I didn't fight it. I sat back and laughed, enjoying the symphony of madness and cheered when it was done. So I *was* mad. I *was* a killer and I *was* looking forward to killing again. I wanted them all, every one of them from bottom to top and especially the one at the top even if I had to go to the Kremlin to do it. The time for that wouldn't be now . . . I'd only get a little way up the ladder if one of the rungs didn't break first and throw me to my death.

But some day, maybe, some day I'd stand on the steps of the Kremlin with a gun in my fist and I'd yell for them to come out and if they wouldn't I'd go in and get them and when I had lined them up against the wall I'd start shooting until all I had left was a row of corpses that bled on the cold floors and in whose thick red blood would be the promise of a peace that would stick for more generations than I'd live to see.

The music gave up in a thunder of drums and I racked my wheels against the kerb outside Velda's apartment house. I looked up at her floor when I got out and saw the lights on and I knew she was ready and waiting.

I went on in.

She said hello and knew that something was wrong with me. 'What happened, Mike?'

I couldn't tell her the whole thing. I said simply, 'They tried again.'

Her eyes narrowed down and glinted at me. They asked the question.

I said, 'They got away again, too.'

'It's getting deeper, isn't it?'

'It'll go deeper before we're through. Get your coat on.'

Velda went inside and reappeared with her coat on and her handbag slung over her shoulder. It swung slowly under the weight of the gun. 'Let's go, Mike.'

We went downstairs to the car and started driving. Broadway was a madhouse of traffic that weaved and screamed, stopped for red lights and jumped away at the green. I let the flow take me past the artificial daylight of the marquees and the signs and into the dusk of uptown. When we came to the street Velda pointed and I turned up it, parking in the middle of the block under a street light.

Here was the edge of Harlem, that strange no-man's-land where the white mixed with the black and the languages over-flowed into each other like that of the horde around the Tower of Babel. There were strange, foreign smells of cooking and too many people in too few rooms. There were the hostile eyes of children who became suddenly silent as you passed.

Velda stopped before an old sandstone building. 'This is it.'

I took her arm and went up the stairs. In the vestibule I struck a match and held it before the name plates on the mail-boxes. Most were scrawled in childish writing on the backs of match books. One was an aluminium stamp and it read C. C. LOPEX, SUPT.

I pushed the button. There was no answering buzz of the door. Instead, a face showed through the dirty glass and the door was pulled open by a guy who only came up to my chest. He smoked a smelly cigar and reeked of cheap whisky. He was a hunchback. He said, 'Whatta ya want?'

He saw the ten bucks I had folded in my fingers and got a greedy look on his face. 'There ain't but one empty room and ya won't like that. Ya can use my place. Fer a tenner ya can stay all night.'

Velda raised her eyebrows at that. I shook my head. 'We'll take the empty.'

'Sure, go ahead. Ya coulda done whatcha wanted in my place but if ya want the empty go ahead. Ya won't like it, though.'

I gave him the ten and he gave me the key, telling me where the room was. He leered and looked somewhat dissatisfied because he wouldn't be able to sneak a look on something he probably never had himself. Velda started up the stairs using her flashlight to pick out the snags in the steps.

The room faced on a dark corridor that was hung heavy with the smell of age and decay. I put the key in the lock and shoved the door open. Velda found the lone bulb that dangled from the ceiling and pulled the cord to throw a dull yellow light in the room. I closed the door and locked it.

Nobody had to tell us what had happened. Somebody had been here before us. The police had impounded Charlie Moffit's personal belongings, but they hadn't ripped the room up doing it. The skinny mattress lay in the centre of the floor ripped to shreds. The hollow posts of the bed had been disembowelled and lay on the springs. What had been a rug at one time lay in a heap in the corner under the pile of empty dresser drawers.

'We're too late again, Mike.'

'No we're not.' I was grinning and Velda grinned too. 'The search didn't stop anywhere. If they found it we could have seen where they stopped looking. They tore the place apart and never came to the end. It never was here.'

I kicked at the papers on the floor, old sheets from weeks back. There was a note pad with pencil sketches of girls doing things they shouldn't. We roamed around the room poking into the remains, doing nothing but looking out of curiosity. Velda found a box of junk that had been spilled under the dresser, penny curios from some arcade.

There was no place else to look that hadn't already been searched. I took the dresser drawers off the rug and laid them out. They were lined with newspapers and had a few odds and ends rolling on the bottoms. There was part of a fountain pen and a broken harmonica. Velda found a few pictures of girls in next to nothing that had been cut from a magazine.

Then I found the photographs. They were between the paper lining and the side of the drawer. One was of two people, too fuzzy to identify. The other was that of a girl and had 'To Charlie, with love from P.' written on the bottom. I held it in my hand and looked at the face of Paula Riis. She was smiling. She was happy. She was the girl that had jumped off the bridge and was dead. I stared at her face that smiled back at me as if there never had been anything to worry about.

Velda peered over my shoulder, took the picture from me and held it under the light. 'Who is she, Mike?'

'Paula Riis,' I said finally. 'The nurse. Charlie Moffit's girl-friend. Oscar Deamer's nurse and the girl who chose to die rather than look at my face. The girl who started it all and left it hanging in mid-air while people died and killed.'

I took out a cigarette and gave her one. 'I had it figured wrong. I gave Pat a bum steer, then when I thought it over I got to thinking that maybe I told the truth after all. I thought that Paula and Oscar planned his escape and Oscar killed a guy . . . just any guy . . . in order to squeeze Lee. Now it seems that it wasn't just any guy that Oscar killed. It wasn't an accident. Oscar killed him for a very good reason.'

'Mike . . . could it be a case of jealousy? Could Oscar have been jealous because Paula played up to Charlie?'

I dragged the smoke down, held it and let it go into the light. 'I wish it happened that simply. I wish it did, sugar. I started out with a couple of green cards and took it from there. I thought I had a coincidental connection but now it looks like it wasn't so damn coincidental after all. We have too many dead people carrying those green cards.'

'The answer, Mike . . . what can it be?'

I stared at the wall thoughtfully. 'I'm wondering that too. I think it lies out West in an asylum for the insane. Tomorrow I want you to take the first plane out and start digging.'

'For what?'

'For anything you can find. Think up the questions and look for the answers. The part we're looking for may be there and it may be here, but we haven't the time to look together. You'll have to go out alone while I plod along this end of the track.'

'Mike . . . you'll be careful, won't you?'

'Very careful, Velda. I won't ask questions if I think a gun will do the job quicker. This time I'm going to live up to my reputation. I've been thinking some things I don't like and to satisfy myself I'm going to find out whether or not they're true.'

'Supposing they make another try for you?'

'Oh, they will, they will. In fact, they have to. From now on I'll be sleeping with my gun in my fist and my eyes open. They'll make the play again because I know enough and think too much. I might run into a conclusion that will split things wide open. They'll be looking for me and possibly you because they know there were two guns that killed those boys in Oscar's room. They'll know I wasn't alone and they may think of you.

'I'll have to keep my apartment and the office covered while I'm away. They'll get around it somehow, but I'll try anyway.'

Velda took my shoulder and made me look at her. 'You aren't sending me out West just so I won't be there if there's trouble, are you?'

'No, I wouldn't do that to you. I know how much it means to be in on a thing like this.'

She knew I was telling the truth for a change and dropped her hand into mine. 'I'll do a good job, Mike. When I get back I won't take any chance on their finding any information I have. I'll tuck it in that trick wall-lamp in the office so you can get to it without waking me from the sleep I'll probably need.'

I pulled the cord and the light did a slow fade-out. Velda held her flash on the floor and started down the corridor. A little brown face peeked out of a door and withdrew when she threw the spot on it. We held on to the banister and went down the steps that announced our descent with sharp squeals and groans.

The hunchback opened his door at the foot of the landing and took the key back. 'That was quick,' he said. 'Pretty quick for your age. Thought ya'd take longer.'

I wanted to rap him in the puss, only that would have shut him up when I had a question to ask him. 'We woulda stayed only the room was a mess. Who was in there before us?'

'Some guy died who lived there.'

'Yeah, but who was in there next?'

'Young kid. Said he wanted a bunk for a night. Guess he was hot or something. He gimme a ten too, plus a five for the room. Yeah, I remember him 'counta he wore a nice topcoat and one of them flat pork-pie hats. Sure woulda like to get that topcoat.'

I pushed Velda outside and down to the car. The MVD had been there. No wonder the search was so complete. He looked and never looked hard enough. In his hurry to find some documents he overlooked the very thing that might have told him where they were.

I drove Velda home and went up for coffee. We talked and we smoked. I laughed at the way she looked at the ring on her finger and told her the next thing she knew there'd be a diamond to match. Her eyes sparkled brighter than the stone.

'When will it be, Mike?' Her voice was a velvet glove that caressed every inch of me.

I squirmed a little bit and managed a sick grin. 'Oh, soon. Let's not go too fast, kid.'

The devil came into her eyes and she pushed away from the table. I had another smoke and finished it. I started on another when she called, me. When I went into the living room she was standing by the light in a gown that was nothing at all, nothing at all. I could see through it and saw things I thought existed only in a dream and the sweat popped out on my forehead and left me feeling shaky all over.

Her body was a milky flow of curves under the translucent gown and when she moved the static current of flesh against sheer cloth made it cling to her in a way that made me hold my breath to fight against the temptation I could feel tugging at my body. The inky blackness of the hair falling around her shoulders made her look taller, and the gown shrouded what was yet to come and was there for me alone.

'For our wedding night, Mike,' she said. 'When will it be?'

I said, 'We're . . . only engaged to be engaged, you know.'

I didn't dare move when she came to me. She raised herself on her toes to kiss me with a tongue of fire, then walked back to the light and turned around. I could see through that damned gown as though it weren't there at all.

She knew I'd never be able to wait long after that.

I stumbled out of the room and down to my car. I sat there awhile thinking of nothing but Velda and the brief glimpse of heaven she had showed me. I tried thinking about something else and it didn't work.

I couldn't get her out of my mind.

CHAPTER NINE

I SLEPT with a dream that night. It was a dream of nice things and other things that weren't so nice. There were a lot of people in the dream and not all of them were alive. There were faces from the past that mingled with those of the present, drawn silent faces turned toward me to see when I would become one of them, floating in that limbo of non-existence.

I saw the bridge again, and two people die while the stern face of the judge looked on disapproving, uttering solemn words of condemnation. I saw flashes of fire, and men fall. I saw Ethel hovering between the void that separates life from death, teetering into the black while I screamed for her not to and tried to run to catch her, only to have my feet turn into stumps that grew from the very soil.

There were others too, bodies of dead men without faces, waiting for me to add that one missing part, to identify them with their brother dead in one sweeping blast of gunfire. I was there with them. They didn't want me because I wasn't dead, and the living didn't want me either. They couldn't figure out why I was still alive when I dwelt in the land of the dead men.

Only Velda wanted me. I could see her hovering above the others, trailing the gown of transparent fabric, her finger beckoning me to come with her where nothing would matter but the two of us.

The dead pushed me out and the living pushed me back. I tried to get up to Velda and I couldn't reach her. I screamed once for them all to shut up before there was only the land of the dead and none of the living.

Then I woke up. My head throbbed and the shout was still caught in my throat. My tongue felt thick and there was an ache across my shoulders. I staggered into the bathroom where

I could duck myself under a cold shower whose stinging chill would wash away the dream.

I glanced at the clock, seeing that the morning had come and gone, leaving me only the afternoon and night. I picked up the phone, asked for long distance, then had myself connected with the hospital outside the city. I hung on for ten minutes waiting for the doctor, told him who I was when he came on and asked him how she was.

The doctor held his hand over the receiver and his voice was a slight mumble of sound. Then: 'Yes, Mr Hammer, I can talk now. The patient has passed the crisis and in my opinion she will live.'

'Has she talked, doc?'

'She was conscious a few minutes but she said nothing, nothing at all. There are quite a few people waiting to hear her words.' I sensed the change in his voice. 'They are police, Mr Hammer . . . and Federal men.'

'I figured they'd be there. Have you said anything?'

'No. I rather believe that you told me the truth, especially since seeing those Federal men. I told them I received an anonymous call to go to the cabin and when I did I found her.'

'Good! I can say thanks but it won't mean much. Give me three days and you can say what you like if it hasn't already been explained.'

'I understand.'

'Is Mr Brighton there?'

'He has been here since the girl was identified. He seems considerably upset. We had to give him a sedative.'

'Just how upset is he?'

'Enough to justify medical attention . . . which he won't have.'

'I see. All right, doctor, I'll call you again. Let me have those three days.'

'Three days, Mr Hammer. You may have less. Those Federal men are viewing me somewhat suspiciously.' We said our good-byes and hung up. Then I went out and ate breakfast.

I got dressed and went straight to the office. Velda had left a note in her typewriter saying that she had taken the morning

170

plane out and for me to be careful. I pulled the sheet out of the roller and tore it up. There was no mail to look at so I gave Pat a ring and caught him just as he was coming in from lunch.

He said, 'Hello, Mike. What's new?'

If I told him he would have cut my throat. 'Nothing much. I wanted to speak to somebody so I called. What're you doing?'

'Right now I have to go downtown. I have to see the medical examiner and he's out on a case. A suicide, I think. I'm going to meet him there and if you feel like coming along you're welcome.'

'Well, I don't feel like it, but I will. Be down in a few minutes. We'll use my car.'

'Okay, but shake it up.'

I dumped a packet of Luckies out of the carton in my desk and shoved it in my pocket, went downstairs and took off for Pat's. He was waiting for me on the kerb, talking earnestly to a couple of uniformed cops. He waved, made a final point to the cops and crossed the street.

'Somebody steal your marbles, Mike? You don't look happy.'

'I'm not. I didn't get but eleven hours' sleep.'

'Gosh, you poor guy! That must hurt. If you can keep awake, drive down to the foot of Third Avenue. How're you making out with Lee?'

'I'll have a definite report for him in a couple of days.'

'Negative?'

I shrugged.

Pat looked at me querulously. 'That's a hell of a note. What else could it be?'

'Positive.'

Pat got mad. 'Do you think Oscar left something behind him, Mike? By damn, if he did I want to know about it!'

'Simmer down. I'm checking every angle I know of and when my report is made you'll be able to depend on its answer. If Oscar left one thing that could frame Lee I'll be sure nobody sees it who shouldn't see it. That's the angle I'm worried about. A smear on Lee now will be fatal . . . and Pat, there's a lot of wrong guys out to smear him. If you only knew.'

'I will know soon, sonny boy. I've already had a few initial reports myself and it seems that your name has cropped up pretty frequently.'

'I get around,' I said.

'Yeah.' He relaxed into a silence he didn't break until I saw the morgue wagon and a prowl ahead of me. 'Here's the place. Stop behind the car.'

We hopped out and one of the cops saluted Pat and told him the medical examiner was still upstairs. Pat lugged his briefcase along and met him on the stairs. I stood in the background while they rambled along about something and Pat handed him a manila folder. The M.E. tucked it under his arm and said he'd take care of it.

Pat waved his thumb toward the top of the stairs. 'What is it this time?'

'Another suicide. Lieutenant Barner is on the case. Some old duck took the gas pipe. They're always doing it in this neighbourhood. Go up and take a look.'

'I see enough of that stuff. Let Barner handle it.'

He would have followed the M.E. down the stairs if I hadn't been curious enough to step up to the landing and peer in the door. Pat came up behind me and laughed. 'Curious?'

'Can't help it.'

'Sure. Then let's go in and see somebody who died by their own hand instead of yours.'

'That's not funny, pal. Can it!' Pat laughed again and walked in.

The guy was a middle-aged average man. He had a shock of white hair and a peculiar expression and colour that come from breathing too much gas. He stunk of whisky and lay in a heap on the floor with his head partially propped up against the cushioned leg of a chair.

Barner was slipping into his coat. 'Damn good thing there wasn't a pilot light on that stove. Would have blown the block to bits.'

Pat knelt down and took a close look at the body. 'How long has he been dead?'

'Few hours, at least. There hasn't been anybody home in this building all morning. The landlady came in around noon and smelt the gas. The door was closed, but not locked, and she smashed a couple of windows out and called a doctor. There wasn't anything he could do so he called us.'

'Any note?'

'Nah. The guy was tanked up. He probably got disgusted with himself and turned on the gas. He used to be an actor. Name's Jenkins, Harvey Robinson Jenkins. The landlady said he was pretty good about thirty years ago, a regular matinée idol. He dropped into character parts, got wiped out when vaudeville went out and picked up a few bucks working in small road shows now and then.'

I looked around the room and took stock of his things. There was a good leather chair by the window and a new floor lamp, but the rest of the furnishings had lost their shape and lustre with age. There were two rooms, a combination sitting-room-bedroom and a kitchenette. A stack of old theatre posters were neatly stacked behind the bed and a new military kit decorated the top of the dresser. The kitchen was big enough to hold one person at a time. A faint odour of gas still hung up high and clung to the curtains. The refrigerator didn't work, but then it didn't have to because it was empty. A jar of jam was on the table next to an empty bottle of whisky. There were a dozen other empties under the table in a cardboard carton.

So this is death. This is the way people die if you don't help them. He was on the long road and glad of it. Too bad he had to leave his most prized possessions behind. The make-up kit was old and battered, but it was clean, unlike everything else, and the tubes and jars inside it were all neatly arranged and labelled. The mirror fastened to the back of the lid was polished clear by a careful hand. I could picture the little guy sitting there night after night playing all the great roles of history, seeing his hand transform him to the glories of his youth.

They were taking the body out in the basket when the land-lady came in to see that that was all they took out. Barner said so-long and left us watching the procession down the stairs. The landlady was a chubby woman whose scraggly hair fell down past her ears. Her hands were calloused and red from work and she kept rubbing them together as though they were cold.

She turned to me, clucking through her teeth. 'There you see the evil of drink, young man. I lost me two husbands that way and now I lose a boarder.'

'Tough. Did he owe you any money?'

'No, not one red cent. Oh, he was an honourable one was Mr Jenkins. Lived here over three years he did, but always paid his rent somehow. Too bad he got that inheritance. It was too much for him who never had any real money. He spent it all on drink and now look at him.'

'Yeah.'

'Well, I warned him, you can't say I didn't try. He was always making those speeches like an actor does and he told me that drink was food for the soul. Food for the soul! He never went hungry then.'

Pat grunted, anxious to leave. 'Let that be a lesson to you, Mike.' He looked at the landlady pointedly. 'How long was he on that binge?'

'Oh, for quite a while. Let me see, the letter with the money came a week after the Legion Parade. That was a Wednesday, the 13th. Yes, that's it, a week later he got the money. He paid me the three months he owed me and for two more months in advance, then he started drinking. I never did see a man drink so much. Every night he'd get carried in still mumbling one of them silly parts of his and messing up my floor.'

Pat nodded thoughtfully. 'See, Mike, that's what you're heading for. An untimely end.'

'Nuts! I don't drink that much. Anyway, I'll shoot myself before I try to get charged up on gas. Come on, let's get out of here.'

The landlady showed us to the door and watched from the stoop as we pulled away. I hunched behind the wheel when I began thinking of the old coot who took the easy way out.

I thought about it for a long time.

I let Pat out at his office, found a saloon that was half empty and perched on a stool where I could think about it some more. The rows of whisky bottles behind the bar gleamed with reflected light. They were like women. Bait. They lured you in where you forgot what you were doing then sprung the trap and kicked you out.

The bartender filled my glass again, scooping up the rest of my change. I watched myself in the back mirror, wondering if I was as ugly to others as I was to myself. I grinned and the bartender scowled my way. I scowled and the bartender started grinning because my scowl isn't as pretty as most. I swirled the drink around in my glass, slopping it over the top so I could make patterns on the bar.

I made rings, ovals, faces, then overlaid the whole picture with a bridge that towered high at both ends. I stared at the hump in the middle and drained the glass in a hurry to get my mind off it.

A lot of it had fallen into place, piece by piece. Things I didn't see before were suddenly clear. It was a gigantic puzzle that only started here in Manhattan . . . the rest of it reached down to Washington, across to San Francisco, then on across the ocean. And onward still until it encompassed the world and came back to where it started.

It was a picture of hate, terror and death that had no equal in history and it was here with us now. I was the only one who could see it. There were still parts of the puzzle missing, but it had a broad, recognizable outline now. I could make up parts that would fit, but that wouldn't do. *I had to know. I had to be sure!*

This time I wasn't dealing in murder, I was dealing in war!

It was a curious puzzle that had two solutions. Every part could fit in different places, fooling you into thinking you had it. They were clever, I thought. They were clever, crafty, cunning, anything you wanted to call it.

They had a slogan that the end justified the means.

They would kill to accomplish a purpose.

They would wreck everything to gain their ends, even if they had to build again on the wreckage.

They were here and they were smart as hell. Even the Nazis were like schoolchildren as compared to them.

But that was the catch. They were smart . . . for them! I could laugh now and think rings around them all because I was smarter than the best they could offer. Torture, Death and Lies were their brothers, but I had dealt with those triplets many times myself. They weren't strangers to me. I gave them my orders and they took them because they had to.

I was a ruthless bastard with a twisted mind who could look on death and find it pleasant. I could break an arm or smash in a face because it was easier that way than asking questions. I could out-fox the fox with a line of reasoning that laughed at the truth because I was the worst of the lot and never did deserve to live. That's what that damned judge thought anyway.

This time I got back in the car and drove over to the building that had the radio antenna projecting up from the roof. There were two police cars parked in front of it and I nodded to the drivers. For once I was glad to have been seen around so much with Pat. I went in and leaned on the railing that separated the room and waited until the cop in the faded alpaca coat and the eyeshade came over to me.

He nodded too.

I said, 'Hello, George. I need a favour done.'

'Sure, Mike. That is, if I can do it.'

'You keep a record of incoming calls, don't you?'

'Yeah, why?'

'Look one up for me. A few days ago a New York prowl car crossed the George Washington bridge.' I gave him the date and the approximate time. 'See if it was on a call.'

He went back to a stall where he rummaged around in a filing cabinet. When he returned he carried a sheet, reading from it. He looked up and raised his eyeshade farther on his forehead. 'Here it is. Unidentified girl called and asked to have a police car meet her. I think I remember this one. She was in a hurry and instead of giving her address she said on the walk of the bridge. A car was dispatched to see what went on and called in that it was a wild-goose chase.'

'That's all?'

'Yeah. Anything to it?'

'I don't know yet. Thanks a lot, George.'

'Sure, Mike, any time. So-long.'

I went out and sat in the car with a cigarette drooping from my lips. Unidentified girl. That car on the bridge wasn't there by chance. I had just missed things. Too bad, too damn bad in one way that the boys in the car had gotten there late. The weather, no doubt. Then again it was lucky they didn't make it.

The engine came to life under my feet and I drove away from the kerb. I took the notebook from my pocket and thumbed the pages while I was stalled in traffic, picking up Paula Riis's address from the jumble of notes. I hoped I had it right, because I had jotted it down after coming from Pat's the time he had thrown her identity at me.

It was a number in the upper Forties just off Eighth Avenue, a four-story affair with three apartments above a shoddy beauty parlour that took up the first floor. A sedan with United States Post Office Department inscribed in the door was double parked outside it. I found a place to leave my heap and got back just as two men came down the stairs and got into the car. I had seen the taller guy before; he was a postal inspector.

A dark, swarthy woman stood in the door, with her hands on chunky hips, muttering to herself. I took the steps two at a time and said hello to her.

She looked me up and down first. 'Now what you want? You not from Post Office.'

I looked past her shoulder into the vestibule and knew why those men had been here. A good-sized rectangle had been torn out of the wall. The mailbox that had been there had been ripped out by the roots and the marks of the crowbar that did it still showed in the shattered lath and plaster.

I got that cold feeling again, of being just a little bit too late. I palmed my buzzer and held it out where she could see it.

'Oh, you the police. You come about the room. Whassa matter with other police? He see everything. These crooks! When that girl comes back she be one mad cookie, you bet!'

'That's right, I came about the room. Where is it?'

'Upstairs, what's left of it. Now there's nothing but junk. Thassall, just junk. Go look.'

I went and looked. I saw the same thing that had happened to Charlie Moffit's room. This was a little worse because there was more to it. I cursed softly and backed out of the room. I cursed because I was pleased that the room *was* like Charlie Moffit's room, a room ripped apart by a search that didn't have an end. They were still looking. They tore the room up then stole the mailbox because they thought that Charlie had mailed his girlfriend the stuff.

Then I stopped cursing because I knew then that they did have it after all. Charlie mailed the stuff and it lay in the mailbox because she was dead. They couldn't get it out so they took the whole works. This time I cursed because I was mad, mad as hell.

I made a circuit of the room, kicking at the pieces with a frenzied futility. Clothes that had been ripped apart at the seams were everywhere. The furniture was broken, disembowelled and scattered across the floor. The bottom had been taken out of the phone and lay beneath the stand by the window. I picked it up, turned it over then chucked it away.

They had come in through the window and gouged hunks out of the sill when they prised up the sash. I threw it up and looked around, saying damn to myself because it had been so easy. There was an overturned ashcan on the ground below. They had stepped on that, then on to the roof of the extension below and right into the room.

Too bad Mr MVD couldn't have tripped over the phone line and broken his lousy neck. I picked up the strand of wire that ran out the window to the pole and switched it out of the way. It was slack, too damn slack. I saw why in a minute. The insulator that had held it to the wall had been pulled out. I climbed out on the roof and ran my hand along the wire and the answer was in the slit that was in the insulation.

Somebody had a tap on that wire and when they pulled it off they yanked too hard and it came right off the wall. Damn! Damn it all to hell and back again! I climbed back in the room and slammed the window shut, still swearing to myself.

The woman still stood in the doorway. 'You see, you see?' Her voice went higher on each word. 'These damn crooks. Nobody is safe. What for are the police? What that girl going to say, eh? You know! She give me hell, you betcha. She was all paid up, too. Now whatcha think?'

'Don't get excited. Whoever searched her room took the mailbox too. They were looking for a letter.'

She made a sour mouth. 'Huh! They don't get it, I tell you that, for sure. She's a lose her key a month ago and I always get her mail personal. The postman he's give it to me every day and I take it inside.'

My heart hammered against my ribs and I heard it send the blood driving into my head. I licked my lips to get the words out. 'Maybe I better take it all along then. She can call for it when she returns.'

She squinted, then bobbed her head. 'That is good. I don't have to worry no more about it. From now on till I get a new mailbox I have to take everybody's mail anyhow. Come inside, I give it to you.'

We went into the beauty parlour on the first floor and I waited with my hat in my hand. She came back with a handful of envelopes and one of them was a heavy job stuffed so full the flap had torn a little. I thanked her and left.

Just like that.

How simple could it get?

The murder and the wreckage that had been caused by this one fat envelope, and she drops it in my hand just like that. No trouble. No sneaking around with a gun in your hand. No tight spots that left you shaken and trembling. She hands it to me and I take it and leave.

Isn't that the way life is? You fight and struggle to get something and suddenly you're there at the end and there's nothing left to fight for any longer.

I threw the works in the glove compartment and drove back to my office. From force of habit I locked the door before I sat down to see what it was all about. There were nine letters and a big one. Of the nine three were bills, four were from female friends and had nothing to say, one was an answer to a letter she sent an employment agency and the other enclosed a Communist Party pamphlet. I threw it in the waste-basket and opened the main one.

They were photostats, ten in all, both negatives and positives, on extra thin paper. They were photos of a maze of symbols, diagrams and meaningless words, but there was something about them that practically cried out their extreme importance. They weren't for a mind like mine and I knew it.

I folded them up into a compact square and took them to the lamp on the wall. It was a tricky little job that came apart in the middle and had been given to me by a friend who dabbled in magic. At one time a bird flew out of the hidden compartment when you snapped the light on and scared the hell out of you. I stuck the photostats in there and shut it again.

There was an inch of sherry left on the bottom of the bottle in my desk and I put the mouth to my lips.

It was almost over. I had come to the pause before the end. There was little left to do but sort the parts and make sure I had them straight. I sat down again, pulling the phone over in front of me. I dialled headquarters and asked for Pat.

He had left for the weekend.

The next time I dialled Lee Deamer's office. The blonde at the switchboard was still chewing gum and threw the connection over to his secretary. She said, 'I'm sorry, but Mr Deamer has left for Washington.'

'This is Mike Hammer. I was there once before. I'd like to get a call in to him.'

'Oh, yes, Mr Hammer. He's registered at the Lafayette. You can call him there. However, you had better call before six because he's speaking at a dinner meeting tonight.'

'I'll call him now, and thanks.'

I got long distance and gave the number and she told me the lines were all busy and I would have to wait. I hung up and went to the filing cabinet where I had the remains of another bottle of sherry stashed away. There was a box of paper cups with it and I put the makings on my desk and settled back to enjoy the wait.

After the third half-cup of sherry I snapped the radio on and caught the broadcast. The boy with the golden voice was snapping out the patter in a tone so excited that he must have been holding on to the mike to stay on his feet. It was all about the stolen documents. Suspicions were many and clues were nil. The FBI had every available man on the case and the police of every community had pledged to help in every way.

He went off and a serious-voiced commentator took his place. He told the nation of the calamity that had befallen it. The secret of our newest, most powerful weapon was now, most likely, in the hands of agents of an unfriendly power. He told of the destruction that could be wrought, hinted at the continuance of the cold war with an aftermath of a hotter one. He spoke and his voice trembled with the rage and fear he tried so hard to control.

Fifteen minutes later another commentator came on with a special bulletin that told of all ports being watched, the round-up of suspected aliens. The thing that caused the round-up was still as big a mystery as ever, but the search had turned up a lot of minor things that never would have been noticed. A government clerk was being held incommunicado. A big-shot labour leader had hanged himself. A group of Communists had staged a demonstration in Brooklyn with the usual scream of persecution and had broken some windows. Twenty of them were in the clink.

I sat back and laughed and laughed. The world was in an uproar when the stuff was safe as hell not five feet away from me. The guardians of our government were jumping through hoops because the people demanded to know why the most heavily guarded secret we ever had could be swiped so easily. There were shakeups from the top to bottom and the rats were scurrying for cover, pleading for mercy. Investigations were turning up Reds in the damnedest spots imaginable and the senators and congressmen who recommended them for the posts were on the hot spots in their bailiwicks. Two had already sent in resignations.

Oh, it was great. Something was getting done that should have been done years ago. The heat was on and the fire was burning a lot of pants. The music I had on the radio was interrupted every five minutes now with special newscasts that said the people were getting control of the situation at last.

Of the people, for the people, by the people. We weren't so soft after all. We got pushed too far once too often and the backs were up and teeth bared.

What were the Commies doing! They must be going around in circles. The thing that would have tipped the balance back to them again had been in their hands and they dropped it. Was the MVD out taking care of those who had been negligent? Probably. Very probably. Pork-Pie Hat would have himself a field day. They were the only ones who knew where those documents *weren't*. Our own government knew where they started to go and still thought they were in their hands. I was the only one who knew where they *were*.

Not five feet away. Safe as pie, I thought.

The phone rang and I picked it up. The operator said, 'I have your party, sir.'

I said thanks, waited for the connection and heard Lee saying, 'Hello, hello . . .'

'Mike Hammer. Lee.'

'Yes, Mike, how are you?'

'Fine. I hear Washington is in an uproar.'

'Quite. You can't imagine what it's like. They tell me the hall is filled to the rafters already, waiting to hear the speeches. I've never seen so many reporters in my life.'

'Going to give 'em hell tonight?'

'I'll do my best. I have an important topic to discuss. Was there something special you wanted, Mike?'

'Yeah, sort of. I just wanted to tell you that I found it.'

'It?'

'What Oscar left behind. I found it.'

His voice held a bitter ring. 'I knew it, I knew it! I knew he'd do something like that. Mike . . . is it bad?'

'Oh, no. In fact it's pretty good. Yeah, pretty good.'

He paused, and when he spoke again he sounded tired. 'Remember what I told you, Mike. It's in your hand. Authenticate what you found, and if you believe that it would be better to publish the facts, then make them public.'

I laughed lightly. 'Not this, Lee. It isn't something you can print in a paper. It isn't anything that you nor Pat nor I expected to find. It doesn't tie you into a damn thing so you can blast 'em out tonight and make it good because what I have can push you right up there where you can do a good house-cleaning job.'

The surprise and pleasure showed in his voice. 'That *is* fine news, Mike. When can I see it?'

'When will you be back in New York?'

'Not before Monday night.'

'It'll keep. I'll see you then.'

I pushed the phone back across the desk and started working on the remainder of the sherry. I finished it in a half-hour and closed up the office. It was Saturday night and time to play. I had to wait until Velda came back before I made my decision. I ambled up Broadway and turned into a bar for a drink. The place was packed and noisy except when the news bulletins came on. At seven o'clock they turned on the TV and all heads angled to watch it. They were relaying in the pics of the dinner in Washington that was to be followed by the speeches. The screen was blurred, but the sound was loud and clear.

I had a good chance to watch Mr and Mrs Average People take in the political situation and I felt good all over again. It was no time to come up with the documents. Not yet. Let the fire stay on full for a while. Let it scorch and purify while it could.

The bartender filled my glass and I leaned forward on my elbows to hear Lee when he spoke.

He gave them a taste of hell. He used names and quotations and pointed to the big whiskers in the Kremlin as the brother of the devil. He threw the challenge in the faces of the people and they accepted it with cheers and applause that rocked the building.

I shouted the way I felt louder than anybody and had another drink.

At midnight I walked back to my car and drove home slowly, my mind miles away from my body. Twice I patted the .45 under my arm and out of force of habit I kept a constant check on the cars behind me.

I put the car in the garage, told the attendant to service it fully and went out the side door that led to the street. When I looked both ways and was satisfied that I wasn't going to run into another ambush I stepped out to the sidewalk and walked up to my building.

Before I went upstairs I checked the little panel of lights behind the desk in the lobby. It was a burglar alarm and one of the lights was connected to the windows and doors in my apartment. They were all blank so I took the stairs up and shoved the key in the lock.

For safety's sake I went through the place and found it as empty as when I left it. Maybe Pork-Pie was afraid of a trap. Maybe he was waiting to get me on the street. He and the others had the best reason in the world to get me now. It wouldn't be too long before they figured out where the documents went to, and that was the moment I was hoping for.

I wanted them, every one of the bastards. I wanted them all to myself so I could show the sons-of-bitches what happened when they tried to play rough with somebody who likes that game himself!

The late news broadcast was on and I listened for further developments. There weren't any. I shoved the .45 under my pillow and rolled into the sack.

CHAPTER TEN

I SLEPT all day Sunday. At six-fifteen p.m. I got up to answer the persistent ringing of my doorbell and a Western Union messenger handed me a telegram. He got a buck for his persistence and I went into the living-room where I opened it up.

The telegram was from Velda. It was very brief, saying the mission was accomplished and she was carrying the papers out on the first plane. I folded the yellow sheet and stuck it in the pocket of my coat that was draped on the back of the chair.

I had a combination meal, sent down for the papers and read them in bed. When I finished I slept again and didn't wake up until twelve hours later. The rain was beating against the windows with a hundred tiny fingers and the street was drenched with an overflow too great to be carried off by the sewers at the end of the block.

For a few minutes I stood at the window and looked out into the murk of the morning, not aware of the people that scurried by on the sidewalks below, or of the cars whose tyres made swishing sounds on the wet pavement. Across the street, the front of the building there wavered as the water ran down the glass, assuming the shape of a face moulded by ghostly hands. The face had eyes like two berries on a bush and they turned their stare on me.

This is it, Judge. Here is your rain of purity. You're a better forecaster than I thought. Now, of all times, it should rain. Cold, clear rain that was washing away the scum and the filth and pulling it into the sewer. It's here and you're waiting for me to step out into it and be washed away, aren't you? I could play it safe and stay where I am, but you know I won't. I'm me, Mike Hammer, and I'll be true to form. I'll go down with the rest of the scum.

Sure, Judge, I'll die. I've been so close to death that this time the scythe can't miss me. I've dodged too often, now I've lost the quick-step timing I had that made me duck in time. You noticed it and Pat noticed it . . . I've changed, and now I notice it myself. I don't care any more.

The hell of it is, Judge . . . your question won't get answered. You'll never know why I was endowed with the ability to think and move fast enough to keep away from the man with the reaper. I kept breaking his hour-glass and dulling his blade and he couldn't do a thing about it.

Your rain of purity has come, and out there in it is the grim spectre who is determined that this time he will not miss. He'll raise his vicious scythe and swing at me with all the fury of his madness and I'll go down, but that one wild swing will take along a lot of others before it cuts me in half.

Sorry, Judge, so sorry you'll never know the answer. I was curious myself. I wanted to know the answer too. It's been puzzling me a long, long time.

I showered and dressed, packing the automatic away in the oiled leather holster under my arm. When I finished I called long distance and was connected with the hospital. Again I was lucky and got the doctor while he was there. I told him my name and that was enough.

'Miss Brighton is out of danger,' he said. 'For some reason she is under police guard.'

'Studious young men?'

'Yes.'

'How about her father?'

'He visits her daily. His own doctor is prescribing for him.'

'I see. My time is up, you know. You can talk if you like.'

'For some reason I prefer not to, Mr Hammer. I still don't understand, but I still believe that there is more to this than I can see. Miss Brighton asked me if you had called and I repeated our conversation. She has taken the same attitude of silence.'

'Thanks, doc. It's going to be rough when it starts, but thanks. Tell Miss Brighton I was asking for her.'

'I will. Good day.'

I put the phone back and shrugged into my raincoat. Downstairs I got my car out of the garage and backed out into the rain. The windshield wipers were little demons working furiously, fighting to keep me from being purified. I drove downtown hoping to see Pat, but he had called in that his car was stuck somewhere along the highway and he might not make it in at all.

The morning went by without my noticing its passing. When my stomach tightened I went in and had lunch. I bought a paper and parked the car to read it through. The headlines hadn't changed much. There were pages devoted to the new aspect of the cold war; pages given to the coming election, pages that told of the shake-up in Washington, and of the greater shake-up promised by the candidates running for election.

Lee had given 'em hell, all right. The editorial quoted excerpts from his speech and carried a two-column cut of him shaking his fist at the jackals who were seeking the protection of the same government they had tried to tear down. There was another Communist demonstration, only this one was broken up by an outraged populace and ten of the Reds had landed in the hospital. The rest were sweeping out corridors in the city jail.

The rain let up, but it was only taking a breather before it came down even harder. I took advantage of the momentary lull to duck into a drugstore and put in a call to Lee's office. His secretary told me that he wasn't expected in until evening and I thanked her. I bought a fresh pack of Luckies and went back to the car and sat. I watched the rain and timed my thoughts to its intensity.

I took all the parts and let them drop, watching to see how they fit in place. They were all there now, every one. I could go out any time and show that picture around and anybody could tell that it was a big Red flag with a star and a hammer and sickle. I could show it to them, but I'd have to have the last piece of proof I needed and I'd have that when Velda got back. I went over it time after time until I was satisfied, then I reached for a butt.

189

There was only one left. I had just bought a pack and there was only one left. My watch was a round little face that laughed at me for thinking the afternoon away and I stared at it, amazed that the night had sifted in around the rain and I hadn't noticed it. I got out and went back to the same drugstore and looked up the number of the terminal.

A sugar-coated voice said that all the planes were on schedule despite the rain and the last one from the Midwest had landed at two o'clock. I smacked my hand against my head for letting time get away from me and called the office. Velda didn't answer so I hung up. I was about to call her apartment when I remembered that she'd probably be plenty tired and curled up in the sack, but she said she'd leave anything she had in the lamp if I wasn't in the office when she got in.

I started the car up and the wipers went back into action. The rain of purity was starting to give up and here I was still warm and dry. For how long?

The lights were on in the office and I practically ran in. I yelled, 'Hey, Velda!' The smile I had ready died away because she wasn't there. She *had* been there, though. I smelled the faintest trace of the perfume she used. I went right to the lamp and opened the little compartment. She had laid it right on top of the other stuff for me.

I pulled it out and spread it across my desk, feeling the grin come back slowly as I read the first few lines.

It was done. Finished. I had it all ready to wrap up nice and legal now. I could call Pat and the studious-looking boys with the FBI badges and drop it in their laps. I could sit back in a ringside seat and watch the whole show and laugh at the judge because this time I was free and clear, with my hands clean of somebody's blood. The story would come out and I'd be a hero. The next time I stepped into that court of law and faced the little judge his voice would be quiet and his words more carefully chosen because I was able to prove to the world that I wasn't a bloodthirsty kill-happy bastard with a mind warped by a war of too many dawns and dusks laced by the criss-crossed patterns of bullets. I was a normal guy with normal instincts and maybe a temper that got a little out of hand at times, but was still under control when I wanted it that way.

Hell, Pat should be back now. I'll let him get the credit for it. He won't like it, but he'll have to do it. I reached for the phone.

That's when I saw the little white square of cardboard that had been sitting there in front of me all the while. I picked it up, scowling at the brief typewritten message. CALL LO 3-8099 AT EXACTLY NINE P.M. That was all. The other side was blank.

I didn't get it. Velda was the only one to have been here and she would have left more of an explanation, at least. Besides, we had memo pads for stuff like this. I frowned again and threw it back on the desk. It was ten to eight now. Hell, I wasn't going to wait another hour. I dialled the number and heard the phone ring a dozen times before I hung up.

A nasty taste was in my mouth. My shoulders kept hunching up under my coat as if I were cold. I went to the outer office to see if she had left a note in her desk typewriter and found nothing.

It wasn't right. Not at a moment like this. Nothing else could come up now. Hell, I was on my way to being a hero. The door of the washroom was standing open a little and I went to close it. The light from the lamp on the wall darted in the crack and bounced back at me with bright sparkle. I shoved the door open and every muscle in my body pulled tight as a bowstring and my breath caught in my throat.

There beside the faucet was Velda's ring . . . the sapphire ring I had given her and her wristwatch!

Velda wasn't here but her ring was and no girl is going to go off and forget her ring! No girl will wash her hands and not dry them, either . . . But Velda apparently had, for there was no crumpled paper towel in the basket under the sink!

Somehow I staggered back to my chair and sat down, the awful realization of it hitting me hard. I buried my face in my hands and said, 'Oh, God . . . oh, God!' I knew what had

191

happened now . . . *they* had her! They walked in on her and took her away.

I thought I was clever. I thought they'd try for me. But they *were* clever when the chips were down and now they had something they could trade. That's what they'd say . . . trade. Ha, that was a laugh. They'd take the documents and when I asked them to give her back I'd get a belly full of slugs. Nice trade. A stupid ass like me ought to get shot anyway.

Goddamn 'em anyway! Why couldn't they act like men and fight with men! Why did they have to pick on women! The dirty yellow bastards were afraid to tangle with me so they decided to do it the easy way. They knew the score, they knew I'd have to play ball. They seemed to know a lot of things.

All right, you conniving little punks, I'll play ball, but I'm going to make up a lot of rules you never heard of. You think I'm cornered and it'll be a soft touch. Well, you won't be playing with a guy who's a hero. You'll be up against a guy with a mind gone rotten and a lust for killing! That's the way I was and that's the way I like it!

I grabbed the phone and dialled Pat's home number. When I got him I said hello and didn't give him a chance to interrupt me. 'I need a favour as fast as you can do it, kid. Find out where the phone with the number Longacre 3-8099 is located and call me right back. Shake it because I need it right away.'

Pat let out a startled answer that I cut off by slamming the phone back. Five minutes later the phone rang and I picked it up.

'What goes on with you, Mike? That number is a pay station in the Times Square subway station.'

'Fine,' I answered, 'that's all I need to know. See you later.'

'Mike . . . hey . . .' I cut him off again and picked up my coat.

They thought they were smart, but they forgot I had a fast brain and a lot of connections. Maybe they thought I wouldn't take the chance.

I was downstairs and in the car like a shot. Going up Broadway I pulled out all the stops and forgot there was such a thing as a red light. When I turned off Broadway onto Times Square I saw a patrolman standing in front of the subway entrance idly swinging his stick in his hands.

Tonight was my night and I was going to play it all the way to the hilt. I yanked out the wallet I had taken from that overturned car the other night, plucked the FBI card from the pocket and fitted it into mine. The cop was coming out into the rain to tell me I couldn't park there when I stepped out and shoved the wallet under his nose.

I didn't let him have more than a peek at it, but it was enough. I said, 'Stay here and watch that car. I don't want it gone when I come back.'

He drew himself all the way up with a look that only public servants old in the service can get and passed me a snappy salute. With the headlines blaring from all the papers he didn't have to ask questions to know what was up. 'I'll take care of it,' he shot back.

I ran down the stairs and slipped a dime in the turnstile. I had fifteen minutes to find the right booth, fifteen short minutes. I made a tour of the place poking my head into the empties, hoping the one I was looking for wouldn't be occupied.

It wasn't. I found it over near the steps that led to the BMT line, the last one on the end of five booths. I stepped into one and shut the door. The light above my head was too damn bright, but one crack with the nose of the .45 took care of that. I lifted the receiver off the hook without dropping a nickel in and started conversation with an imaginary person on an imaginary phone.

At five minutes to nine he walked up to the end booth, obviously ignoring the others, and closed the door. I let the minutes tick off until the hands of my watch were at right angles to each other, then shoved a nickel in the slot and dialled LO 3-8099.

It rang just once. 'Yes?'

I forced a bluff into my voice, keeping it low. 'This is Mike Hammer. Who the hell are you and what's this business with the card?'

'Ah, yes, Mr Hammer. You got our card. That is very fortunate indeed. Need I tell you who is speaking?'

'You damn well better, friend.'

'No, certainly not a friend. Just the opposite, I would think. I'm calling about a matter of documents you have, Mr Hammer. They're very important documents, you know. We have taken a hostage to ensure their safe delivery to us.'

'What . . .'

'Please, Mr Hammer. I'm speaking about your very lovely secretary. A very obstinate woman. I think we can force her to talk if you refuse, you know.'

'You bastard!'

'Well?'

My voice changed pitch and stuttered into the mouthpiece. 'What can I say? I know when I'm licked. You . . . can have them.'

'I was sure you'd see the light, Mr Hammer. You will take those documents to the Pennsylvania Station on Thirty-fourth Street and deposit them in one of the pay lockers at the end of the waiting-room. You will then take the key and walk about on the streets outside until someone says, "Wonderful night, friend," and give that person the key. Keep your hands in plain sight and be absolutely alone. I don't think I have to warn you that you will be under constant observation by certain people who will be armed.'

'And the girl . . . Velda?' I asked.

'Provided you do as you are told, and we receive the documents, the girl shall be released, of course.'

'Okay! What time do I do all this?'

'Midnight, Mr Hammer. A fitting hour, don't you think?'

He hung up without waiting for an answer. I grinned and watched him squirm out of the booth, a guy who fitted his voice to perfection. Short, soft and fat, wearing clothes that tried without success to make him look tall, hard and slim.

I grinned again and gave him a good lead, then climbed out of the booth and stayed on his tail. He hesitated at the passages, settled on the route that led up the north-west corner of the block and started up the stairs. My grin like to have split my face open. The famous Hammer luck was riding high, wide and handsome. I could call his shots before he made them and I knew it.

When he reached the street I brushed by him and gave him the elbow for luck. He was so intent upon waving to a cab that he never gave me a tumble. I waited for him to get in then started my car. The cop waved me off with his night stick and I was on my way.

Three hours before the deadline.

How much time was that? Not much, yet plenty when it counted. The cab in front of me weaved around the traffic and I stayed right with it. I could see the back of his head in the rear window and I didn't give a hoot whether or not he turned around.

He didn't. He was so sure that I was on the end of the stick that it never occured to him that he was being tailed. He was going to get that stick up the tail himself when the time came.

So the judge was right all the while. I could feel the madness in my brain eating its way through my veins, chewing the edges of my nerves raw, leaving me something that resembled a man and that was all. *The judge had been right!* There *had* been too many of those dusks and dawns; there *had* been pleasure in all that killing, an obscene pleasure that froze your face in a grin even when you were charged with fear. Like when I cut down that Jap with his own machete and laughed like hell while I made slices of his scrawny body, then went on to do the same thing again because it got to be fun. The little bastards wanted my hide and I gave them a hard time when they tried to take it. Sure, my mind was going rotten even then. I remember the ways the guys used to look at me. You'd think I had fangs. *And it hung on and rotted even further!* How long had it been since I had taken my face out of the ground? How long had it been since they handed me the paper that said it was over and we could go back to being normal people again? And since . . . how many had died while I backed up the gun? Now who was I trying to fool – me? I enjoyed that killing, every bit of it. I killed because I had to and I killed things that needed killing. But that wasn't the point. *I enjoyed killing those things and I knew the judge was right!* I was rotten right through and I knew that at that moment my face was twisted out of shape into a grin that was half sneer and my heart beat fast because it was nice sitting back there with a rod under my arm and somebody was going to hurt pretty quick now, then die. And it might even be me and I didn't give a good damn one way or another.

I tried to figure out where the hell we were. We had passed over a viaduct and a few other things that were vague outlines, but I couldn't tell where we were. If I didn't see the name on the movie house I would have been screwed up, but I caught it in time along with the smell of the river and knew we were some place in Astoria heading down toward the water where the people gave way to the rats and the trash that littered the shore.

There wasn't much more to the block. I cut my lights and drifted in to the kerb, snatching the keys out of the ignition as I opened the door. Ahead of me the tail light of the cab was a red dot getting smaller and for one second I thought I had been too soon.

The red dot stopped moving away from me.

Of all the fates who were out for my skin, only one backed me up. It was a lovely fate that turned over a heap and spilled the pair of studious-looking boys out, the ones who had the FBI cards and that gorgeous black tommy-gun that was still in the trunk of my car. I held the lid open and yanked it out, shucking the case on the pavement. It nestled in my hands like a woman, loaded and cocked, with two spare clips that made a pleasant weight in my pocket.

I got in close to the buildings and took off at a half-trot. A drunk watched me go by, then scurried back into his doorway. The dot up front disappeared, turned into two headlights on dim and came back and past me.

I ran faster. I ran like a guy with three feet and reached the corner in time to see the guy angling up the rutted street that paralleled the river.

How nice it is when it gets dark. It's all around you, a black coat that hides the good and the bad, and lets you stay shouting distance behind somebody else and never gives you away. My little man stepped right along as if he knew where he was going.

There weren't any houses now. There was a smell of decay, noises that didn't belong to a city. Far away the lights of cars snaked along a bridge happily unaware of this other part of New York.

Then the rain began again. The glorious rain of purity was nothing but light tears . . . the sky protesting because I was walking and thinking when I should be dead. Long dead. I spit on the ground to show what I thought of it.

My little man was gone. The constant, even grinding of his shoes in the gravel had stopped and now there was a silence that shut out all other noises, even the rain.

I was alone in the darkness and my time had come. It had to come, there was only an hour left and never time to undo it if it had all been a mistake! For about ten seconds I stood still, watching those cars in the distance. They wormed ahead, they disappeared as if going into a tunnel, emerging again many seconds later. I knew where my little man was now.

Not far off was a building. That was what stopped those lights. There was a building and I saw it when I took a dozen more steps. It was the remains of a building, anyway. Three floors staggered up from the ground in uneven rows of bricks. Only the windows on the top floor showed a few panes whole and unbroken, most likely because they were beyond stone's throw. The rest were plastered with boards that seemed to be there to keep things in rather than out.

I was back in the jungle again. I had that feeling. There was a guy at my shoulder in deeper black than the night and he carried a scythe and a map to point out the long road. I didn't walk, I stalked and the guy stalked with me, waiting patiently for that one fatal misstep.

He was Death and I knew him well. I had seen him plenty of times before and I laughed in his face because I was me, see? I was Mike Hammer and I could laugh because what did I give a damn about death? He could laugh back at me with his grisly, bony laugh and even if we didn't make any sound at all my laugh was louder than his. Stick with me, man in black. Stick close because some customers are going to be made that should have been made a long time ago. You thought I was bad when there was a jungle around me for cover and I learned how to kill and kill and kill and walk away and remind myself that killing was nice. Yeah, you thought I was a wise guy. Stick around, old man, maybe you'll see me for the first time doing something I really enjoy. Maybe some day I'll pick on you and we'll have it out, a hot .45 against that blade of yours.

All the instincts came back. The chatter gun was slung just right for easy carrying and quick action. Without me telling it to, my hand had scooped up gobs of mud and daubed my face and hands, even blanking out the luminous dial of my watch.

The pleasure of the hunt, the wonderful knowledge that you're hot and right! The timing was there, that sense of alertness that gets bred into you when there's blood in the air. I liked it!

I stood in the shadow of the building, melting into the wall with the rain, watching the two men. One was there at the doorway, an invisible figure I sensed rather than saw. The other was coming toward me just as I planned it. It had taken a long while just to get this far. I knew without looking that the hands of my watch would be overlapping. Somewhere back in Manhattan a guy would be looking for me to call me friend. Somewhere inside Velda would be sitting, a hostage who would never talk.

The guy came nearer and I knew he had a gun in his hand. I let him come.

Now I could see him plainly. He stopped three feet away and looked back uncertainly. I had the tommy-gun in one hand and the nose of the .45 in the other. I let him look back again and this time I let him see me.

No, it wasn't me he saw, it was the other guy, the one with the cowl and the scythe. I swung that gun butt so hard it made a wet smack and almost twisted out of my hand. The guy didn't have any forehead left. There was nothing but a black hole from his eyes to his hair and I was grinning. I eased him down without a sound and picked up the tommy-gun. Then I started around the building.

It goes that way. One guy makes one lousy error and everybody falls into the trap. The guy at the door thought it was the other one when I walked out of the murk. He grunted the last sound he ever made because I wrapped my arm under his neck and started bending him over backwards. I had my knee in his spine, pulling him into a living bow that clawed at my hands to release the scream that sudden fear had driven into his throat.

The goddamn grin wouldn't come off my face even when I heard his spine snap and felt that sickening lurch that comes when the bow is bent too far. Two of them. A pair of bastards who had wanted to play in the Big Game. Slimy, squirmy worms who had visions of being on top where they could rule with the whip.

I went into the building with Death at my shoulder and he was mad because I was giving the orders. He was waiting for the mistake he knew I'd have to make sooner or later.

My breath wasn't coming easy now. It was hot and coarse in my throat, rasping into my lungs. I stood inside the door, listening, waiting, letting my eyes use precious seconds to orient themselves to this new gloom. My watch made a mad ticking to remind me that now it had to be quick. Time, it had gone. There was nothing left!

I saw the empty packing-boxes that had been smashed and left to rot. I saw the welter of machinery, glazed with rust, lying in heaps under the high, vaulted roof. Long ago it had been a factory of some sort. I wondered incongruously what had been made here. Then the smell of turpentine gave it to me. Paint. There was three hundred feet of length to it, almost that in width. I could make out the partitions of wood and brick separating it into compartments.

But I didn't have time to look through it all, not all three floors of it!

The sons-of-bitches had picked the best spot on earth – not a sound would penetrate these walls! In that maze of partitions and cubicles even the brightest beam of light that could escape would be dulled and unseen. I wanted to pull the trigger of the gun and blast the whole dump to bits and wade into the wreckage with my bare hands. I wanted to scream just like the guys outside wanted to scream and I couldn't.

Another minute to make myself cool off. Another minute to let instinct and training take over.

Another minute for my eyes to see and they picked out the path that led through the rubbish, a path I should have seen sooner because it had been deliberately made and often used. Old paint cans had been pushed aside and spilled their thick, gooey mess on the floor. The larger drums had been slop pails for left-over stuff and marked the turns in the trail.

My eyes saw it, my feet followed it. They took me around the bend and through a hall then up the stairs.

And the path that was cleared through the dirt on the floor led to the middle, then the top story. It led to rooms that reeked of turpentine so strong it almost took my breath away. It led to a corridor and another man who stepped out of the shadows to die. It led to a door that swung open easily and into a room that faced on other rooms where I was able to stand in my invisible cloak of blackness with barely the strength to hold the gun.

I stood there and looked at what I was, hearing myself say, 'Good God, no, please . . . no!' I had to stand there for a moment of time that turned into eternity while I was helpless to intervene and see things my mind wanted to shut out . . . hear things my ears didn't want to hear.

For an eternal moment I had to look at them all, every one. General Osilov in a business suit leaning on his cane almost casually, an unholy leer lighting his face. My boy of the subway slobbering all over his chin, puking a little without noticing it, his hands pressed against his belly while his face was a study in obscene fascination.

And the guy in the pork-pie hat!

Velda.

She was stark naked.

She hung from the rafters overhead by a rope that chewed into her wrists, while her body twisted slowly in the single light of the electric lantern! The guy in the pork-pie hat waited until she turned to face him then brought the knotted rope around with all the strength of his arm and I heard it bite into her flesh with a sickening sound that brought her head up long enough for me to see that even the pain was dulling under the evil of this thing.

He said, 'Where is it? You'll die if you don't tell me!'

She never opened her mouth. Her eyes came open, but she never opened her mouth!

Then there was only beauty to the nakedness of her body. A beauty of the flesh that was more than the sensuous curve of her hips, more than the sharp curve of breasts drawn high under the weight of her body, more than those long, full legs, more than the ebony of her hair. There was the beauty of the flesh that was the beauty of the soul and the guy in the pork-pie hat grimaced with hate and raised the rope to smash it down while the rest slobbered with the lust and pleasure of this example of what was yet to come, even drooled with the passion that was death made slow in the fulfilment of the philosophy that lived under a red flag!

And in that moment of eternity I heard the problem asked and knew the answer! I knew why I was allowed to live while others died! I knew why my rottenness was tolerated and kept alive and why the guy with the reaper couldn't catch me and I smashed through the door of the room with the tommy-gun in my hands spitting out the answer at the same time my voice screamed it to the heavens!

I lived only to kill the scum and the lice that wanted to kill themselves. I lived to kill so that others could live. I lived to kill

because my soul was a hardened thing that revelled in the thought
of taking the blood of the bastards who made murder their busi-
ness. I lived because I could laugh it off and others couldn't. I
was the evil that opposed other evil, leaving the good and the
meek in the middle to live and inherit the earth!

They heard my scream and the awful roar of the gun and the slugs tearing into bone and guts and it was the last they heard. They went down as they tried to run and felt their insides tear out and spray against the walls.

I saw the general's head splinter into shiny wet fragments and splatter over the floor. The guy from the subway tried to stop the bullets with his hands and dissolved into a nightmare of blue holes.

There was only the guy in the pork-pie hat who made a crazy try for a gun in his pocket. I aimed the tommy-gun for the first time and took his arm off at the shoulder. It dropped on the floor next to him and I let him have a good look at it. He couldn't believe it happened. I proved it by shooting him in the belly. They were all so damned clever!

They were all so damned dead!

I laughed and laughed while I put the second clip in the gun. I knew the music in my head was going wild this time, but I was laughing too hard to enjoy it. I went around the room and kicked them over on their backs and if they had faces left I made sure they didn't. I saved the last burst for the bastard who was MVD in a pork-pie hat and who looked like a kid. A college boy. He was still alive when he stared into the flame that spit out of the muzzle only an inch away from his nose.

I cut her down carefully, dressed her, cradled her in my arms like a baby and knew that I was crying. Me! I could still do that. I felt her fingers come up and touch one of the wet spots on my cheek, heard her say the three words that blessed everything I did, then I went back to the path that led out into the night that was still cold and rainy, but still free to be enjoyed. There was a soft spot on the ground where I laid her with my coat under her head while I went back to do what I had to do. I went back to the room where death had visited and walked under the rafters until I reached the pork-pie hat that lay next to the remains of the thing that wore it. I lifted his wallet out of his back pocket and flipped his coat open so I could rip the inside lining pocket out along with some shreds of the coat fabric. That was all. Except for one thing. When I went down the stairs once more I found a drum of paint whose spilled contents made a sticky flow into some empty cans. When I built up a mound of old papers around the stuff I touched a match to it, stood there until I was satisfied with its flame, then went back to Velda. Her eyes were closed and her breathing heavy. She came up in my arms and I fixed my coat around her.

I carried her that way to my car and drove her home, and stayed while a doctor hovered above her. I prayed. It was answered when the doctor came out of the room and smiled. I said another prayer of thankfulness and did the things that had to be done to make her comfortable. When the nurse came to sit by her side I picked up my hat and went downstairs.

The rain came down steadily. It was clear and pure. It swept by the kerb carrying the filth into the sewer.

We know now, don't we, judge? We know the answer.

There were only a few hours left of the night. I drove to the office and opened the lamp. I took out the two envelopes in there and spread them out on my desk. The beginning and the end. The complexities and the simplicities. It was all so clever and so rotten.

And to think that they might have gotten away with it!

It was over and done with now. Miles away an abandoned paint factory would be a purgatory of flame and explosions that would leave only the faintest trace of what had been there. It was a hell that wiped away all sins leaving only the good and the pure. The faintest trace that it left would be looked into and expounded upon. There would be nothing left but wonder and the two big words, WHY and HOW. There were no cars at the scene. They wouldn't have been foolish enough to get there that way. The flames would char and blacken. They would leave remains that would take months to straighten out, and in that straightening they would come across melted leaden slugs and a twisted gun that was the property of the investigation bureau in Washington. There would be cover-up and more wonder and more speculation, then, eventually, someone would stumble on part of the truth. Yet even then, it was a truth only half-known and too big to be told.

Only I knew the whole thing and it was too big for me. I was going to tell it to the only person who would understand what it meant.

I picked up the phone.

CHAPTER ELEVEN

THE sixth time it rang I heard it come off the cradle. A sharp click was the light coming on then Lee Deamer's voice gave me a sleepy hello.

I said, 'This is Mike Hammer, Lee.' My voice had a tired drag too. 'Hate to call you at this hour, but I have to speak to you.'

'Well, that's all right, Mike. I was expecting you to call. My secretary told me you had called earlier.'

'Can you get dressed?'

'Yes. Are you coming over here?'

'I'd rather not, Lee. I don't want to be cooped up right now. I need the smell of air. A hell of a lot has happened. It isn't anything I can broadcast and I can't keep it to myself. You're the only one I can talk to. I want to show you where it started and how it happened. I want you to see the works. I have something very special to show you.'

'What Oscar left behind?'

'No, what somebody else did. Lee, you know those government documents that were copied?'

'Mike! It can't be!'

'It is.'

'This is . . . why, it's . . .'

'I know what you mean. I'll pick you up in a few minutes. Hurry up.'

'I'll be ready by the time you get here. Really, Mike, I don't know what to say.'

'Neither do I, that's why I want you to tell me what to do. I'll be right over.'

I put the phone back slowly, then gathered the envelopes into a neat pack and stuck them in my pocket. I went downstairs and stood on the sidewalk with my face turned toward the sky.

It was still raining.

It was a night just like that first one.

The rain had a hint of snow in it.

Before I reached Lee's house I made a stop. The place was a rooming house that had a NO VACANCY sign in front and a row of rooms with private entrances. I went in and knocked oil the second door. I knocked again and a bed squeaked. I knocked the third time and a muffled voice swore and feet shuffled across the floor.

The door went open an inch and I saw one eye and part of a crooked nose. 'Hello. Archie,' I said.

Archie threw the door open and I stepped in. Archie owed me a lot of favours and now I was collecting one. I told him to get dressed and it took him about two minutes to climb into his clothes.

He waited until we were in the car before he opened his yap. 'Trouble?' That was all he said.

'Nope. All you're going to do is drive a car. No trouble.'

We went over to Lee's place and I rang the bell. They have one of those speaking-tube gadgets there and Lee said he'd be right down. I saw him hurry through the lobby and open the door.

He grinned when we shook hands. I was too tired to grin back. 'Is it pretty bad, Mike? You look like you're out on your feet.'

'I am. I'm bushed but I can't go to bed with this on my mind. My car is out front.'

The two of us went down the walk and I opened the door for him. We got in the back together and I told Archie to head for the bridge. Lee sat back and let his eyes ask me if we could talk with Archie in the car. I shook my head no, so we just sat there watching the rain streak across the windows.

At the entrance to the bridge I passed Archie a half a buck and he handed it to the cop on duty at the toll booth. We started up the incline when I tapped him on the shoulder.

'Stop here, Archie. We're going to walk the rest of the way. Go on over to Jersey and sop up some beer. Come back in a half-hour. We'll be at the top of the hump on the other side waiting for you.' I dropped a fin on the seat beside him to pay for the beer and climbed out with Lee behind me.

It was colder now and the rain was giving birth to a snowflake here and there. The steel girders of the bridge towered into the sky and were lost, giant man-made trees that glistened at the top as the ice started to form.

Our feet made slow clicking sounds against the concrete of the walk and the boats on the river below called back to them. I could see the red and green eyes staring at me. They weren't faces this time.

'This is where it started, Lee,' I said.

He glanced at me and his face was puzzled.

'No, I don't expect you to understand, because you don't know about it.' We had our hands stuffed in our pockets against the cold, and our collars turned up to keep out the wet. The hump was ahead of us, rising high into the night.

'Right up there is where it happened. I thought I'd be alone that night, but there were two other people. One was a girl. The other was a little fat guy with a stainless-steel tooth. They both died.'

I took the fat envelope out of my pocket and shook out the pages inside. 'It's amazing, isn't it? Here the best minds in the country are looking for this and I fell right into it. It's the detailed plans of the greatest weapon ever made and I have it right here in my hand.'

Lee's mouth fell open. He recovered and reached for it.

'How, Mike? How could this come to you?'

There wasn't any doubting its authenticity. He shook his head, completely bewildered, and gave it back to me. 'That's the story, Lee. That's what I wanted to tell you, but first I want to make sure this country has a secret that's safe.'

I took my lighter out and spun the little wheel. There was a spark, then a blue flame that wavered in the wind. I touched it to the papers and watched them smoulder and suddenly flame up. The yellow light reflected from our faces, dying down to a

207

soft red glow. When there was nothing left but a corner that still held the remnants of the symbols and numbers, I flicked the papers over the edge and watched them go to the wind. That one corner I put in my pocket.

'If it had happened to anyone else, I wonder what the answer would have been?'

I shook my head and reached for a Lucky. 'Nobody will ever know that, Lee.' We reached the top of the hump and I stopped.

The winter was with us again. The girders were tall white fingers that grew from the floor of the bridge scratching the sky open. Through the rift the snow sifted down and made wet patches on the ground.

I leaned on the handrail looking out over the river. 'It was the same kind of night: it was cold and wet and all alone. A girl came running up that ramp with a guy behind her who had a gun in his pocket. I shot the guy and the girl jumped over the railing. That's how simple it was. The only things they left behind were two green cards that identified them as members of the Communist Party.

'So I was interested. I was interested in anything that toted around a green card. That's how I got interested in Oscar. The guy he killed had a green card too. Hell, you know the rest of the story. There's a few things only I know and that's the main thing. I know how many people died tonight. I know what the papers will look like tomorrow and the month after. You know what, Lee, I killed more people tonight than I have fingers on my hands. I shot them in cold blood and enjoyed every minute of it. I pumped slugs in the nastiest bunch of bastards you ever saw and here I am calmer than I've ever been and happy too. They were Commies, Lee. They were Red sons-of-bitches who should have died long ago, and part of the gang who are going to be dying in the very near future unless they get smart and take the gas pipe. Pretty soon what's left of Russia and the slime that breeds there won't be worth mentioning and I'm glad because I had a part in the killing.

'God, but it was fun! It was the way I liked it. No arguing, no talking to the stupid peasants. I just walked into that room

208

with a tommy-gun and shot their guts out. They never thought that there were people like me in this country. They figured us all to be soft as horse manure and just as stupid.'

It was too much for Lee. He held onto the rail and looked sick.

I said, 'What's the matter, Oscar?'

His eyes were glazed and he coughed. 'You mean . . . Lee.'

'No, I don't. I mean Oscar. Lee's dead.'

It was all there, the night, the cold and the fear. The unholy fear. He was looking at my face and he had the same look of unholy fear as the girl had that other night so long ago.

I said it slow. I let him hear every word. 'The girl that died here that night was Paula Riis. She was a nurse in an asylum for the insane. I had it wrong . . . she didn't help Oscar to escape . . . she just quit and Oscar escaped later by himself. Paula came to New York and got tied up with a lot of crappy propaganda the Commies handed out and went overboard for it. She thought it was great. She worked like hell and wound up in a good spot.

'Then it happened. Somehow she saw the records or was introduced to the big boy in this country. She knew it was you. What happened, did she approach you thinking you were Oscar's brother? *Whatever happened she recognized you as Oscar and all her illusions were shattered. She knew you were Oscar Deamer and demented as hell!*

'That's why you were a Commie, Oscar, because you were batty. It was the only philosophy that would appeal to your crazy mind. It justified everything you did and you saw a chance of getting back at the world. You escaped from that sanitarium, took Lee's private papers and made yourself a name in the world while Lee was off in the woods where he never saw a paper of any kind and never knew what you did. You must have had an expert dummy the fingerprints on that medical record . . . but, then, you had access to that kind of expert, didn't you?

'It was rough when Paula recognized you. She lost her ideals and managed to contact Lee. She told him to come East and expose you, but she did something else first. She had a boyfriend in the Party. His name was Charlie Moffit and she told him the story hoping to drag him out of the Commie net.

'Charlie was the stupid one. He saw a play of his own and made it. He saw how he could line you up for some ready cash and gave you the story over the phone. It was right after the Legion Parade, the 13th, that you had a heart attack according to your secretary . . . not because your brother contacted you because his ticket was dated the 15th, a Friday, and he didn't arrive until the day after. *You had a heart attack when Charlie Moffit called you!*

'You contacted the torpedo that went under the MVD title and you worried about it, but there was no out until Lee arrived himself and gave you a buzz. That was the best touch of all! Then you saw how you could kill Charlie yourself, have the blame shifted to your brother with a reasonable story that would make it look good. You knew you had a way to kill two birds with one stone . . . and get rid of a brother who could have stood in your way. There was only one thing you didn't foresee. Charlie Moffit was a courier in the chain that passed along those documents. During one of his more lucid moments he recognized that they were important and held on to them for life insurance. He mailed them to his girlfriend, Paula, to take care of.'

He was white. He hung on to the rail and shook. He was scared stiff.

'So you waited until Charlie called again and arranged to meet him. You had it all figured out beforehand and it looked good as gold. You got hold of an old actor and had him impersonate you while you went out and killed Charlie Moffit. The actor was good, too. He knew how to make speeches. You paid him off, but you didn't know then that he liked to drink. He never did before because he had no money. Later you found that he had a loose tongue when he drank and he had to go too. But that was an easy kill and it's getting ahead of the story.

'You killed Charlie, switched with the actor at the dinner

210

meeting, and made yourself a wonderful alibi. It happened after the supper when you were going around speaking to the groups, a time when nobody would be conscious of the switch, especially since none of them knew you too well anyway.

'I don't know what the play was at your brother's place when Pat and I went after him, but I'll try to set it up. See if I'm right. Mr MVD went there first and got him running. He got him in the subway and shoved him under the train so his identity would be washed out.'

As casually as I could I took Yelda's envelope from my pocket and fingered out the sheet inside. He didn't bother to look at it.

I said, 'My secretary dug up this story. She went back to your home state and went through the records. She found out that you and your brother were twins, all right, but you weren't identical twins. *You were fraternal twins and he didn't look like you at all!*

'But to get back to the beginning. You knew when Lee called you that there was more to it than you thought. You knew Charlie wasn't smart enough to dig up the stuff by himself, so you and fat boy did some fast snooping and found out about Paula. During that time she saw you or the other guy and got scared. She wanted to talk and called the police, asking them to meet her on the bridge where they could be alone.

'Your MVD pal was a little shrewder. He tapped her phone line and moved in to intercept her, but she moved a little faster and got out of the house before he came around. She had just enough lead to make it to the top of the bridge right where we're standing when he arrived. It was pretty – you should have been here. You should have seen what I did to him. The sour note was Paula. She thought I was one of them looking for a cut of the loot or something, because she couldn't picture any decent person hauling out a rod just like that and blowing a guy's face off. She went over the bridge.

'It would have been so nice for you if I hadn't had a conscience and wanted to find out what the green cards meant. You knew my reputation, but never thought I could go that far. You hired me so you could keep tabs on me and now look what happened.

'Maybe nothing would have happened if those documents hadn't turned up missing. Those people would have died just to keep your identity a secret. But one of those dead men was a critical link connected with the missing documents, so you cooked up the story of your brother's having left something incriminating behind him, thinking that maybe I'd come across the documents and hand them over to you. Well, Oscar, I did. You had your boys try to run them down first, but they didn't quite make it.

'I got to be a very dangerous guy in your little game. I was all over the picture with my nose picking up a lot of smells. You passed the orders to get me out of the way at any price and damn near succeeded. Too bad your new MVD boy didn't get me instead of Ethel Brighton up in the cabin there. She was dangerous too. She finally got wise to how foolish she had been and talked to the right people. She was even going to turn me in, but your MVD boy stopped that.

'You know, I thought Ethel put the finger on me when she saw my identification in my wallet. But it wasn't Ethel, it was you. You fingered me because I was getting in there. You thought that I had gone too far already and didn't want to take any more chances. So out comes the strong-arm boys and the MVD lad.

'He sure was a busy little beaver. He wanted to kill me in the worst way. When you guys discovered that I had those documents you must have gone nuts. Maybe it even occurred to you that in the process of getting them I would have uncovered all the angles to the thing. I did that, little man, I did just that.

'You got real gay at the end though. You pulled a real smartie when you put the snatch on Velda. For that there was only one answer . . . I wanted to see you die. I saw them die. You should have seen what I saw and you would have died yourself even before a bullet reached you.

'But none of that is bad when you compare it to the big thing. That's you, Mr Deamer. You, the little man whom the public loves and trusts . . . you who are to lead the people into the ways of justice . . . you who shouted against the diabolic policies of the Communists . . . you are the biggest Communist of them all!

'You know the theory . . . the ends justify the means. So you fought the Commie bastards and on the strength of that you hoped to be elected, and from there the Politboro took over. With you in where it counted you could appoint Party members to key positions, right in there where they could wreck this country without a bit of trouble. Brother, that was a scheme. I bet the boys in the Kremlin are proud of you.'

I saw the gun snake out of his pocket and I reached over and plucked it out of his fingers. Just like that. He stared after it as it arched out and down into the river.

'Tomorrow,' I said, 'the boys in the Kremlin are going to be wondering what the hell happened. They'll wonder where their boys are and they'll put up a yell, but there will be fear behind that yell because when they learn what happened they'll have to revise their whole opinion of what kind of people are over here. They'll think it was a tough government that uncovered the thing secretly. They'll think it was one of Uncle's boys who chopped down that whole filthy mob, and they won't complain too much because they can't afford to admit those same boys who were here on diplomatic passes were actually spying. The Kremlin mob will really stand on their heads when they get my final touch. It's a beauty, Mr Deamer. Do you know what I'm going to do?'

He was staring at my face. His eyes couldn't leave my eyes and his flesh was already dying with the fear inside him. He tried to talk and made only harsh breathing sounds. He raised his hands as if I were something evil and he had to keep me away. I was evil. I was evil for the good. I was evil and he knew it. I was worse than they were, so much worse that they couldn't stand the comparison. I had one, good, efficient, enjoyable way of getting rid of cancerous Commies. I killed them.

I said, 'The touch is this, Oscar. You, the greatest Commie louse of them all, will be responsible for the destruction of your own Party. You're going to die and the blame will go to the Kremlin. I'm going to stick a wallet and some shreds of cloth in your fist when you're dead. In your other hand will be the remains of those documents, enough to show what they were. Enough to make the coppers think that somehow you alone, in a burst of patriotic effort, managed to get hold of those important papers and destroyed them. It'll make them think that just as you were destroying them the killer came up and you fought it out. You came out second best, but in the struggle you managed to rip out the pocket that held his wallet and the cops will track it down thinking it came from your murderer, and what they find will be this . . . they'll find that it came from a guy who was an MVD man. He'll be dead but that won't matter. If they manage to tie it in with the bodies in the paint shop they'll think that the killer went back to report without the papers he was sent after and the Party, in their usual manner of not tolerating inefficiency, started to liquidate him and they smeared each other in the process. No, the Kremlin won't think that. They'll think it was all a very clever plan, an ingenious jumble that will never be straightened out, which it is. You're going to be a big hero. You saved the day and died in the saving. When the news is made public and the people know their favourite hero has been knocked off by the Reds they'll go on a hunt that won't stop until the issue is decided, and brother, when the people in this country finally do get around to moving, they move fast!'

The irony of it brought a scream to his lips. He made a sudden mad lurch and tried to run, but the snow that came down so white and pure it tripped him and I only had to reach out to get his throat in my hand.

I turned him around to face me, to let him look at what I was and see how I enjoyed his dying. The man who had thrown a lot of people on the long road to nowhere was a gibbering idiot slobbering at the mouth. I had his neck in my one hand and I leaned on the railing while I did it. I squeezed and squeezed and squeezed until my fingers were buried in the flesh of his throat

214

and his hands clawed at my arm frantically, trying to tear me away.

I laughed a little bit. It was the only sound in the night. I laughed while his tongue swelled up and bulged out with his eyes and his face turned black. I held him until he was down on his knees and dead as he was ever going to be, then I took my hand away and watched while he fell forward into the snow. I had to prise his fingers apart to get the wallet in them. I made sure he had a good hold on the thing then I laughed again.

Maybe Archie would guess I thought. He could guess all he wanted to, but he couldn't talk. I was holding a murder over his head, too. A justified killing that only he and I knew about. I saw the headlights of my car coming from the other end of the bridge and I walked across the steel walk to be there when Archie drove up.

The snow was coming down harder now. Soon that dark mass over there would be just a mound. And when the sun shone again the thaw would provide the deluge that would sweep everything into the sewer where it belonged.

It was lonely standing there. But I wouldn't be here long now. The car had almost reached the top of the ramp. I saw Archie bent over the wheel and took a last look around.

No, nobody ever walked across the bridge, especially not on a night like this.

Well, hardly nobody.